First Feast

Thanksgiving's Predecessor

First Feast

Thanksgiving's Predecessor

A novel by Mark T. Bueltmann

An experience by those passed

© 2022 by Mark T. Bueltmann

ISBN 979-8-9864025-0-5
A publication of MTI Ventures
MTI Ventures: Venturing from unknown unknowns

Additional copies are available from www.amazon.com.

Correspond with the author at mbueltmann@att.net

For Trese & Ian

the 'T' & 'I' of MTI Ventures

Tyranny & Turmoil

It was getting to be too much. Taxation, harassment, intolerance. 'Where were the freedoms of yore?' thought Tom, a scraggly-haired plotter, young in age, and seasoned in dreams. As each day passed and the harassment — deemed enrichment by the current campaign — grew; Tom's plotting, planning, and — dare we say conniving — increased accordingly. Sitting idly by as his world changed was neither a strength nor a desire of Tom.

If still among the living, Tom's mum would have told us that Tom's propensity against sitting idly started before his birth. From the time of Tom's decision to enter this world, to his emersion into the daylight, took an agonizing 21 hours. 21 hours of near-constant assaults on Tom's mum's body by the soon-to-be-born Tom. Assaults whose sole intent was allowing no one — less a mere woman — to delay his exit. Worn and weary from the racking, Tom was born. And sit idle he did not — not on his day of birth and not on this day.

The adjectives used to describe Tom varied from youth to now. Passionate was one of the kinder terms, addressing Tom's endless energy. Hoodlum was the most repeated. As a toddler, there were no words for Tom. Before walking, he found it amusing to rock himself back and forth until dizziness and bodily control ceased — a joy for all within the four walls. When rocking became toddling, Tom found humor in rushing at a full toddler tilt into walls. Meeting the immovable boundary, he would fall back, flail about, shake it off, stand and repeat. In his early years, Tom's litany of talents favored destruction and damage; whether his home, the neighborhood cat, or the freshly laundered clothes upon which he tossed mud. School years brought the beginning of official documentation of truancy, petty theft, and uncountable other offenses. Offenses which were due in part to Tom's fondness for hurling rocks through windows, burning crops, public indecency, or appropriating village possessions for his own purposes. For these and more, as a teenager, Tom was the most known person in the village of Cromwell Crossing — a distinction to which his Aunt Polly was not endeared. Aunt Polly was Tom's guardian and parental stand-in. Considering the genteel nature of Polly, inquiring minds often asked how Tom came to be such a dynamo. If the truth were known, Tom's rambunctious and rebellious nature did not fall far from the family tree. Before Tom reached the tender age of five, his mum succumbed to the plague, resulting in the guardianship and raising of her dear boy by her closest friend, a woman who Tom came to know as Aunt Polly. One whom the village of Cromwell Crossing knew as — his mum.

Descriptors of 'devil child' or 'the one from hell' were not entirely devoid of truth. Chronologies and records show that Tom's mum was the blood sister of Eliza of York, a victim of the Witchcraft Act of 1563. Accused and barely escaping death, Eliza's charge resulted in imprisonment. Fortunately, more sane minds had prevailed since the initial passing of the Act in 1542, an Act that punished invocators with death. Unfortunately for many; curses and incantations can be interpreted broadly and are often indefensible. A conviction against the 1542 Act would have resulted in the death of Eliza and her kin. A result that would have erased Tom from all accounts of Cromwell Crossing and this world.

Having escaped that potential turn of events, Tom vowed to live his life jubilantly and to the fullest — disregarding all who interrupted his journey. Tom viewed challenges to his freedom as both unwelcome and disrupters to his jubilation. Harassment and intolerance were not a part of the itinerary for Tom's journey; however, the Crowne ensured that disembarkment from their itinerary would be nearly impossible. This newly crafted world posed an ever-tightening daily embrace. A constriction that stirred Tom's rebellious genes and fostered thoughts of change. Change which at this precise moment was but a foggy sub-thought — not one which was in any manner nor means clear. All Tom knew was that the freedoms of yore were slowly disappearing. The breaths of Tom's freedom were being quaffed by the very rules alluded to in public broadcasts — rules touted to increase the prosperity of the masses. The broadcasters of this new paradigm boasted of more ale, less toil, and a better life for all protected by Crowne. These were the lofty aspirations promised to the minions of Cromwell Crossing and those residents of the neighboring shires. Despite the Crowne's sincerity, most viewed these proposed aspirations as unachievable; achievement would be for the few with delusions of loftiness.

As with most recent Crowne campaigns, those grounded in reality would not be partaking or benefiting. As Tom had learned, change brought both winners and victims. For this mounting change, Tom sensed himself as amongst the victims. Don't be mistaken. On a superficial level, the promise of being able to drink more ale would seem the attributes of a winner; but Tom had too much doubt to stop at the superficial rewards of the plan. If Tom could make his voice heard — and chances for that were an overwhelming 'not' — Tom would advocate to stay the course and change nothing. For as long as he had a roof over his head, an ale in his hand, and a few farthings in his pocket; he needed naught. This was Tom's itinerary — his raison d'existence.

A detail not uttered by the promoters was that while the cost of ale consumption could drop, the steps to that drop would be unpleasant and, for several, unpalatable. True, the current seemingly innocuous events were subtly small in scope as compared to the massive change of which these daily events were both a part and foreshadowing. The plan called for raising the cost of ale to a ha'penny. After the cost increase was accomplished, a subsequent price decrease would occur However, the timeliness of this decrease was not widely publicized. In reality, the increased cost of ale, that ha'penny, was an hour's wage for Tom and his fellow commoners.

As Tom consumed his less than ha'penny ale, his thoughts continued to return to the nearing fact that a morning's wage would barely quench his thirst. Tom's new reality would be the spending of his morning's wage to drink, followed by his afternoon's wage for lodging and food. The thought of drinking less in barter for better food and housing was not a palatable position for Tom and his tavern-mates.

It was on this eve that one of many planned outcomes came to bear. Reduced stock. A concept sold to the Crowne by educators of the day as *calculated quantity deprivation.* The achievement would aid in limiting the imbibing; a routine practice that negatively affected the productivity of the masses. As planned, the Cromwell Crossing Corner Cantery ran out of ale; an event occurring only once prior in its glorious 80-year reign. Granted, restocking would occur within four hours with the morning delivery. Yet the fact remained — the Cantery ran out of ale. This atrocity, this violation of nature, had never happened in any of those present's alcohol imbibed minds. An event viewed as so vile that its occurrence would surely cause that infamous drunk Lord Falstaff to roll over in his grave. If this cessation of ale was not enough, tonight marked an increase in the presence of constables. Not only were you paying more for consuming, but if one chose to drink a bit too much, you may find yourself in Cromwell Crossing's newest detainery — a constabulary crowning achievement complete with pillory.

'Where are the freedoms of yore?' Tom thought again. Aye, to drink away your worries and make an unfettered crawl home to start another glorious day. This repeated routine of the masses was both undervalued and ignored by both educators and the Crowne. The beginnings of this grand plan were sold to the unaffected as a win for the commoner — an opportunity for increased acceptance of the current campaign. More drink, less cost — where was the question? If opposition by any dared to raise its head to promoters of the plan, the potential charge would be the 't-word' — Tyranny. Few words were as powerful. Few words bear such dire consequences for those accused of it either blatantly or in a mere utterance. Conviction bore the possible penalty of removal from the landscape and lexicon. Tom had heard the horrors of other offenders and adding his name to the list of treasoners was neither a goal nor a desire. For tonight, while he yearned for more ounces of brain-numbing alcohol; the effects of taxation, oversight, and general commoner harassment were becoming visible through this calculated quantity deprivation.

The centre of the campaign lay in the principle that there would be more productivity for Crowne-worthy activities if the minds of the masses focused more on work and less on frivolity. A decision to increase the cost of ale would surely render quantities of spirits consumed fewer. To those in the hallowed halls of Merton, their texts espoused an equation of cost and demand.

> *Where wages are stable, and costs of necessities are known, the remainder known as discretionary will only purchase the quantities allowed. If the cost for discretionary quantities is raised; volumes of consumed quantities will be reduced.*

Simple yet evolutionary. However, the equation viewed by Tom would have fewer factors.

> *Higher cost results in less drink. Less drink means less happiness. Less happiness means more unrest.*

"I swear, I know not the Crowne's intent. What do they mean fewer pints consumed equals more energy available for Crowne-worthy activities? Hmmppfff. Who writes this rot? I'll show them a Crowne-worthy activity," slurred a drunken Tom as he headed to the bath.

Naively, the creators thought these principles would meet little resistance. Offering more ale for fewer coins, who would complain? However, in the infancy of this campaign, the reality was an increase in cost and a decrease in availability. Not the dream for the masses, as poetically preached. As the text of the educated birthed a burgeoning reality, Tom and his mates began to see their world change. As the restrictions became more apparent, the need for the detainery became more evident. Cromwell Crossing House No. 2 was built to accommodate the 24 hours stay of the increasing numbers of the inebriated. Unfortunately for some, a stay in the House could cause losing their meager employment. With no job nor shillings, the vicious circle of desperation would begin; desperation which could be avoided by the simple act of compliance.

"Aye, a ha'penny . . . for the privilege of drinking, one's own pint? A pint produced in me own village, by me kinfolk and neighbor. Next, ye know they will tax the milk of me mum." This was the rant du jour by Tom to the assembled few. Unfortunately for those few, these rants were not new, nor was Tom's presence at the Cantery.

Tom was the fourth son born of Elizabeth Harkin. Now, in his 23rd year, he viewed his perspectives as affirming and not a mere annoyance as perceived by a post-teen rebel. Others, perhaps not the majority — but certainly a few of the Cantery's patrons — shared Tom's conversations and views. As the ale began its familiar effects, Tom chanted under his breath.

"No more, no more . . . we want no'or. No'or tax, no'or rule . . . yea, no pompous rule. No more, no more . . . we want no'or."

Again and again, the cadence grew in intensity with each gulp of ale. The intensity increased with the beginning of the percussion; a distinct and staccato pounding of Tom's beer mug in time with the 'no more, no more . . . we want no'or'. The meter had begun slowly, but now the composition in Tom's mind was reaching a frenzied pace; a pace which returned Tom to the reality of multiple stares and the voice of his friend, Eric. From the depths of Tom's senses came the words of another.

"Ssshhhh," followed by, "why dost ye insist on annoying the tapster?" were the words which became audible to Tom, and in an instant, the cacophony stopped.

"Huuugh?" asked Tom in a drowsily near-drunk manner. "Ye say something?"

"Er, Scotland to Tom. Didst thou hear?"

"Hear what?"

"That ale has definitely affected yer hearing; I've been shouting for the last few minutes. Did ye not see the pissed and exasperated look of the tapster? It be not likely he consider ye a favorite patron." Letting that thought ruminate, Eric continued. "Hast ye forgotten already yesterday's lecture condemning yer rants and prohibiting that jumping about favored by ye? Yea, those distractions we were told effects negatively the drinking and profits of his Cantery. Dost thee want to be banned, facing the devil of sobriety every night? Tell me . . . dost thee?"

"Huumph," grunted a slightly inebriated Tom. "Methinks ye and my fellow patrons would heartily enjoy a bit of entertainment and frivolity with these distilled beverages . . .." As if on cue from the pregnant pause, Tom continued.

"Eric?"

"Yea, Tom . . ." replied Eric, sensing an approach of foolishness.

"Dost thou believe tis called dis-stilled cause thee cannot be still if thee doth drink too much?" Before Eric could answer, a more serious situation was about to occur.

"Oh no . . . here comes der tapster."

"Ah lads, this be no music hall nor den of the arts . . . I want to hear the clanking of mugs. Mugs filled with yer drink. Not chanting and noises more likely found in yonder barnyard. Doth thee understand? I trust I be speaking in a dialect understood by thou and thee mates? Know ye that Dawson would take great pleasure in hoisting yer drunken ass off that stool and transporting ye to his place of incarceration. Keep up the racket and noises of the barn and I'll make sure the pillory is ye's next stop."

With this warning, Tom was left contemplating the words of the tapster. Contemplation soon led to Tom departing the Cantery for a clearing a hundred feet away; his mind slowly filling with thoughts of escape — escape from the taxes, the tyranny, the Crowne. What right-minded man would orally allude that there was more than that which the present bore? Talk of this nature, talk of unhappiness with the present, came only from a public insurrectionist; one who most likely would find himself confined to leg irons, icy cinder walls, and malnutritious gruel.

Although not a full thought, the initial seeds of separation from the Crowne began their maturation — maturation fueled by the ale and the growing fear of the times; times which had not always been this way. The Crowne had been wonderful to be under. The protection, the gallantry, the acceptance — or maybe it was tolerance. In the moment, acceptance and tolerance often look the same. It is only after a few years of deprivation that hindsight shows the true colors of previous events. A careful review of history would show that the terms religious and freedom were never joined in word or concept. History would find that one's religious beliefs were an area of the Crowne's omission. Not mentioned in speeches, nor perceived to be criminal, this 'freedom' was, shall we say, constructively allowed. That's right — allowed. However, could we also infer acceptance? Acceptance is a powerful sentiment and one which Tom and his friends were feeling a tad uncomfortable about.

Unfortunately, the new reality of the day meant one would mind their public orations and concur not with those who voiced dissent against the Crowne. In previous tirades, Tom had come too close to being on the wrong side and had even received a few warnings to bide his manners and refrain from behavior that one could construe as instigation — instigation of others to his point of view. Unfortunately, Tom's point of view could be misconstrued — or intentionally construed — as resembling a host of nebulous crimes. Incitation, mass hysterics, treason, endangering the public — all being litigious terms designed to address those in dissent. The mere utterance of the word 'aye', in the proper setting, in response to a rant, could find one imprisoned if the local authority saw fit. Arrests increased by the week as the Crowne felt an uneasiness in the populace and the need to control instigators whom they viewed as a threat.

And so, it was on that evening of the 23rd of October 1587 that a tree stump near Cromwell Crossing became the pulpit for Tom's latest oration. What started as an inquiry asking why so many did blindly follow the order of one who had never been outside of England drew 25 and was logged in the constabulary minutes as a mass citation. The number of this gathering of the masses — an arbitrarily defined count — was deemed on this evening to meet the definition, resulting in the arrest of one Thomas J. Smythe under the mass hysterics law of Salem Proper. An arrest which began seasoning the plot du jour as Tom spent the night and next morn in Cromwell Crossing House No 2. His first time as a guest in a house designed to serve the swindlers, petty thieves, drunks, and any other who had committed an offense deemed to be against the Crowne.

Plans

The walk had been far from pleasant. The night air was brisk, the stones unlevel, and Tom's state of agility impaired. With the constable's hand on his shoulder, and his arms fixed in irons behind his back; Tom was led to Cromwell Crossing House No 2, a mere one-mile walk from the Cantery.

"Come on, come on . . . a crusade, this be not. Me Gammer can walk faster than thee," chided Constable Dawson, glad to be awakened by the walk and equally pleased to be delivering another hipper to the House.

Hipper was constabulary slang for thripp'nce or thripper. For each arrest and delivery to one of the holding houses, the constable received three pence; a thirpp'nce in additional pay. Four arrests earned the constable an extra shilling in pay. There was a catch. The arrestee had to remain in custody until formally charged, which could only occur during daylight hours. If the one charged escaped custody before a record could be created, the constable forfeited his thripp'nce. A slogan reminded the constables of this rule. If the hipper should hop; thripp'nce be not.

Needless to say, constables were more careful about how they left their arrestees. Left in a secured state with iron cuffs attached to a suitable structure would ensure that when the morning light came, the hipper had not hopped. Left unsecured by a lazy or inebriated constable, the hipper would hop.

Slightly sniggering at the phrase, the constable returned to business. "Is this yer first time at the House? Methinks an outspoken lad of yer likes has been a previous visitor to this fine facility."

"No, Sir. . . fiiirrrssst tiimme," stuttered Tom in uncharacteristic politeness. Tom's stutter was enhanced and prolonged because of the unexpected chill from the walk.

"Well, hope ye don't mind if I don't provide a proper tour. More hippers to be got as yer pals consume more and become annoyances to der tapster and neighboring folk. Nothing like a few ales to make drunkards think the neighbor's flowerbed is their personal bath. Those of ye who loudly water the flowers before the cock crows usually find themselves here."

As the ungainly couple rounded the bend; before them stood the House in all its glory. Cromwell Crossing House No 2 would eventually find itself to be a House of Correction; however, at present, it was merely a brick structure constructed to hold the perpetrators of minor crimes. On the outside, the house resembled the few surrounding structures. Two stories of red clay, hand-hewn brick, windows of leaded glass, doors of walnut. For those having business within, a pronounced knocker was present on the main door. During the day, with the leaden windows opened, a recessed set of bars prevented the escape of those held within its walls. Once inside, the similarity of nearby establishments ended. A large open area with benches, several iron rings set into the floor, five holding cells for night visitors, an area for the warden to take a brief rest, and several desks for conducting the administrative duties. On most evenings, the House was unmanned, and the overnight guests were strongly warned to conduct themselves in an orderly manner. Complaints from the neighbors of excessive noise or other sleep-depriving activities were dealt with harshly; a brief stay became longer for those who wished not to obey the establishment's rules.

As Tom's mind cleared, he slowly realized that he was in the doorway of the House. As Constable Dawson's keys jangled while unlocking the door, Tom heard the noises of another.

"Be still in there . . . ye be having some company for the evening," commented Dawson in an unimpressed manner; not realizing that history was about to be made and Tom's life would not be the same from this moment on.

For it was in Cromwell Crossing House No. 2, that an overzealous and less inebriated Tom met Lawrence Bonham Appleton IV – Lars. A frequenter of holding houses, and a man whose visions usually surpassed those with whom he associated. Lars was a reader and listener. His driving thoughts were inspired by the words and views of others. His latest source of creation could be found in one Walter Raleigh, recently knighted and now known as Sir Walter Raleigh. The tales of Sir Walter Raleigh, adventurer, writer, and nobleman were legendary and devoured in print and tale by Lars. Plans of others to further explore the lands to the West drove Lars to an almost frenzied obsession with plans for joining these sea-farers and escaping his less than noteworthy existence.

History will show, and records of the day will confirm, that Lars and Tom shared an evening of incarceration; Tom for crowd incitation, Lars for public intoxication. Lars had the distinction of also being charged with the attempted beaning of an officer of the law with a brick.

"I be told I'd have the house to meself," slurred Lars to Dawson.

"I made no such promise . . . and besides, what are the chances of ye being the only drunkard out there tonight? Now keep yer voice down and be the cordial mate I know ye to be; else this stay will become quite unpleasant and ye's next . . . more so."

"Urrrgggg," growled Lars in a quasi-menacing manner.

"Urgggg be at ye," retorted the unimpressed and slightly annoyed Dawson. "Now make proper introductions, and I'll be back in a few hours. If yer both civil, I'll see that yer able to work for a day's wages tomorrow."

With that instruction; Tom received Lars' outstretched hand, marking the beginning of their fast friendship.

"Lars is me name . . . what be yer's?"

"Thomas Smythe, er . . . Tom," was Tom's hesitant reply to the offering.

"What did ole' Dawson bring ye in for?"

"Incitation . . . to be precise . . . incitation of man and beast." To which Tom proudly added, "to my count, there were 5 persons . . . and perhaps 3 bored cats."

"Inciting a cat . . . Now that's a skill!" commented a slightly awe-struck Lars.

"Well, Dawson here claims it was 25 . . . methinks he failed grammar school math."

"Maybe he was counting hands and paws," offered Lars, bringing some levity to the room.

"Me shaketh all over in laughter . . . ho, ho, ho," countered Dawson in a forced laugh.

During the exchange, Dawson was securing Tom's leg irons to a ring on the floor and bringing over a chamber pot.

"Well boys, enjoy yer evening and get a bit of rest. Remember, if thee dost wake the neighbors, thou shall rue that decision fer many a day."

With that warning; Dawson left the main room, closed the substantial walnut door, turned the iron tumblers, and returned to the Cantery. His job for the rest of the evening was to ensure the safety of the public and protect the image of the Crowne.

Lars — ever the engager — began his assessment of his housemate. "So Tom . . . incitation, eh? What be yer cause?"

"Well, it's not really a cause, it's more of an annoyance. I be a lowly thatcher trying to enjoy some ale, and the Crowne is interfering with me consumption. It's just not proper, as them Lord's say, 'a man be entitled to his ale' — doth not thee agree?"

"That be right mate, one has got to drink," responded Lars, who was also in a state of slow detoxication from his evening's binge with the spirits. "How dare the bastards tell me how much I can drink! Not the Crowne nor the tapster! Not even that son of a loon, Dawson!"

"Ale doth cost me too much of me wage. Takes a good part of me coins to enjoy an evening of drinking with me mates. The Crowne should recognize the value of comradery and lower the cost," Tom recited, surprising himself at the simplicity and brilliance of the words. "Yea . . . that's what should happen, the price of ale should be lowered to allow for more comradery. Comradery and fellowship . . . that's how we commoners can support the Crowne," rambled Tom as he further explored this new perspective.

"I like yer thinking mate, comradery for the Crowne . . . sounds angelic. How doth we accomplish that feat? Seems them signs over yonder speak of quantity deprivation, not yer comradery. Heard one bloke say this will keep one's head clear for the Crowne's current campaign . . . what rot." After a moment of silent contemplation, Lars continued. "Someone seems a wee bit confused. Keepin' one's head clear does not always promote acts of benefit. I dare say that what be good for the Crowne is not always good for me and my mates. At least I don't recall being asked . . . I must have been in the parlor when the inquisitor came." As if on cue, the snickering began.

"Perhaps if the Crowne drank more, they would know our wants," offered Tom as a simple solution to the created problem, "seeing the day from our perspective, if ye will."

"I like where this is going, me friend, but have ye a solution?"

"Own a tavern and drink for free?" Tom offered brightly, followed by a dose of reality, "But that will never happen." The last statement changing Tom's mood to one of loss.

"Now, now . . . all is not for naught . . . has ye ever heard of Sir Walter Raleigh?" offered Lars as he saw on opening on his favorite topic.

"If thee be a Sir . . . doth that mean he be another of those Crowne cronies?"

"Well, never really thought of him that way . . . but he doth provide a way out."

"I'm listening . . . please proceed," Tom responded cautiously.

"Sir Walter Raleigh has considerable favor with the Crowne; seems he suppressed a rebellion a few years back and, as a reward, became a Lord of the confiscated property. Because of his success with land, the Crowne . . . that be Queen Elizabeth . . . charged him with exploring the lands out West."

"West as in Western Ireland?" Tom naively asked.

"Oh, more West than that," Lars nonchalantly retorted.

"So, like an island or something off the coast?"

"One of limited thought could say that . . . I be speakin' of many weeks from the coast!" Lars clarified with an emphasis on the word weeks.

"Weeks . . .? I be not sure if there be land weeks west of England."

"Aye matey . . . me uneducated young friend. Has not thee heard of the ventures of Columbus and his discovery of lands across the sea? Terra firma for those of the explorer variety."

"Name rings a distant bell, but I don't know a lot of him . . . is thou sure he too be not imagined? There doth seem to be a bit of activity above yer neck.

"Oh no . . . this be real . . . more real than thou can imagine!" Lars responded, his enthusiasm growing by the minute.

"Imagine a land of towering trees and no belching smoke. A land of crisp air and no crime. A land where one is rewarded for his work and there be no Crowne tellin' thee how to live . . . would ye be interested in that reality?"

Tom responded to Lars' description in an almost gibberish manner, "Truth and reality . . . this cannot be . . . sounds as if this be the talk of an idiot."

"Oh no mate, truth indeed . . . are ye interested?"

"Oh yea, if I be not, may I fall off me next roof!" cursed Tom.

"Hear me now . . . last year, Sir Walter Raleigh and another sailed from London Bridge to explore that same West."

"How doth thee know this?" challenged Tom.

"I was there. Me cousin Guppy was a hand on the supply ship . . . I saw him sail off into the sunset. Aye, Guppy, the lad always enjoyed sailing amongst the bigger fish."

"Did he make it?" asked Tom incredulously.

"I . . . I . . . I hope so! Haven't seen him since."

And with the effect of a bucket of water on a raging fire, the enthusiasm of the last hour was instantly lost. For Lars had no answer whether his cousin was safe. However, he had no proof that he wasn't. Did he and Tom want to waste their lives in nowhere jobs, listening to another's view of the world and sit idly by while others more committed strove for a change?

Lars explained that Guppy was a hero. He had chosen to stand tall and escape his mundane existence . . . electing to go where few ventured. Risking all for the greater good; he had escaped, and in escape, he had taken control of his life.

With this logic, Lars reignited the flame. "Tom, me mate, that could be us! We could be there, and not here in this cold, damp, Crowne-controlled world."

Silence again, and as Tom and Lars were left to their thoughts, history began its initial fermentation. In that cell, removed from the rest of those quietly sleeping; Lars continued to portray to Tom a land where rules were formed by the laborers, and open land stretched forever. A land where the only smoke came from a fire and not a stack. A virgin land upon which new beginnings could be forged and past offenses left to whither in the brains of those who chose to remain in the past.

As the cadence of opportunity grew, Tom's eyes got wide . . . wide as a school youth at his first comprehension of a teacher's lesson.

"Let me understand ye, there would be no Crowne . . . we would rule ourselves, establish our society, create our norms? There'd be none to monitor our ale consumption and none to impose taxation on our meager wages and profits?" Tom asked in affirmation as his brain began to comprehend the previous hours of Lars' selling.

"Heard me right . . . wouldn't that be the expectation for a couple of explorers of freedom like ourselves? We and Sir Walter Raleigh . . . pursuers of the same path!" Lars offered with a magical lilt as he brought up his hero's name.

It was then, after hours of emotional and verbal oration — verbiage worthy of Parliament — that Tom performed a final overt act. Looking ceiling-ward, he bellowed into the chilled air, "I'm in! How dost me I make this happen?"

His task complete, Lars began the reparations. "Thou won't regret this mate, here's to thee and yer new life," Lars affirmed as he lifted an imaginary mug in the air and toasted his fellow adventurer. Lars' next statement was made, almost as an afterthought — although the substance was far greater. "Aye mate and this grand adventure will be yers

for a mere five pounds . . . that be the fare for transport to yer new life."

"Let me fetch that from under me bed at home . . ." replied Tom, almost choking at the sudden turn in the conversation. "Me mate, that be a year's wages . . . dost I look to have coins of that color?" grimaced Tom as his lofty spirits began their swan dive to reality.

"Don't give up yet . . . we don't need it now. Let me find out when they sail again. I'm sure we have a few months . . ." Lars offered convincingly.

"A few months . . . a few years. It be all the same to me and my nonexistent stack of silver."

"A few months means a few months of planning and succeeding," Lars replied to his skeptical friend. "If there is one challenge we're both good at, it's solving problems . . . this be just another problem."

And so began a few hours of thinking, countering, querying, and hope generation. Sleep was not in the equation for this evening, which was a new beginning for the newly formed comradery of Lars and Tom.

As the light of dawn broke, Dawson returned to check on his charges and confirm his night's extra payment. "I hope ye hippers weren't up all night . . . I'd hate to charge ye for sleeping in the square."

Sleep was far from Lars' or Tom's minds; for their thoughts were consumed with planning their future and beginning their new life.

The Preparation

"Art thou witless?" Tom's Aunt Polly asked in utter disbelief. "Didst thou fall off the roof again? If thou sells yer bed and shelf . . . thou shan't be getting another!"

"It's me bed, and I have plans more important than sleep!" Tom stubbornly responded, countering Polly's obvious annoyance.

"Plans . . . whether they be large or small, seems foolish for ye to be selling yer bed. Methinks that most of ye mates have beds. . . well, except for that Barnaby chap . . . he smells like he sleeps in a barn."

"It's me bed and I'll sell it if I want!" Tom replied in a louder tone.

"Go ahead . . . but I won't be helpin' ye get another . . . sleep on the roof, if ye want!" With that final rant, Polly left the room.

Polly's annoyance with Tom was becoming greater. Over the past few weeks, she had noticed his personal effects disappearing. At first, the disappearances were but fuzzy memories — didn't Tom's prized ball rest on the shelf? Where did that go? That hand-crafted stoker that always stood in the corner — haven't seen that recently. These and assorted prized bounties of boyhood left the house, never to be seen again. However, the bed and shelf were too large and too — let's say — necessary to be overlooked. Polly did not realize that Tom's possessions, large and small, were becoming cash for his developing plan; a plan created with Lars during that brief stay in Cromwell Crossing House No. 2. Tom often remembered how, in that cell, Lars had portrayed a land like none he had ever heard or dreamed of. Open land for new beginnings; a permanent separation from the past. Total life changes were usually viewed as the stuff of folklore, not much different from dragons and magic. However, Lars had portrayed and — more importantly — sold this vision as reality.

Since meeting Lar's, Tom's goal had been the acquisition of 5 pounds, nearly a year of thatcher's wages. As of February, four months into Tom's crusade, Tom had only managed to save 5 shillings. This meager effort was partially because of Tom's mental sloshing from incredible excitement and motivation to an abysmal acknowledgment of the impossibility of the task before him.

This changed in early March. It was then that Tom transitioned from mentally doomed to one who was pointedly focused on his goal. March 9th, 1588 would forever be known as the day Thomas Smythe began his new life. On that day at approximately 8:15 pm, one hour into his nightly routine of plotting and planning, Tom's life changed — shall we say, forever.

"How to earn money? . . . Is it even possible? . . . Do I want to go? . . . Of course, I want to go . . . how can I earn money?" This was Tom's current carousel of quandaries. These were the answers sought this evening. This night, as was the same as most others, Tom sought his insight through the power of the pint.

"Here . . . here, thee be!" gasped an out of breath disheveled and dirty worker akin in cleanliness to a chimney sweep. It took Tom a moment to realize that the filthy laborer stumbling into the Cromwell Crossing Corner Cantery was Lars. "I . . . I was hoping to find ye . . . news me mate . . . news to change our lives!" were the uttered words before Lar's near collapse.

"Lars! . . . why so flustered?" asked Tom, seeing his mate in both distress and excitement.

"Couldn't be better . . . wait till ye hears me news!" spoke Lars in a clearer manner as his breathing resumed a normal rhythm. "We. . . we sail in May . . . we sail the end of May!" Lars repeated, as if not believing the news himself.

"May? . . . this May mate? . . . surely not this May!" Tom asked in a disbelieving tone.

"Right ye be, as sure as I stand before ye . . . this May, not nearly eleven glorious weeks from now!"

"Ugh . . . Lars . . . I may be reconsidering," Tom replied as he experienced a serious dose of lucidity.

"What . . . oh no . . . I won't let ye . . . remember our oath?" Lars retorted to the hesitant Tom in an anxious, yet challenging, manner. "We made an oath that night so many moons away that rest would not grace our mortal bodies until we were upon that ship of dreams — that ship of our dreams. How could ye forget so soon?"

"Of course not . . . I haven't forgotten that glorious night, but I still wonder where I am to get those pounds . . . me mind cannot fathom success," admitting his failure aloud to Lars.

"Have faith, me fellow explorer . . . we too will conquer this obstacle," spoke Lars in a lulling tone of confidence.

"Obstacle? Tis not like those 5 pounds will just magically appear, or that the ship captain will say 'yo boys, passage for ye is free . . . I be unsure how to get that much money," Tom presented as his recurring logical argument. "That be a year of me wages — I don't make the money of yer Sir Walter Raleigh."

"Me mate, we discussed this that night," reminded Lars. "Dost thee recall how we agreed we could sell, work, beg and borrow for this opportunity. Art thee working two extra jobs? That be the plan ye proposed," reminded Lars in case Tom had forgotten.

"Well I was gonna," smirked Tom, "and then I decided I was gonna drink more."

"Tom, me pal, me mate . . . yer letting me down! Yer abandoning our oath! Seems thou wishes to remain here forever and not experience those glorious lands . . . to never smell that pristine smell or be the ruler of yer own destiny."

"I hear . . . really I do . . . I'm just at a loss of how to make that money. I've saved 5 shillings . . . maybe that will help pay for me piece of the sail . . ." Tom began as his tone and thoughts began to turn towards the positive.

"Have confidence . . . where is that planner I met in October? Hast ye been beaten down by the very rules thee seeks to escape?" chided Lars. "Have thee no desire to escape this rot and be yer own person . . . or would ye rather succumb to the

Crowne and cronies, controlled by their notions of what is best for ye? What be yer desire, mate?"

Slowly, Tom's heartbeat rose, his fingers fidgeted, his face flushed. "Right ye be . . . right again!" exclaimed Tom, leaping to his feet and smashing his mug on the bar top, only to be interrupted by . . .

"Break that mug lad, and ye be floor-sweeping," bellowed the tapster in an annoyed tone.

As quickly as his emotions rose, Tom managed to halt their escalation. "Sorry Tapster Darwin, I shall be more careful," groveled Tom in a tone quite the departure from his normal response.

"Earn that money mate . . . we sail in eleven weeks!" This retort was Lars' last instruction before disappearing into the night air.

As the gravity of the situation became more refined in Tom's mind, so too was the solution more intensely sought. 5 pounds — well actually 4 pounds 15 shillings. The lesser number sounded easier to achieve than the 95 shillings he needed to amass. Considering he collected 2 shillings a week, Tom had a better chance of having Sir Walter Raleigh bequeath him a homestead — or hamlet — in his name. In Tom's mind, the goal to be achieved with these shillings was, in fact, quite noble. One might say worthy of Sir Walter Raleigh's generosity, and not nearly as pompous as a self-named hamlet. Surely Sir Walter Raleigh would applaud one who would use these shillings for passage to the lands West — those wondrous lands o'er the magnificent, seemingly boundless sea. Lost in his own mental morass, Tom continued to plot and plan.

For the next week, Tom was continuously plagued with his plight, one which once again began to climb into the category of insurmountable — with once again, no solution in sight. That was until an evening at the Cantery provided an interesting instigator of an idea.

Seated just behind Tom were two of the shire's business owners. Two men with more wealth than Tom would ever acquire in 100 of his lifetimes. Tom overheard them discussing business expansion and the borrowing of money from an endower of the arts and trade. Borrowing money from someone other than a friend or relative was a concept Tom had never considered. Listening furtively, Tom took in their words. Upon the conclusion of their conversation, Tom understood that their trade model involved pleading one's current case to the endower; and, if successful, funds would be conveyed. It was as if ye were speaking personally to Sir Walter Raleigh himself.

Tom began to perspire in unbelief at this option. His mind flashed from scene to scene as he attempted to get a grip on a possibility . . . a possibility previously believed to be unattainable.

Returning to reality, Tom saw the gentlemen were wrapping up their business. It was now or never if Tom wished to have a remote chance at success. Turning in his chair, he looked squarely at the finely dressed gentlemen and uttered a weak greeting.

"Uh, Sirs . . . I may have overheard a bit of your conversation . . . not intentional, mind ye." With that confident opening, Tom continued his dialogue in a dazed and somewhat confused state, "if . . . if one would want to visit this endower of the trades as ye called it . . . where would one go?"

Tom couldn't believe he got that sentence out, and now he waited seemingly minutes for a reply. The gentlemen were not expecting such a question from a lad the looks of Tom — unkempt, dirty, tattered clothes and obviously inebriated. The gentlemen looked at each other — smirked a bit — and responded momentarily.

"Glad to help! Yer destination would be 2 New Street in Plymouth. Ask for Mr. Hoare, tell him Cuthbert Houblon sent ye."

With their good deed done, or so it appeared; Cuthbert and his companion turned, walked out of the Cantery, and almost immediately broke down in laughter. The mere thought of Tom heading into the well-heeled establishment on New Street and requesting a meeting with one of the most powerful financial advisors to the Crowne was cause for a guffaw the likes they had not experienced in weeks. The only vision which would surpass their present mental image would be the sight of the constables removing Tom from an establishment for which he had no earthly business, not now nor foreseeably ever.

Tom, however; believing the gentlemen to be genuine, finished his final ale and headed home to prepare for his journey the next morning to Plymouth. Tom's pre-dawn hours were filled with optimism — an optimism not experienced since the inception of the plan that night in the House with Lars.

Tom rose early this Tuesday. Normally, he would head into the outskirts of Cromwell Crossing for a day of thatching the roofs of several dwellings. However, this day would have him travel in the opposite direction toward Plymouth. As a drunk, Tom was annoying and undesired. As a thatcher, Tom was actually proficient and admired — no fear of heights nor complaints of the weather. Tom's employer appeared satisfied with his work; satisfied to a level that Tom believed a day away could be explained and his source of ale consumption would not be disrupted. This was the hope of Tom.

After an hour's walk and a few hours as a passenger on a wagon, Tom made it to Plymouth. Ah, Plymouth, the famed seafaring city which was the center of business for the area and a world apart from Tom's reality. Street after street of 2 story granite and limestone dwellings, all with stoned chimneys, and ornate signage designating the owner or the services offered. The air was heavy with the smell of the sea, and the slosh of water could be discerned from the city center.

Determined to have success, Tom walked the streets of Plymouth until he found New Street. On the corner stood Number 2, a building equally majestic as the others, constructed of the best which could be imported from throughout the Empire. Cocking his hat and adjusting his cloak, Tom walked up the granite stairs and made his way into the building signed: W. Hoare, Esq. - Proprietors & Trades.

This is what a palace must look like, thought Tom as he gazed upon the pristine foyer; sunlight streaming through the leaded glass, warming the interior. Not a sack or straw to be found. However, it was the voice behind Tom which caused a disruption to his gawking and a return to reality.

"Thou dost appear to be quite lost. Where did thee plan to go? I doubt it be here," came the voice of one who spent a majority of the day greeting others. That voice belonged to Miss Chilson, keeper of all that is to be kept, whether record, schedule, or entry.

"If you please . . . I'm here to see Mr. Hoare," responded Tom in a polite tone and manner that he had been practicing since nightfall.

"So says thee!" came the response on the verge of laughter, "dare I say that just because thee have fowl for the office, doth NOT mean that they are to be delivered in person . . . our barn is two streets over."

"Oh, thee be mistaken. I be here on an urgent financial quest. I was personally sent by Cuthbert Houblon!" Tom asserted in a manner also practiced repeatedly over the last 24 hours.

"So thee be not here with fowl?" inquired Miss Chilson. "Do know that thee doth appear to be one quite familiar with those of the barnyard variety. As for seeing Mr. Hoare, that will not be happening. If indeed thou did meet Mr. Houblon, I fear he has played a joke on thee. It be yer ill-luck that his trick was successful."

"Oh please mum, just a few moments. I have traveled from Cromwell Crossing for this meeting and must make Mr. Hoare's acquaintance. Please, I implore thee!"

Miss Chilson was beginning to lose her patience with Tom's persistent resistance. Tom's level of adamancy was rarely encountered by Miss Chilson, especially from one of the lower classes. "I believe I have made myself clear, thou will NOT be seeing Mr. Hoare and thee will be leaving . . . now . . . understood!"

At that moment a large mahogany door opened and a youthful, bearded gent exited, smoking a rather exotic pipe and holding a heavy leather-bound book. "Miss Chilson, who will NOT be seeing me today?"

Sheepishly replying, Miss Chilson offered, "Sir, this deliverer of fowl wishes to have a meeting with thee. He claims to know Mr. Houblon."

The day had started well for Mr. Hoare. Besides having an opportunity for additional wealth acquisition; he was enjoying the unseasonably warm weather. It was indeed Tom's lucky day for instead of a dismissal — as would be the norm — instead, Mr. Hoare extended his hand. "I feel thee have been the butt of a joke by Cuty, but I shall have the last laugh. I shall give thee five minutes . . . that be five minutes, no more," Mr. Hoare stated in a commanding tone. A tone of ultimate authority rarely encountered by Tom. As Mr. Hoare returned to his office, he beckoned Tom to follow. With that instruction, Tom followed Mr. Hoare, a titan of industry and advisor to the Crowne, into a large room and behind the heavy door which shut as he entered.

Five minutes became 25 and when the door opened, Tom was beaming. His countenance had assumed a pallor that he had previously not known.

Those viewing Tom saw his smile stretching to the breaking point and his feet ready to break into a jig at the slightest instigation.

"Now remember, interest on that pound is due every month. If I'm not paid in full after 18 months, thee shall be jailed — understood?" The words flowed from Mr. Hoare's mouth in an obviously rote manner. The same terminology and request for understanding appeared to be uttered many times a day and many more times a month.

"Aye Sir, Aye . . .thank thee Sir . . . thank thee again . . ." stumbled Tom in disbelief and shock.

With this meeting; Tom exited one pound richer and substantially closer to his dream of escape. This newfound enthusiasm prepared him for his next pound's acquisition.

⁎⁎   ⁎⁎   ⁎⁎

As if struck by lightning, Tom's eyes were opened as he waited for a refill of his ale. Tottering between bravery and historical ambivalence, Tom opted for the former and arose to converse with the tapster.

"I'm coming . . . I'm coming!" panted Darwin. "If'n ye roams about, thou shall never get yer ale."

"No . . . Not here . . . no complaints here," began Tom, "rather an offer if ye have a moment."

"If I talk with ye, yer fellow imbibers will get more vocal, as I deprive them of their pints and ale. As for no complaints — complaints is all ye do lad!"

"Uuggghhh," started Tom, "I guess I can be a bit of an annoyance, but it was the ale talking. Forgive me, please . . . I meant ye no personal grief."

"I have no response. I be viewing a scene not of this world. Thomas Smythe apologizing . . . what more will this evening bear? Well, what be yer query, as ye put it — be quick about it?"

"Iiifff thee be willing, I could help ye . . . serve ale, clean the tables, keep me mates happy."

"And fall, and spill, and curse at me customers — not a chance."

"Ohhh, no . . . that was the old Tom . . . as I speak here before ye, I am a new man. I swore to my Aunt Polly that I would change and ye would be helping me with me change."

"I don't believe ye, once a drunk, always one — can't take the risk mate."

At that very moment, a customer shouted for Darwin. "Where's me ale?!" bellowed a burly customer, clearly able to instigate a riot and lay waste to the whole tavern. Sensing the urgency of the situation, in a mere moment, Tom grabbed an ale from Darwin and presented it to the eager requestor. "So sorry, Sir, just having a chat with me friend," began Tom. "Please Sir, accept me apology for the delay." Noting the heraldic ring on the man's finger, Tom continued, "If I may, Sir . . . doth yer ring bear the crest of the House of Lancaster? A stately ring it be!"

Calming almost immediately at the service and smoothness of Tom's discourse, the patron had trouble finding words. "Aye, that it is! Eagle eyes have ye. Me kin were guards at the Abbey and they gave this ring for years of service to me father. Thank ye for the ale and thank ye for giving notice to me ring."

Darwin stood amazed, not sure how to assess the site before him. Seems Tom had an unknown communication gift that may exceed his gift for ale consumption and lethargy. "I swear this be just luck, but if ye help me tonight, I'll consider yer offer. No payment tonight, but I'll buy ye another on the house for yer help."

"Done," replied Tom, feeling the inner glow of another positive change. While not quite the bequeath of a homestead, the possibility of additional income helped to focus Tom on the prospect of earning more shillings. While this brief glimmer could only partially offset the ominous task of earning nearly a year's wages in ten short weeks, the compass of Tom's life was pointing properly. A fact that was not so true a few days prior.

The Final Weeks

No one could recall when the stranger entered the shire; not an inquisitive youth, not one of the alert elderlies sitting in their favorite spot — no one. Yet, one ominous in personality and dark of shadow visited Cromwell Crossing for several days in March of 1588. An uncharacteristically frigid rain greeted the stranger for his arrival; continuing until his departure. Joining the rain was a chilling breeze; not merely a seasonal wintery breeze, but a breeze with a bone-chilling grasp, engulfing the wayward and serving as a reminder of the stranger's visit.

Answering a rap at her door, Aunt Polly did not realize that her exact locale was the destination for the dark being. Introducing himself as Hopkins, guardian of Chelmsford, the cloaked man with the top hat asked if one Thomas Smythe, nephew of Eliza of York, resided there. As Tom's behavior frequently resulted in formal visitors knocking at the door — whether truant officer, constable, or enraged merchant — a stranger of the likes of Hopkins was still unnerving.

"I be Tom's Aunt; how may I assist?" Polly inquisitively asked the stranger while remaining surprisingly protective.

"My dear lady, I have traveled far for a discussion regarding young Thomas' kin. I would prefer to have this discussion with the lad," responded Hopkins in a dismissive manner. "Is he home?"

"Well . . . the lad," Polly started, emphasizing the word lad, "is 23 and I would hope he would be working at this time. If thou must speak with him, I'm quite confident he will be at the Cantery consuming ale and serving others."

"That be the tavern across the square?" queried Hopkins.

"That be the one," responded Polly, tiring rapidly of the stranger and ready to relieve herself of the chill in the air. "If that be all . . . I have cleaning to do.

"Grammercy Ma'am," Hopkins replied in his domineering tone before turning and disappearing into the mist. A mist fast becoming a miserable rain.

As Polly re-entered her home, an unshakeable chill followed her, causing her to pause and wonder about her visitor and his search.

Hopkins had spoken the truth. He had come a great distance to see Tom. A purveyor and collector of articles of wizardry and the occult; Hopkins had set his being on acquiring a ring. Not just any ring, but one which graced the finger of Eliza of York, a suspected witch, and survivor of the trials at Essex. Hopkins had been told that Eliza possessed a ring that contained a fiery red stone. A stone so red it appeared to have been forged from the very depths of Hades. Before her inquisition, it was purported that Eliza twisted the ring twice upon her finger while uttering the words 'in sanguinem nostrum ingentius' with each rotation — loosely translated as 'from our bloodline'. Whether the ritual had legitimacy is not the question; the fact remains, Eliza survived her tormentors. Her survival, whether luck or occultly aided, had brought Hopkins in search of Tom. Hopkins believed that if Eliza could survive the inquisition as a witch; that he could market the ring to provide protection from lesser challenges for quite a price. These were the thoughts that graced Hopkins' mind as he traversed the town square toward the Cantery.

Entering the purveyor of brews and ale, a chill fell over the crowd. Many looked up. Some shivered. Yet others were unaffected, continuing their consumption. Moving definitively in an almost ethereal manner, Hopkins inquired of a semi-sober patron if he knew of a Thomas Smythe.

"That be him . . ." the man replied, finishing the sentence with a gaseous belch, and pointing a finger toward Tom standing at the end of the counter.

"Thank ye," replied Hopkins, and moved effortlessly through the patrons toward his intended.

"Mr. Smythe . . . Mr. Thomas Smythe?" inquired Hopkins in a tone indicating this was not a question.

Surprised at being called Mr. and equally annoyed at the distraction from his duties, Tom looked up, surveyed the inquirer, and grunted a semi-intelligible . . . "ya".

"Me lad, I have come a long distance to pay my respects . . ." began Hopkins to the less than impressed Tom.

"Respects . . . to me?" Tom asked as he looked around to see if another had joined the conversation.

"Yes, to ye, my fine fellow . . . I wish to speak with ye of yer Aunt Eliza Harkin. Me name be Hopkins, and I have a great interest in yer storied kin."

"Huh," was all that Tom could muster to this totally surprising line of conversation.

After a few moments' pause, and the delivery of a pint to an over-imbibing patron, Tom responded to the stranger. "Ye doth know Aunty Liza is no longer in this world?"

"And a sad state of affairs it be . . . my condolences," replied Hopkins almost reverently.

"Actually . . . never met her," Tom replied in an almost contemplative manner, "but me mum has told me stories . . . horrifying stories . . . stories which no one should know of . . ." As Tom's story continued, he began to drift from the present. "It be said me aunty was a witch. They tried to prove she had these, uh, powers. Yea, they tried . . . but failed," concluded Tom with his head slumped and his eyes tearing.

"Who be the 'they', ye speak of?" inquired Hopkins, fully knowing the answer.

"The Crowne — the Crowne tried to kill me Aunt! The Crowne . . . them bastards!" replied Tom, full of emotion. A draining emotion that for the next minute found Tom sinking back into silence while mentally adding this charge to his reasons for departing the Crowne.

Bringing Tom back to the present, Hopkins began, "A tragedy . . . should never happen to anyone . . . especially not kin. Do ya have any memories of yer Aunt Liza?"

"Yea . . . a ring, delivered to me a few years back. They say I am her sole remaining kin . . . why do ye ask?"

"What might this ring look like?" inquired Hopkins, taking all his might to stop the salivation which was beginning.

"Nothing special . . . gold band, reddish stone . . . won't fit me . . . keep meaning to add a chain and wear round me neck," responded Tom in an uninterested manner, a manner quite the inverse of Hopkins.

"Really . . . I collect old rings . . . think ya might consider selling it?" Hopkins asked with each word being carefully formed and each emotion carefully checked to avoid suspicion.

"Sell . . . definitely not . . . it's me auntie's . . . it's all I got . . . me last memory."

"Ah, lad . . . gold and red stirs up the interest of folks . . . sure I couldn't tempt ye?"

At that moment, Tom was summoned from across the room for another ale in payment for a lost wager. Returning to the counter, Tom provided his less than eloquent answer.

"Nay . . . I couldn't sell me Auntie's ring . . . not for a shilling, not for a pound!" Tom asserted; quite certain the conversation would end there.

"Would ye sell for two?" Hopkins proposed, again using carefully crafted words.

"Two . . . two shillings?" certainly not.

"Two pounds, my fine lad . . . two English pounds," countered Hopkins.

Tom hesitated a noticeable time, "Did ye say two pounds, Sir?" Thomas asked, trying to hide his incredulity. As Tom's mind began to process how those two pounds would help his current monetary needs . . . in fact, with the pound he received from

Mr. Hoare, and his savings to date, he would have only two pounds to amass. Considering a few hours ago he had nearly 4 pounds to acquire, not quite two pounds in 6 weeks seemed on the verge of possible.

"What thinks thee lad . . . two pounds for the ring?" asked Hopkins again, retaining his controlled speech.

"Well . . . I suppose if thou wish to possess the ring . . . I may be persuaded to sell it . . . to preserve me auntie's memory."

"Of course . . . a fine choice, Master Tom. Can I trouble ye to bring the ring tomorrow for me inspection?"

"I shall bring auntie's ring as ye request . . . ", responded Tom.

With this parting promise, Hopkins arose and departed the Cantery as mysteriously as he had entered it.

Tom was still shaken by his quite unplanned acquisition of wealth, an acquisition which equaled ten weeks of thatcher wages. The earlier events made Tom nearly unable to provide the last pints and ales of the night. Upon completion of this provision, and the nightly floor swabbing and counter wiping; Tom departed the Cantery, returning home through the unearthly fog and mist.

The following eve, before journeying to the Cantery; Tom opened a nondescript box in the corner of his room and removed a patched cloth that one could easily mistake as a scrap to be tossed. Within the scrap lie the Ring of Eliza, its blood-red center appeared to pulse, its golden band capturing the ring's stray light fragments; magnifying them to brilliance. It was this linen wrapping and this ring that Tom placed in his pocket to finance his escape.

As promised, Hopkins returned in the same eerie manner as the night prior. The still of the night returned, coupled with his unearthly maneuvers toward the bar; the recurring chill emanating from his being.

"Mr. Hopkins, here I be. Good to see ya again . . ." began Tom, as if seeing a long-lost relative.

"Ye has the ring?" inquired Hopkins in a droll, uninterested tone.

"Ya, here she be," replied Tom as he drew the linen from his pocket and placed it upon the bar top, only to be stopped by Hopkins.

"Shall we conduct our business in yonder corner, away from the prying eyes of them who have no part of our transaction?" Hopkins offered in a businesslike tone.

"If ye insist . . ." said Tom as he rose and followed Hopkins to a table in the dimly lit corner.

As Tom unwrapped the ring, the gold band gathered the few fragments of light in the Cantery, causing it to erupt in brilliance. Once again, the stone beckoned those nearby to examine its contents closer — as if drawing the viewer into a portal of Hell.

Hopkins fell backward in shock; not expecting such a spectacular show from the aged jewel.

"May I . . .?" asked Hopkins as he gazed at the ring.

"Surely . . . it will soon be yers," replied Tom, not aware of the spell which the ring cast upon the buyer.

As Hopkins reached for the ring, he experienced a shuddering of his body similar to none he had previously encountered. His hands shook, his glands opened in blatant perspiration, his ears rang, and his muscles convulsed.

"Ye . . . a thing of beauty she is," Hopkins hypnotically stated, quickly returning the ring to Tom to regain his faculties. "I do have a condition for the purchase . . . I will pay the pound now; however, I need the ring's authenticity verified by one in Totnes. If permitted . . . I would like to take the ring for verification and return the day after 'morrow with the remaining pound. If the ring shall not pass, I will return it and ye may keep 10 shillings for the bother."

Tom took this in. "Is't thou saying I shan't get two pounds in total till the day after 'morrow and I won't have me ring?"

"Ye lad. If ye wish the two pounds . . . that be the terms."

Tom's being convulsed in thought, for never had a decision been so life-changing. Failure to deliver the ring assured that he would not be leaving in May. Delivery of the ring brought him very close to his goal; however, a failure of Hopkins to deliver the final pound meant that the goal of 5 pounds would be quite difficult to achieve. Realizing that the delivery of the ring provided a chance, a greater chance of success. Refusal to part with the jewel almost certainly guaranteed failure and acceptance of this existence for the rest of his days. Seeing no genuine option, Tom did the latter and handed the ring to Hopkins. Upon the transference of the ring, a loud and almost ceremonial clap of thunder erupted from distant land within that fiery red portal. From that ring — nay from the Netherworld itself — came a violent shaking of the earth. This tremor was so pronounced that its tale would be told for months to come. Many a misfortune were attributed to the unearthly tremor — a fallen tree, a failed birthing, a clock stopping . . . yea, even a near-permanent deafening. These were all attributed to the shock. A shock traced to a transaction between the nephew of a convicted witch and a denizen, not of this locale — perhaps not of this world.

Immediately upon transferring the prized Ring, Tom sensed an overwhelming regret and darkness engulfing his very soul. Tom's looking out the window momentarily to determine whether the darkness was real allowed a brief lapse for Hopkins to disappear into the mist in a manner quite similar to his arrival.

"I'm not sure if I want to do this . . ." Tom started as he slowly turned toward what was Hopkins. However, Hopkins had been replaced by a foggy chilled air bearing no living being.

"Hopkins!" Tom bellowed as he became more aware of his reality. "Hopkins . . . where ye be?" To which there was no reply by the fog.

Tom looked in his hand at the pound coin and made a mental note of the day Hopkins promised he would return with another. A day conveniently deemed as April 1st. Convenient for Hopkins, as he had promised delivery on All Fools' Day. A day which would forever take on a new meaning to Tom, for at this moment Tom may have become the most fool-hardy of all in the shire.

Upon Hopkins' departure, Tom slowly returned to fetching ale, engaging customers, and constantly amazing Darwin. During these previous two weeks, Tom had been a new man — bright, cheerful, full of mirth and goodwill. Quite the opposite of the annoying loafer and lazy drunk who previously had patronized the Cantery. Amazingly, Tom found that, while working at the Cantery, he didn't need to be drinking. It was as if merely being around the ale and pints served the purpose for which Tom had been spending three ha'penny a nite for hundreds of cock crows. What Tom thought necessary for waking to another morning of thatching was — for at the least the time being — not a necessity of life.

Darwin, like the tablemates who knew Tom, was astounded. Quick, polite, congenial; not a single word uttered by anyone to describe Tom just a month prior. And the most surprising — the patrons enjoyed him. They enjoyed the attention. They marveled at his wit; and, most important to Darwin, they did not bolt from the Cantery in anger or annoyance. A few days into Tom's sobriety and nightly assistance at the Cantery, Darwin approached Tom after the last customer crawled out of the pub on his way to what would become his earthy pillow.

"Tom . . . can we talk?"

"Aye Mr. Darwin."

"Darwin is appropriate, me lad. I really cannot believe I am saying this, but yer quite the bar hand . . . the customers love ye," began Darwin, "I'm now believin' yer services be worthy of pay. What say ye to a shilling a week for helping me as ye have been?"

"Aye . . . I accept, Thank Ye Sir. . . er Darwin, I will not disappoint," Tom replied with sincere appreciation.

And hence began Thomas Smythe's 10-week employ as a helpmate at the Cromwell Crossing Corner Cantery, an engagement which would bring him 10 shillings closer to this goal of 5 pounds. The 5 pounds, which needed to be raised by the end of May, a date approaching far too fast. To secure those prized shillings, Tom spent each night hoisting ale, entertained patrons, and sweeping at opening and closing. All who knew Tom were amazed. He worked by day; he worked by night; and most surprising of all; he complained not.

While Tom worked each night, he kept an eager eye on the front door of the Cantery for the return of Hopkins. Night after night, not a sign. April 1st had come and gone and Tom remained 30 shillings shy of his goal — 20 of those owned by Hopkins. Certainly, he was proud of the 70 shillings he had gathered, nearly 9 month's pay earned in but 10 weeks was a task to be envied; yet Tom needed the complete fare and as the days of May disappeared, the need for the final shillings began to take its toll.

To Tom's dismay, the hope of Hopkins returning was now lost, for it was 45 days since he was to return. Compounding matters, Tom needed to be in Plymouth by noon of 'morrow. Tom had been so busy worrying about Hopkins that he nearly forgot about the other 10 shillings he needed. That be assuming that Hopkins would magically appear in the next 12 hours.   It was in the desperation that Tom sunk to a new low in his otherwise storied existence as ruffian and jailee.

It had been a good evening at the Cantery, with many patrons, many rounds, much frivolity, even more shillings. "Tom, me boy, methinks there be over two pounds in me coin sack," Darwin stated in an unbelieving manner.

"Ya! . . . lots of ale . . . and several bottles of wine thanks to the governours sitting in the corner," Tom added.

"Are ye sure it's over a pound?" Tom asked in a surprised tone.

"How's ya Math? . . . Count if ye wish," offered Darwin.

"Don't mind if I do," and with that, Tom laid out the contents of the sack on the bartop, beginning his count by separating the ha'pennys, tuppences, and pennies.

At 8 shillings, Tom's eyes caught a glimpse of gold under the coinage. Someone had paid with an angel, that coveted angelic 10-shilling coin whose name echoed its appearance. At that moment, Tom lost all self-respect and realized this golden coin — this angel — would be his passage and escape. Looking about, he saw Darwin in the other corner. Reluctantly and shaking, Tom pocketed the angel, the remaining 10 shilling needed for passage. Tossing the coins in the sack, he replied to Darwin. "Lots of smaller coins, only a pound and a half . . . still quite good Sir."

"Really?" asked Darwin in a questioning manner . . . I would have thought more."

"Well, I be off . . . see ya tomorrow." And with that unceremonious exit, Thomas J Smythe would never again grace the premise of the Cromwell Crossing Corner Cantery. Yea, Tom would never again see Darwin nor be able to repay his debt for the angel he stole from his friend, his employer, his mate. These were the thoughts that plagued Tom's mind as he ventured home for the last time.

Returning home after spending several hours wandering Cromwell Crossing, Tom returned to his room and his mattress. From under that mattress lay his sole remaining possession of note — his ledger and sack of coins. Tom retrieved the ledger, his beacon of hope, complete with a notation of the source., to which he added a notation for the 10 shillings just gained. An acquisition he designated 'a shameful act'. The act being the till theft from Darwin earlier that night. The notation of that act appearing blotted and brighter than the others — both as a tormenter and as a physical feature of drying ink.

5s	*sales*
6s	*ale reduction (the Crowne be happy... Tom not)*
20s	*Mr. Hoare loan*
20s	*Hopkins ring payment*
10s	*Cantery wages*
8s	*Higgins farming help*
1s	*bed & shelf sale*
10s	*shameful act*
80s	

With that, Tom grabbed his bags, crumbled the ledger and tossed it into the fireplace edge, and headed toward the front door; his entryway to the future. On route, he passed Aunt Polly's room, her door ajar. Polly was deep in slumber and didn't see Tom pause, look long at his current reality, and take a deliberate step into the early morning air. A step from the known into the unknown; an unknown full of fear, promise, and a new birth for Thomas J. Smythe.

The Flight

During the coming months and weeks, how would he remember that chilled morning in May? Would he see this as a life-changing day? At this moment Tom did not feel any different; however, Tom sensed that he was changing. Changing from a lad in Cromwell Crossing to a man . . . a man of the West. Just an hour prior, he had taken his last walk from his Aunt Polly's house; heaving his lone sack of earthly possessions over his shoulder. This act had begun the nearly 25-mile journey to the shores of Plymouth.

Early morning in Cromwell Crossing brought a chill in the night air as the horizon prepared for the transition from the moon to the rising sun. 10 minutes into the walk, Tom's mind began to wander, for it would be nearly two hours before a chance of transport would avail itself. With a bit of luck, Tom believed he would make Plymouth by 9.

Tom was used to walking. Nearly all his journeys were on foot. However, this was a different walk. This would be a walk of remembrance; a walk of anticipation. With each step, Tom's brain added a beat, and with each beat, a fresh memory. The memories started slowly as the previous 10 weeks replayed themselves in random confusion — memories of the Cantery, of the ledger, of his conversation with Hoare. As Tom walked still further, his mind filled with memories of Hopkins and his promise of payment, of the promise to Higgins, and his promise to Lars. As Tom walked, each of these individual thoughts cascaded one after the other; each fighting for space in Tom's consciousness. Each thought being interrupted by the chill of the pre-dawn air.

So much had happened since Lar's visit in March. Tom recalled the feelings of fear and utter weakness at realizing he had only until the middle of May to raise 5 pounds. The remembrance of that insurmountable feat made Tom pause in his step, and shudder again. Yet here he was, walking to the finish line. Some would wonder why. Considering he traveled with only 4 pounds — a situation he knew not what the resolution would be. Still, he moved forward — not letting a few shillings deter his goal, nor affect his future.

For a moment, Tom's brain cleared of thought; this mental clearing being caused by an encouraging sight. 'Mary Tav ahead' — stated the broken wooden sign at the bend. Three miles down, twenty-two to go, mused Tom as his thoughts returned to the days of April, to his meeting with Mr. Hoare.

Hardly believing his luck at actually meeting this titan of England's financial structure, much less being invited into his office, Tom remembered the conversation as if it were yesterday. Upon being summoned by Mr. Hoare, Tom slowly crossed the threshold of the heavy mahogany door, and at his crossing, the door swung shut, beginning the ensuing conversation. "Mr. Smythe . . .", Mr. Hoare started, "I trust that is your preferred manner of address?"

Unbelief was my memory of the moment. Before me was this man . . . this leader of industry who had no earthly reason for sharing more than three words with me. Those three being — 'off you be' — whether being told to get off his land, chair, or cart. Instead, Mr. Hoare had continued, " My apologies for any ill caused by the likes of Cuthbert Houblon. I view him and his associates as blemishes upon this society. There be no excuse for one who intentionally intends to waste the time of a respected worker like yourself. Please know a majority of my acquaintances are not at all like him."

Tom remembered he was still in unbelief at the respect being offered and, for a moment, feared the current conversation was an ale-inspired dream; one from which he would awaken at any moment. Respect was not a term ever associated with Tom's being; especially when spoken by one of Mr. Hoare's standing in the community.

"It would seem you came for assistance . . . perhaps a venture? Pray tell me your plans," were the words which Tom heard as his mind returned to the present after realizing this was reality.

"Well, Sir . . .", Tom began, "I wish to venture to the West . . . to start anew . . . to be an influencer. In short Sir, I feel predestined with no foreseeable hope for a future." Predestined and foreseeable were terms he learned from Lars, the use of which made Mr. Hoare's eyes twitch and take a keener note at the one before him.

"Predestined, eh? Well, Mr. Smythe, no one should be in a box, society should encourage flourishment . . . I applaud you, young man!" was the unexpected response received from Mr. Hoare.

"How can I help you escape predestination and make your future, shall we say . . . positively foreseeable?"

"Well Sir, I have amassed 2 of me required 5 pounds for passage to the West. I came to you upon Mr. Houblon's suggestion that I may borrow some of my necessary funding." Tom recalled how surprised he was at how naturally this request left his lips. It was as if requests for sums of this size were a common part of his day. Upon this revelation, I spent the next few minutes describing my meeting of Lars, our adoration of Sir Walter Raleigh, and our fixation with the Crowne. After providing these details, I spoke of my encounter with Hopkins and other bits of gleeful discourse, all of which ended with the single phrase. . . "I shall pay ye back Sir".

Mr. Hoare had politely taken in the narrative of Tom's life and after a brief staring out the window at the horizon, he chuckled and replied, "No worries there Mr. Smythe, I can see you are a man of integrity, and yer word is ye bond."

As Tom walked, rethinking this discourse, he remembered how stunned he was that Mr. Hoare did not challenge his ability to repay the loan. Not wanting to change the course of the conversation, Tom had continued the discussion. "Aye, Sir . . . that I be. Doth thou think ye can assist?" This was the hesitant inquiry that Tom had made. Tom recalled the growing pit in his stomach as every inch of his being strove to hear the words emitting from Mr. Hoare's lips. At that very moment, Tom's ears could only hear ringing bells announcing the 10:00 hour. No matter how hard he discerned, he could not hear Mr. Hoare's answer to his plea. The pealing of the bells forced Tom to ask, "perchance Sir could you repeat your answer, the bells of yonder St. Paul's disrupted me hearing."

A brief second passed and Mr. Hoare briefly chuckled, responding, "Mr. Smythe, it would be me honor to assist an adventurer like yourself in the fulfillment of a dream. . . in declaring your predestination moot."

And with that remembrance — those few words of trust, those words of aspiration, those words with unknown meanings, Tom returned to the present. A present which presented a sign for Plymouth in the distance. A discolored stone reading, 'Plymouth, 20 mi'.

Am I a simpleton? Perhaps Polly was right. Maybe I am witless, yet another common fool? These were the thoughts that came to Tom as the light of day began with the sun's glimmer of orange, making its daily presence known. The sun's rising marking a more symbolic morn than most, and by its light, Tom continued his pace; noticing with greater intent all that would soon be behind him.

Passing a fully developed oak, one which had been spared when the road was established, Tom could only imagine that trees of this age were commonplace in the West and that if felled, he might well be the feller. He would be creating the society, a society that differed greatly from the one of which he currently was a part. Tom desired to change society. For a change meant that youths of the future would not be put in a position to leave all they knew — nay to escape all they knew. Not only was Tom's mind flitting about at a dizzying pace, but his senses were also overly aroused, noting the arboreal world surrounding him. As with the oak, which Tom observed the likes of regularly but had never contemplated; this early morn rewarded Tom with a similar awareness of the passing streams, flowers, and fauna. Which of these species would he see again in the land out West? He believed it safe to say that he would encounter again the willowy morning mist or light as air butterflies. What was he leaving? Should he stop and return home? 4 pounds would be a wondrous windfall for himself and Aunt Polly. So much could be fixed, so much could be provided. The roof would not leak, the windows would be clear and unbroken, their beds more than smashed feathers which had long given up their fluff. These were the contemplations of Tom as he continued his pace towards Plymouth — the gateway to His West.

'One thousand and two'. . . 'one thousand and three'. This was the mental exercise of the moment. A mile back, Tom had decided that counting would be an interesting diversion. After all, he had extinguished memories of acquiring the money, of flora and fauna, and his future lodging. It was during his progression to ten thousand that he was interrupted by a familiar sound that began to rattle his facilities — that long-anticipated cadence of horse hooves to the road. The familiar clickity-clack was finally heard by Tom's ears. A sound that swiftly and instantly brought him back to reality. Re-engaged, Tom stopped and looked toward the sound.

Paying closer attention, Tom heard an even more joyous sound, for along with the horse hooves came a dull sound, the sound made by a wheel against the earth. A cart! The still unviewed horseman was towing a cart! Tom could hardly contain his glee.

Closer and closer came the sounds until finally rounding the bend a black aged barb with an equally aged rider came into view. Behind the pair was towed a rickety cart partially filled with lamps, knockers, and others of the metallic variety. Tom's transport plans now rested with a seller of all that be metallic. Snickering at this thought, Tom stood silent, looking toward the rider, and waved his hands in the event the rider was sleeping or distracted. Meeting his eyes, the rider saw Tom and the single bag he had slung over his shoulder. "Whoa, Archer," came the call which broke the silence of the dawn.

"A tad early, is not it boy . . . heading to work, are ye?"

"Aye good Sir, that I be. Perchance are ye going as far as Plymouth, Sir?"

"As sure as a toad is slimy, I be."

Tom's heart raced, "mind you good Sir, would ye entertain the thought of me riding in your cart to Plymouth? The road is long and I shall be quite exhausted and unable to work if I make the entire journey on foot."

Hesitation which seemed a fortnight followed, and then a grin followed by "surely lad . . . welcome aboard."

And with that beckon, Tom crawled into the rickety cart, joining the castoffs of others — now prizes of their new purveyor. "Comfy are ye, the road is rocky and there be nearly 18 miles in travel to Plymouth . . . but it shall be better than a 6-hour walk."

"Finer than the Palace of Westminster, good Sir . . . again me thanks ye for providing me passage."

"Then off we go."

As the cart moved forward, Tom's brain returned to revisiting his exploits of the previous weeks. With the repetitive cadence of wheels turning, cart rocking, and almost cyclic bumps; Tom's brain was recollecting a conversation held at the Cantery some 2 weeks prior. A conversation that resulted in 8 more of his shillings. Tom recalled clearing a table on an otherwise uneventful Tuesday night. He had turned to return to the counter only to find a gent immediately behind him.

"You be Tom?" the stranger asked.

"That I be . . . for whom do I have this honor?" Tom responded in his new persona, reeking of properness and politeness.

"My name be Higgins, and I hear you're a changed man . . . a man who now possesses strong work morals. I have a proposition for a man with your ethics and morals." With that opening, the request began, "May I interest you in assisting with a farming venture in 8 weeks? I need me beans harvested. Seems to be a robust crop, and I need dependable help. I shall pay 6 shillings for your time, and shall pay in advance to reserve your person for the 3 sessions in July. What say ye . . . doth ye have interest?"

"Aye, Mr. Higgins, I appreciate your seeking me out, but as you can see with yer own eyes, I be employed by Mr. Darwin. I can't just abandon me good tapster." Pausing a moment, Tom continued. "However, . . . you are giving me several weeks' notice. Would ye consider 8 shillings payable this week to reserve my time and talents for this noblest of tasks?" Tom uttered to the stranger, not believing the eloquent prose being uttered from his lips.

Several words were exchanged and ultimately, Higgins accepted and placed 8 shillings in Tom's hand, putting him nearer his goal. With that, Tom began to once again mentally count his shillings. With each count came the rhythm of the wheels, ruts, and trots sounding in unison, lulling Tom to sleep. What seemed like only a moment passed before Tom felt a shaking on his shoulder. "Lad we be here. Welcome to Plymouth . . . that be your destination, be it not?"

Struggling to wake when Tom heard the word Plymouth, a bolt of lightning struck through his body. "Whhhaaa . . . whaaatttt time would it be good Sir?" inquired Tom in a groggy manner, emitting noises of one who had either just awoke or was still half snockered.

"From the look of the sun and the shadows drawn; I would say close to 9 am," replied his driver.

Jumping up, Tom grabbed his bag, ensured he had his sack of coins, and bid the cartman adieu; dropping a farthing into his hand for appreciation.

Seeking his orientation, Tom headed toward a profound smell of fish and salt. Seeing a trio of well-dressed businessmen, Tom approached them with his recently acquired air of achievement. "Excuse me fine Sirs, where would the docks be?"

Looking first at Tom and then around their surroundings, they first snickered and then pointed to the West. "Bout 3 streets that way . . . over three and ye shall fall into the drink."

"Thank ye," replied Tom and made his way the last blocks from home to port.

So engaged was Tom that when he arrived at the docks of Plymouth at 5 minutes till 9, he almost walked past Lars as he headed toward a crowd.   Not thinking of what to expect in Plymouth, Tom was a bit surprised by the crowd. Slowly forming, Tom beheld a group of 50 men, women, and children who were forming a line near the plank of the single ship tied to the mooring.

"Yo Tom . . . Tom, over here mate . . . don't you recognize me?" joked Lars as he waved his arms, trying to attract Tom's attention over the din of those assembling.

Consciousness immediately became reality and Tom's cacophony of thoughts screeched to a halt as he heard Lar's voice and saw his smiling face and waving arms.

"Oh . . . sorry mate . . . kind of preoccupied," Tom offered as his excuse. "Is Plymouth always this busy early on a Tuesday morn?"

"Well, it is not every day that the dreams of these fifty are about to be met."

"Fifty? . . .What fifty?" asked Tom, initially believing Lars to be joking until he began taking further notice of the assembling men, women, and children milling about the docked ship.

"Tom, me boy . . . all these fine folks . . . just like you, wish to begin a new life in the lands out

West. Unlike you . . . they will not be governours. Look upon your charges for ye be their protectorate."

Comprehending this for the first time, Tom could only survey the crowd and utter a weak . . . "me".

"Ya, you . . . tis a grand day for the governours of the West. Speaking of grand. Can't believe you earned those 100 shillings — that's quite the feat, me mate," responded Lars with a smile that covered his face.

"Uhhh . . . about that."

"About what?" Lars asked, his tone changing as the words exited his mouth. As joy changed to fear, Lars' next words were spoken with chilling precision. "Have ye the 100 shillings, or have ye not?"

Silence.

"Tom . . . you have 100 shillings? Please tell me you do?" inquired Lars in a now severely serious tone. A tone verging on fear.

"Well . . . almost," replied Tom in a tone far too casual and cavalier for the importance of the ask.

"Almost! . . . Almost will get you passage to the tip of England, but not beyond! Almost will find you walkin' on those white caps toward the West! Almost means . . . that I be going alone." Lars retorted angrily to Tom in growing annoyance with each word.

"I'll do something," said a dazed and partially confused Tom. "Do ye know the captain?"

"I do . . . old cuss goes by McGuilocutty. He'll drink you under the table and takes no disrespect, not from man, nor beast. It be his ship and if you don't like it, he will make you leave . . . whether near shore or leagues from land. You get no second chance." Allowing these words to sink in, Lars continued his previous rant, "How could you do this to yer pal . . . yer mate?"

However, Tom was too distracted and dare we say, on the verge of giddy to appreciate the gravity of the situation. His mind was soaring over those white caps and flying free as a bird of the air toward a new destiny. As Tom turned toward the ship, the words of Mr. Hoare resounded in his brain, serving as an irrevocable act of encouragement. 'It would be my honor to assist an adventurer like yourself in the fulfillment of his dream . . . in declaring your predestination moot.' Armed with this confidence, Tom turned toward the lone ship, unaware of Lars' continued verbal assault.

Tom now gazed upon his vessel to freedom. In her youth, the carrack would have been a stately gem. Tom could envision the imposing frame rising nearly 130 feet from the waterline, the billowing sails filled with gusts driving the vessel effortlessly toward her destination. The myriad of ropes, almost web-like, traversing sail and deck pulley. Aye, a true ship of dreams she would have been. But now, her spritely youth had vanished and her stateliness deteriorated with a patchwork of repairs. Her sails mending lacked uniformity, her rigging knotted in repair, nearly half of her glassed windows wooded, and the most notable repair of all, the plank which bore her name. During a repair, one had consciously — or unconsciously — affixed a board from a shipping box. For now, and perhaps for the rest of her sea-going life, my vessel to freedom, my ship of dreams, was to be known as — Figs. Emblazoned upon her hull, where others had affixed a nom d'elegance or a whimsical phrase, my ship bore the name 'Figs'. I can only presume one who repaired the ship needed a final board and, looking about, had spotted one which dimensionally was correct. Yes, the single word 'Figs' greeted all who sought the name of their transport. 'Figs' would be taking Tom, Lars, crew, and passengers to the land out West. 'Figs' would be their chariot to freedom.

Beginnings

In his excited and tired state, Tom almost fell on the rickety gangway — a gangway serving as the portal to his dreams. Unfortunately, at that moment, observing his gangway acrobatics stood Captain McGuilocutty, surveying his kingdom and exerting control over all within.

"Aye lad . . . only crew now . . . me hourglass is not yet empty," his authoritative voice boomed from the deck.

"I be a governour, Sir . . . I was told I could board," Tom hesitantly responded to the commanding voice.

"Thou speak the truth . . . had me concerns for a wee moment . . . thought ye be a new crew member who had over-imbibed. I'll have no ruffs nor netherstocks sailing on me ship. Those who work on me ship are real men, and I don't take kindly to landlubbers sailin', swabbin' or even sittin' on me ship if they be not here to work." Enjoying his authority, the captain continued, ". . . part of ye job governour will be to keep these non-workers — these Londoner's — away from me and my crew. I'll provide them passage . . . but they must stay out of me way." Realizing that he still did not know the identity of the one before him, McGuilocutty asked . . . "What be yer name?"

Hesitantly Tom began . . . "Sir, I be Tom Smythe, of . . ."

"You? You be Smythe . . . if that be true, your mate Lars be a liar!" McGuilocutty expounded, almost tripping over his own words. "The Tom Smythe I was told of was a seasoned adventurer . . . a conqueror of obstacles . . . a sea-faring lad with experiences beyond his years. The boy before me can barely climb a gangway! Surely you must be another Smythe? I promised Lars passage for Smythe at 100 shillings . . . that be because Lars said you were experienced and could help me crew if need be. If you can't even walk me entry plank, you be useless . . . no better than a gross o gobermouch."

Tom was taking this all in and getting even more anxious. "Aye Sir . . . I be that same Smythe and Lars spoketh the truth . . . adventures I welcome. Me lead in life has been Sir Walter Raleigh, the esteemed explorer, and adventurer . . . surely you've heard of him?"

A hearty laugh ensured, "Ah boy, I has heard and has met the great Sir Walter Raleigh, and may I suggest if adventure it is you seek, that you seek at a location beside me gangway. You be blocking the plank and halting me crew."

Tom turned around and saw 4 snarling lads smelling of the sea and wearing hats adorned with large fish hooks. Each were holding large crates which they were trying to bring onto the ship; but for Tom blocking the sole entrance.

"Move it Raleigh," one lad said in a snide, laughing tone. "If ye want adventure, I'm sure I can find you some exploring the bowels of this here ship as ye try to escape one of these crates."

"Yea boy, if adventure ye wish, I'll be glad to acquaint you later with the adventurous innards of a freshly caught marlin." An abundance of raucous laughter ensued as the crew made sport of Tom.

"Better move boy, me mates are tiring of that crate weight and unless you want to lug them by yerself, I strongly suggest you move forward onto me ship."

Following the directions of the captain, Tom finished the final foot-long walk of the gangway with a confidence that would make that sea dog Drake proud. Just off the gangway and on the deck, Tom stood face to face with Carmine McGuilocutty, his present obstacle to his westward dream.

"So, you be Smythe? . . . yer mate Lars speaks highly of ye. But your performance on me gangplank was not the most assuring. Sell yerself boy . . . why should I take you West? Lots of folks would wish passage for a mere 100 shillings. Why should I take ye?"

Before answering, Tom's life flashed before his eyes as he remembered parts of how he got here. There were Mr. Hoare, Hopkins, and Darwin. He mustn't forget Dawson and Aunt Polly, nor earning nearly a year's pay in 3 months. Where to start, thought Tom; and then, as if inspired by Sir Walter Raleigh himself, he began.

"Good Sir . . . a year ago I was a ruffian thatcher, a hard worker spending each day atop houses, climbing ladders in fit weather and bad. Twas my job to mud and thatch through scorching sun and driving rain. Working for ale money was me life. Till last year, that be all I knew . . . climbing, thatching, and aleing. Then I met Lars and heard of the opportunities in the lands to the West. It was

Lars who gave me vision. It was Lars who led me to you . . . the realizer of dreams. Three months ago, I had five shillings to me name as I had consumed the rest in weekly bouts at me local Cantery . . . me provider of ale. Then Lars reentered me life and intensified me dream of escape, me dream of starting a new life, me dream of one-day meeting Sir Walter Raleigh, himself. It was this dream which led me to Mr. Hoare, a banker some three blocks from this site and the acquisition of another pound. Another two pounds were to be received from the sale of an esteemed family possession to a trader and scoundrel who promised payment in full. I too indentured meself to another for farm labor, and took on a second job where I consumed ale nightly." Catching his breath, Tom concluded. "A survivor of all; I stand humbly before thee seeking passage on your stately vessel."

Pausing for a moment, McGuilocutty did a final mental inspection of Tom before stating, ". . . well that be quite the story and quite the work ethic . . . I applaud thee. Almost made me flush with pride. Almost . . . I say. Therefore, as I be a man of me word for payment of 100 shillings, I accept you onto me ship and wish you good fortune for your future." Reaching out his hand, McGuilocutty made the request that Tom had been avoiding. "The 100 shillings, if ye will, Master . . . or shall I say Governour Smythe."

With that, Tom's stomach sank to a previously unknown depth. "Well Sir . . . about that."

McGuilocutty immediately changed his tone. The tone of his voice deepened, his stature stiffened and his words more direct.

"The 100 shillings . . . you do have the payment . . . don't you boy?"

"Nearly . . . good Sir."

"How nearly?"

"Eighty Sir."

"Last I checked eighty did not equal 100. Unless you know some higher mathematics than I and Copernicus."

"No Sir . . . that it is not."

"Heavens to Murgatroyd . . . why be you wastin' me time? Off me ship . . . off me ship now or I shall have me crew toss ye into these chilled waters."

"Oh, please Sir. A scoundrel took me family heirloom . . . me mum's ring, he promised me 2 pounds payment in full and only delivered 1 pound. I waited some 45 days for his return. Please Sir can't we barter or come to an agreement?"

"Not me issue lad . . . you have nothing I need. No is what I said — no is what I mean," McGuilocutty said in his firm and authoritarian voice. "Not 100 shillings, not 100 feet shall ye go toward the West."

"But Sir . . ."

"Doth thee really wish me crew to deposit ye on the shore? I have a feeling they may not treat you as gently as you would like."

"But . . ."

"Off!"

And with that, Tom's hopes and dreams immediately emptied. His bucket of hope had sprung an irreparable leak and his hopes and dreams drained to the earth, en route to the cistern which epitomized Tom's existence. How could he face Darwin? Would his employer take him back after failing to show? What will Polly say? How will... Alas, the Crowne had won. Tom was indentured for life . . . indentured to a life of no purpose . . . a life of no hope. Turning his back on his dreams, Tom entered the gangway and proceeded in the wrong direction . . . the direction of failure . . . the direction of loss . . . the direction of defeat. Just a few feet from shore, a shout distracted Tom during his mental disassembly of plans made.

"Yo boy . . . this could be your lucky day."

As if a charging stallion had encountered the end of a forged chain, Tom's mental gymnastics immediately ceased; nearly causing him to fall and, for a moment, taking away his voice.

"Uhhh, uuuhh, wha . . ." was all Tom could muster. Still questioning whether this moment was real, Tom looked toward the voice.

"Did ye say your job had you climbin'?"

Returning to mental clarity, Tom replied, "Aye Sir, daily . . . up and down . . . sometimes 10 or 20 times in a single day."

"Turns out me topper got a case of the consumption, and won't be joining us. You know what a topper is?"

"One who climbs to the top?" Tom said in a slow response as he chose each word precisely, trying to hide his ignorance of his role. During his brief response, he pointed to the spar, hoping to provide some moniker of knowledge.

McGuilocutty snickered a snotty partial laugh. "There ye be, acting like you 'ave skill where ye have none. But I do say, a worthy attempt ye make." McGuilocutty continued, "A topper be the one who climbs to the spars to furl and unfurl the sails. He'll work in pleasant weather and he'll work in bad. In storms that try the souls of the most seasoned, me topper is up there ensuring our safe passage. Won't lie . . . is a dangerous job and one which no one wants nor wishes for their worst foe . . . hence, the opening. No one wants to be the topper. Doth thee?"

In this split-second, Tom realized his response would separate his life of mediocrity and certain dissatisfaction from that of a founder. Would his life be a shilling-less one or a life of potential fortune? Would his life be one of an unknown or would he separate himself from others? Finally, would his life be one that Sir Walter Raleigh would take notice? To all these, Tom provided the only acceptable response — "Aye Sir . . . I be your topper!"

"Then stop yer lollygagging! Figs awaits yer boarding. Payment for the topper be 25 shillings. Mr. Smythe, you'll be entering your new world with 5 shillings in yer vest. Welcome to the crew of Figs . . . welcome to your transport to lands West. Stow ye bag for we be needing you soon."

Receiving his first command, Tom officially boarded his ship of dreams. With each step, Tom left behind another part of his Cromwell Crossing life. Gone were Tom the bar assistant, the thatcher, the nephew, the drunk, the ruffian, the . . . thief. He regretted the last descriptor; however, bad as he felt, if not for that act of thievery, his feet would not be on the rocking rickety deck of this soon-to-be seafaring vessel. At this moment, Tom vowed to make amends 10-fold when an opportunity presented himself for funds to be provided to one returning Eastbound. But for now, Tom began another phase of this life's journey. "Topper Tom", would be his new moniker. A temporary one it would be, as Tom foresaw upon arrival in the West an exchange of this title for one of Founder. As Lars had explained, each of the governours who entered the new land would be christened with the elite title, Founder of the West. A title worthy of praise from all, including Sir Walter Raleigh — the ultimate Founder.

Upon officially boarding Figs, Tom provided his sack of coins to the outstretched hand of McGuilocutty. A nod of approval was the sole indication of this transfer of Tom's wealth. Walking past the captain, Tom began following his first official order — the stowing of his meager belongings. In searching out a door or hatch to the lower levels, Tom came upon another of the crew. However, instead of growling threateningly, this sailor was humming a tune and looking quite happy. Quite the opposite of the crew members encountered minutes before. As he neared, Tom extended a hand of civility. "Aye mate, I be Tom . . . you be part of the crew?"

"Aye . . . I be Quibbs. Figs be me home, so I guess I be crew," replied the sailor, almost whimsically, while accepting Tom's handshake.

"Quibbs, me mate, can you lead me to where me bag goes? Cap said to stow it below . . . I be looking for a hatch."

"Follow me . . . I'll show ye," replied Quibbs as he motioned for Tom to follow.

Following Quibbs to the lower level, Tom was first struck by the noises — of which there were several. The loud creaking of wood, the whistling of the wind, the sounds of water lapping the sides of Figs. Some sounds were gentle, others harsh; all emanating from the carrack. Observing these, Tom had to wonder whether Figs was seaworthy. An inopportune snap or a deluge of water from a hole could mean the demise of Figs like her majesty's Mary Rose. Tom wanted not to be memorialized on a plaque reserved for those lost at sea; rather, he desired notoriety as that of Founder. With this in mind, he continued to follow Quibbs past what he would soon learn to be the capstan and steerage rooms.

"What brings ye on board?" inquired Quibbs, a lad of probably 20, with a complexion salted from days at sea and hair bleached from wind and sun.

"A change," Tom replied tersely, not providing near the rationale to satisfy Quibbs.

"Change, eh . . . you didn't just want to move to Scotland?"

"Aye, the Crowne would follow me there," sighed Tom, providing Quibbs a bit more context.

"Follow you . . . are you wanted? Did ye filch the Crowne Jewels?" asked Quibbs, half hoping he was in the presence of one on the lam.

"Not quite . . . just want to be free to drink a pint for a fair wage and not have to endure a campaign for economic reform," lamented Tom in a voice indicating both annoyance and impending defeat.

"Glory be!" a surprised Quibbs exclaimed, "you be lordship material. I know no one who has ever uttered the word economics. Are you one of those uvarsity types?" asked Quibbs, emphasizing the 'var' in uvarsity. Only equation I know is that the 70-day war was longer than the 10-week war."

"You do know they lasted the same amount of time?" snickered Tom, beginning to enjoy the company of Quibbs.

Arriving at their destination, Quibbs asked, "Which bunk do you want?" Quibbs' inquiry returning Tom to the reality of his new home in the rear of Figs. The room was a palatial 15 feet long. Affixed to the walls were 10 bunks with hooks and netting tween each for the worldly goods of those who called it home.

"Choose a bunk, me lord. Which would be worthy of an economic master like yerself? You should know that yer bunk may be another's. When you sleep, he be awake; when you toppin', he be at rest."

Taking in the majestic offerings before him and briefly reminiscing of the considerably more space he had at Aunt Polly's, Tom replied, pointing to the top bunk on the far wall, "this be my new home."

"Seems right for our topper," snickered Quibbs.

"What do I do with me possessions?" Tom asked as he surveyed the room, still holding his bag.

"This all we get, bunk and hook . . . nothing more. I be happy there ain't water on the floor like some of me other sleeping areas," offered Quibbs in explanation.

"I'll take the bunk right under ye. Please try not to step on me face as you ascend to the lofts."

Tom was still taking in the reality of the accommodations when he was disrupted. Suddenly the noise level on Figs rose as confused commoners began to swarm the corridors of Figs.

"'Cuse me Sirs, where be the Sleeping Rooms? I be told they were down here," inquired an older gent with a hesitant lass peeking behind his shoulder.

"Other end of the ship. Go back to the deck and head down a level. There ye shall find the grande parlour," Quibbs replied with a flourish of his hands pointing in the proper direction.

"Thank ye," responded the gent.

"Guess they be letting the frolickers on," replied Quibbs in anticipation of further interruptions.

"Why do ye call them frolickers?"

"They do no work, they eat the food, they gaze over the rail, and they expect us to get dem to der next home . . . Sounds like the life for me. What thinks thee, Tom?"

Before Tom could answer, another crew member appeared at the door.

"There be a Tom here? Tom the Topper. I be lookin' for Tom the Topper . . ." bellowed another sandy-haired seaworthy lad also not more than 20 years of age.

"That be me," responded Tom in a voice that belied his true capabilities.

"Cap wants you on deck . . . sails need unfurled and checked before sailing . . . we sail within the hour."

"Coming mate," replied Tom, fearing any delay would expose his farce and lose his dream forever.

Setting his bag on the bunk, Tom hesitated only long enough to grab a single possession., an innocuous glass bottle.   Heading to the deck, Tom began his adventure, one which he hoped he had not over-committed. Reaching the deck, Tom peered over the rail. Spying a young lad on the shore, he called to the boy. "Eh lad, me mate, up here . . . catch this bottle and deliver it to my Aunt Polly. Her address be on the bottle."

"Surely Mister!" the boy replied, as if the King of England had just tasked him with delivering a crucial battle plan.

Mister, thought Tom . . . that's a first . . . surely a harbinger of good luck and new beginnings. Perhaps the boy mistook him for one of the ship's officers. Hmmm, thought Tom, Captain Smythe — I like it. Returning to the present, Tom hurled the bottle to the boy, who handily caught it and read the address.

"I won't let you down, Sir," responded the lad affirmatively.

Furled within that bottle was the last text that Tom would write from English soil.

Aunt Polly,

I be off to the lands out West.
As one of the first upon those shores,
I be told I shall be called Governour,
Therefore, upon your visit, I,
Governour Tom, shall be able to care
for you, just as you have cared for
me. I look forward to meeting up
with you at Candlemas next.

Tom

Glorious Beginnings

$\mathfrak{T}$he approaching shouts brought Tom back to reality; shouts that increased by the moment. "Topper! . . . When we call, ye need to come quicker . . . Now climb those ropes and ensure all is secure on the main!" bellowed a ship's officer Tom would later find to be one Cornelius Sark. Cornelius Sark was a man without an original idea who only echoed loudly the commands of others.

"Sorry Sir . . . I had to send a note home to me Aunt . . . Not sure when I will see her again."

"Do you wish to stay with ye Aunt? If not, then do as I say . . . otherwise, I'll rid this ship of you before we pull anchor . . . understand?"

"Aye . . . Sir," responded Tom in a voice more meek than manly.

"Now get to it! Those sails need securing. If ye didst not know, our sailing awaits you!" exclaimed Sark, putting Tom's task in perspective.

With that, Tom grabbed the halyard in one hand and the shroud in another; proceeding to climb as if it were a solid rung. The difference being, a ladder is sturdier than a rope; especially a rope billowing in the wind. As a gust caught the sail and reverberated through the ropes, Tom felt his ladder giving way and, with it, his arms. Upon encountering the foreign force of physics; Tom fell backward, making quite the thud on the deck, causing the observing crew to laugh a raucous laugh.

"Yo boy, ever climbed a ladder?" mused a crew member.

"He must think the job was fallin' and not climbin'," chimed in another.

"Up . . . not down, boy, you do know sky from the sea, don't ye?" echoed yet another at Tom's expense.

Frustrated at his failure, Tom rose and began the ascent a second time. This time, Tom made it halfway up the sheeting attached to the spar. Resting for a moment; Tom took a breath before reaching for the next rung of rope. He missed.

The crew on deck watched with humor and horror as Tom fell backward, only catching himself at the last second before the 20-foot fall would have surely resulted in Tom's demise or a disabling injury sending him ashore and ending his noble aspiration. Through all the laughter, catcalls, and joking, a single powerful voice made it to Tom's ear.

"Look up boy . . . don't look down." It was the voice of the captain. The voice bore no humor or chastisement, only direction, guidance, and a hint of empathy.

Tom heard the direction loud and clear and affixed his eyes on the target — the spar closest to the lift. Once again, Tom began the ascent; however, this time he successfully completed the final 7 feet of his climb. Reaching his target on the mainmast, he looked down at those on deck. Reveling in his accomplishment, he charged his naysayers in an appropriately challenging manner.

"Come on ye landlubbers . . . I be waitin' fer ye to take out the slack . . . the West awaits."

"You heard our topper . . . he did his job . . . now you do yours," commanded McGuilocutty; his voice rising from the din and causing frivolity to cease as the work of sailing began.

Immediately those on deck began their tasks, ignoring Tom as he descended. Reaching the deck, Tom was met by McGuilocutty, who put an arm on Tom's shoulder, looked him in the eye, and began, "Lad, you've never done this before, have ye?" a slight snicker enunciating the spoken words.

"Er . . . climbed a ladder . . . oh Sir, I've climbed many a ladder," began Tom thinking quickly in his response.

"On a ship, boy . . . you've never climbed on a ship," continued the captain, knowing the answer.

"A ship? Well, er, ah . . ." stumbled Tom.

"Don't need an answer lad. I know the answer. I'm not going to take back me generous offer . . . you'll still have passage West. You got more courage than most, and I admire that," McGuilocutty said in an almost paternal manner.

"But ye has to ask if ye don't know. I alone have control over ye body be. If I see fit for ye to walk that there plank . . . so be it. But I also have the power to keep ye safe . . . despite the caterwauling of these here sailors. Understand?"

"Aye," Tom said shakily, "Gramercy . . . Thank ye Cap."

"Well, go on and spend some time watching how a ship works."

"Aye Sir . . . Gramercy . . .."

"One more task, Mr. Topper. I suggest a visit to the head . . . or as you may call it . . . the loo. I detect a soiling stench that be coming from no fish."

With that, Tom completed his first task as a topper. A story he would repeat often in the coming weeks . . . a story he would hold in his memory for retelling to Aunt Polly upon their reuniting.

As Tom gathered his thoughts upon exit from the head and began to take in the surrounding activities, Figs moaned and creaked, pulling at her tethers awaiting release. As Tom studied the assorted ropes, he heard a familiar voice.

"Still aboard . . . I would have lost that bet," began Lars. "You boarded with only 80 shillings, you got yerself a job as a topper, you failed twice in your ascent, and after a talk with the Cap, yer still here. I surely be in the presence of one with the spirit of the great Sir Walter Raleigh."

"Aye, you know what them challenges be . . . a plot . . . yea, a plot by the Crowne," Tom replied, looking directly at Lars and trying to put the events of the last hour into perspective. "Just another opportunity for the Crowne to further their shadow over all in their kingdom. The Crowne wants me not to succeed. Those heathens wish me not to be governour. The Crowne . . ."

"Aye my friend, I doubt if the Crowne is personally trying to ruin your life, but if that be yer belief, what better reason to escape," replied Lars with a touch of rationalization for his clearly annoyed and slightly delusional friend.

"Aye but remember, the Crowne . . . those bastards were planning to control me liquor consumption by fixin' me wages. Did they not?" Not waiting for a response, Tom continued his rant. "Now the Crowne be ensuring I don't make it to the western world. Aye, if I fall and break me back, the Crowne has won. You know what this means . . . I must be a genuine threat! The Crowne wants me gone," replied Tom in a calculating, almost psychotic manner. A manner which, after listening to his own words, caused Tom to assume a slight smirk and mischievous glimmer.

"Yep, Sir Walter Raleigh was probably discussing you at the palace just last night," mused Lars as he saw that sense was slowly returning to his shipmate. "Before your heroics affect your delusional abilities, can ye spare a bit of time to meet your fellow governours?"

"Ah, where be me mates?" asked Tom, registering excitement at meeting his fellow leaders.

"We meet in the storage area for the barrels of food . . . few visit that area," mused Lars.

And with that Tom followed Lars out the door, through the steerage and capstan room, across the deck, and into the galley, a room now occupied by a mismatched group . . . a group to be known as . . . governours.

Entering the room, Lars proclaimed, "Aye mates, greetings to ya. You have before ye one Thomas J. Smythe. Tom and I spent a night in the House at Cromwell Crossing. Me for public intoxication and Tom for public incitation. Those 'in's' will get you every time." Lars's emphasis on the word 'in' brought muffled laughter from those assembled and a delayed bellow by another.

"Easy Barns, tis not that funny," said Lars in response, to which the bellowing abruptly stopped.

Lars began, "We have the 6 of you assembled for the first time. As recorded history shall affirm, the first meeting of the governours of the New World occurred on May 24th, 1588, onboard Figs en route to the lands out West. Congrats me fellow governours!" With that flourish of pageantry, Lars brought the assembly to order.

"Gents, please say your name and for those with a colorful moniker, please add that. Let's start with you Barns."

In the back of the room, there sat a giant of a man with a bright red nose and wisps of red hair poking out from beneath his cap. Even while sitting, the man rose a full head above the others. "I be Bertram Gleissen. They call me Barns . . . don't know why . . . but that's what I go by."

"Would it be because ye es big as a barn?" offered a lad seated by the stove.

"Thank ye Barns . . . since Squint is so quick-witted today, he can go next."

"That be me . . ." Quinton Partridge, at your service. "They call me Squint, as me eyes aren't what they used to be. Too many days making dem hats."

"Despite his lack of vision, Squint be quite adept at seeing futures," added Lars.

"Next man," Lars added to keep the meeting going.

Laughter was followed by a squeak. "Uh, next be me. I be Timothy O' Toole, but you can call me Mouse, as these old goats seem to have trouble hearing me speak."

"Did ye say speak or squeak?" to which laughter erupted again.

The next man to speak was Titus Mongier. A man whose sole comment was a single word, "Mon."

Finally, introducing the quietest but most influential of the horde, Lars began. "You may have noticed there be one lad remaining. Know ye that this trip would not be if it were not for Sir Rodney Grenville, known to one and all as Peti G . . . and if ye know him well . . . just Peti." Lars explained that while Peti G referred to the smaller G, that the G — emphasis added — was his uncle THE Sir Richard Grenville. "If ye did not know when Sir Richard . . . Uncle G . . . returned to England from the newly established Roanoke colonies; his plan was to return with supplies. Yet the Crowne's bloody battle with Spain ceased that effort."

"Am I correct Peti?" inquired Lars.

"Aye, continue," confirmed Rodney.

"It doth appear that Peti convinced, connived, con-something and Uncle G agreed to assist with financing this voyage aboard Figs . . . allowing this task to be performed outside the . . . let us say . . . direct purview of the Crowne. So here we be!"

"So are the others on the ship stewards of the Crowne?" Tom quizzically asked with a bit of confusion.

"Oh no," began Lars. "Peti and I presented our plan to Uncle G. We mentioned we would seek volunteers to deliver the supplies. What we left out is that after delivering those supplies that we would be staying. Staying and creating our own community . . . nay, our new world."

With the intent of the meeting met, and contemplation beginning, Lars charged the group,

"Now mates, you have met. I expect you to have more conversations over the following days, for ye are the leaders of these on this ship. Those heading towards their new life. This is your charge . . . this is your challenge." And before Lars' last words to the group had finished, he urged the group to focus on the words being spoken outside of their gathering.

Outside the room and in the halls of Figs, all could hear a continuous stream of conversation and noise. Far be it from nautical talk; instead, the fragments of words heard related to the size of the quarters, what was forgotten and what awaits them in a land far from their birth. The passengers were boarding. Like Tom and the fellow governours, these 53 folks who were seeking freedom were ready for a change. The need for change was so great they had each paid 200 shilling for transport to a land far from Plymouth . . . far from the Crowne. Emitting from them were sounds of anticipation, sounds of nervousness, sounds of discovery. All of which Lars brought to the attention of the assembled. "Those be your charges, mates. Those questions, comments, and exclamations belong to the men, women, and children who will look to you for guidance . . . who will look to you for sustenance . . . who will look to you for success."

In a final motivational rally, Lars challenged the gouvernours present to not let down their fellow governours or themselves. Departing the room, the governours' journey formally began with its realities, dreams, and unknowns. At this moment, the dreams of the past were now meeting the visions of the future. A future where Tom and his mates were at the apex looking forward. The excitement of the moment resulted in Tom once again being quite engrossed in thoughts far from the deck of Figs. A mental exercise that resulted in a resounding crash of baggage and personal possessions. For as he exited the galley, Tom walked forthright into a young lass of 20, her vision limited by the baggage she was carrying in both arms. Baggage which toppled, filling the aisle upon contact with Tom.

Returning immediately to the current reality, Tom shook his head, appraising the site before him while he unconsciously began gathering the strewn parcels and sacks.

"My apologies Miss, I was in me own world . . . are ye hurt?"

"Oh no, I'm uninjured. Tis my fault kind Sir. I wish't not to make multiple trips. It's not easy carrying this many parcels and packages while your floor is rocking about."

"That movement under yer feet . . . it doth take a bit of getting used to," Tom added as he gathered the packages.

"Oh please, kind Sir . . . I can do that; I mean not to distract you from your tasks, for it appears we are preparing to sail."

"A true gentleman would never put a minor detail like sailing ahead of a lady's wellbeing."

Giggling, the lass offered, "surely ye jest, if we don't mind to that minor detail of sailing, we shall never leave Plymouth . . . never reaching our destination."

As Tom picked up the last of the packages, he looked at the lass and replied, "how right you are, where were ye heading Miss before our mishap?"

"Well kind Sir, if truth be told, I keep getting lost . . . I believe our quarters be yonder," the lass stated in a confused manner as she pointed down the alleyway. "It be a rather large room . . . a room nearly as large as some of our houses."

"Allow me to lead you to your home for this journey," Tom offered in his most gallant voice.

What could not have been more than 50 feet away was the entrance to a large room, already crowded with men, women, and a few children establishing their home for the coming month.

There were boxes and bags, parcels, and chests all seeking a logical order. Amid the chatter, a voice got closer.

"Rachael . . . Rachael . . . where have ye been? We thought ye may have changed yer mind and we would see you from the deck waving to us," was the welcome I heard from a red-haired man of middle age whose anxiety level dropped when he saw the woman he had been seeking.

"Ah fear not Uncle . . . here I be . . . ready for adventure," replied Rachael in a voice teetering between excitement and uncertainty.

Turning to Tom, Rachael's uncle offered, "Thank you, kind Sir, for delivering me niece . . . she can at times be a bit of an adventuress and we be not always sure where she will land."

It was in this moment that Tom realized that his escape from the Crowne was not a lone sojourn. Nay . . . it was a journey he shared with several. One could say it was more a movement than a journey. A movement westward by those in this room and by those on the ship. A movement to freedom — freedom of religion, of taxation. A movement whose result would be purity of land, mind, and soul.

". . . your name," were the lone words Tom heard as his mind cleared and he began to appreciate more the grandeur and pomp of the impending journey.

To this, Tom responded with an unpompous, "Huh . . ." as he mentally returned to the present.

"Your name kind Sir? What shall I call you when we pass in the alleyway?" Rachael asked.

"Tom . . . me name be Tom . . .and you Miss? So as not to be rude . . . how shall I acknowledge ye?"

"Rachael. Rachael of Ivybridge. Well . . . formerly of Ivybridge," was Rachael's reply; a hint of mourning of her previous life present in her voice. "A pleasure to meet ye . . . Tom. What may I ask are your plans for the new colony? Are ye a builder, hunter, mason, perhaps a cooper?"

"I be one of the governours," Tom replied, feeling the first strand of pride at uttering that phrase.

"Oh, Sir, how wonderful for you . . . I had no idea," gushed Rachael emoting the emotions of one who was standing in front of one truly great. But before Rachael could say more, Tom in his usual distracted manner began looking about the room and towards the door.

Rachael, sensing Tom wished to be elsewhere, began the departure exchange. "Thank you again,

kind Sir . . . I shall let you return to your duties. I
believe I heard we are sailing soon."

  With those parting words, Rachael turned,
disappearing into the masses within the overcrowded
room. Tom turned, exiting the room to the deck; a
deck swarming with activities of a crew preparing for
departure.

First Days

To the uninitiated, the activities before Tom's eyes seemed disjointed and not at all in unison. However, as Tom would soon learn, each activity was planned and together a beautiful orchestration culminating in the vessel beginning her journey. As a young bride beginning her married life with her betrothed; the vessel's separation from the parental mooring marked a milestone of life's journey for the many onboard. This journey would transport 53 to a land of opportunity. The conveyance of that dream would be Figs and her crew of 30. Commemoration of this event coincidently occurred during the hourly tolling of the bells of St. Andrews, producing a beautiful departure serenade . . . an ode to the Western lands.

As Tom surveyed the situation, he felt a hand on his shoulder. "Good job lad! Each of me crew has a task and together if they perform their tasks we succeed." The speaker of these words was none other than the captain. "Watch thee jobs . . . learn thee jobs . . . and there may be more work for ye." With those words and a paternal pat, the captain left Tom to piece together the unfolding actions.

Unfortunately, after watching briefly, Tom's initial observations led to some unpleasant sensations. Never having been on a ship, Tom's uneasiness was based on the movement of the surface upon which he stood, a movement which was far from gentle. As the ship moved away from the dock and into gradually deepening waters; the rocking increased and with it the uncertainty of Tom's innards. The uncertainty was not solely physical. Mentally, Tom wondered if he was making the right decision. With the pier still in sight, a dive and a brief, albeit chilly, swim would return Tom to the known. A return to his home, a return to his aunt, a return to . . . a return to the tyranny, a return to the control, a return to all that deprived him of his freedom.

As Tom harbored these thoughts, he made the ultimate commitment. A commitment to not look back. A commitment to face forward, looking toward the future . . . whatever it may hold. Tom made this commitment by a single overt act — turning his back on England and facing his new home. His home in the West.

For nearly an hour, Tom stood mesmerized by the actions occurring before his eyes. As time passed, so too did the duties of the crew change. Men who were coiling lines became men who minded the sails. Men who had helped hoist the anchor became men who swabbed the deck. Passengers, who were originally many huddling for space along the deck rail, slowly diminished until only the most inquisitive youth remained. Behind him, the town which was Plymouth shrank until the towers of Plymouth Castle, the guardian of the port, were mere specs on the elongated horizon.

Turning to determine what his days would now hold, Tom encountered Squint.

"Tom, is it?" Squint asked.

"Aye, and you be Quinton?" Tom asked in an equally hesitant voice.

"Squint, if you will. First time on a ship?"

"That it be, trying to convince me innards that all is well," Tom responded with a gentle laugh.

"Hate to say this, but it will get worse before it gets better. In me venture to the Irish shores, me innards didn't calm till the trip was nearly done. That be three days of, at times, wishing death on meself. So me fellow governour, be strong. Remind yourself how grand our futures shall be. It may not calm yer stomach, but it will provide a worthy distraction."

"Thank thee Squint, I'll abide by ye words, although I can't say I'm looking forward to this feeling for three days." Walking less steadily, Tom left Squint and headed toward the floors below to assess the activities occurring in other areas of Figs.

For the next few hours, Tom ventured from capstan to whipstaff, from hold to tiller. Each room bore an activity; each a uniqueness for Tom to learn. Tom had already met Captain McGuilocutty, Master Mate Salk, and Quibbs. It was during these initial hours that Tom started learning of a world he had not previously known. Each man is beholden to duty no matter how large or small, and each contributes to a greater life for one and all. For Tom, that greater life was the escape from his previous existence. A life that was greater than one of thatcher, field plower, or bricklayer. Through observation, Tom learned the roles of the crew. There were Master Mates like Salk, a surgeon, a copper, four quartermasters, a cook, a gunner, a boatswain, a carpenter, and 14 sailors. Each with a task, each contributing to the success of Figs.

Aside from his designation as governour, Tom needed to remember that for this journey, he was also a part of the crew. Captain McGuilocutty had entrusted him with responsibility — a responsibility already shown to be a bit more difficult than he anticipated. Additionally, Tom had received payment for these responsibilities. If not for McGuilocutty, Tom would be returning to Cromwell Crossing at this very moment. Tom decided that he would have to practice his required tasks before needing to make the ascent in the future. Another potential mishap like earlier might not end so well for his fellow passengers or his own being. As glee visibly erupted upon Tom's face, borne by the thought of his meaningful contribution to the journey, another familiar face was approaching — that of Lars.

"Aye mate, what think thee?" inquired Lars, seeing Tom's flushed cheeks and erupting smile.

"Methinks you be right . . . I am a governour." Tom replied proudly to Lars. "As you directed us earlier, it is my task to guide these folks."

"Aye mate, appreciate the confidence you put in me choice, but no reason to take on the whole of that task's success yourself. The team of governours is a 'we', and 'we' will establish the new world. We shall provide to our fellow citizens what they had not under the Crowne; the ability to conduct life in their manner . . . with their rules . . . in their time. Just remember, these tasks cannot be done by 'ye', and 'ye' cannot do it without us! We be a team . . . and this part of the team wants a bit of sustenance," snickered Lars.

As Tom had learned from his earlier exploration of the ship; just below the main deck lay the galley. Peaking his head in, Lars noticed no crew.

However, amidst the boxes and barrels, he spied a lone barrel with the lid ajar. The barrel was marked 'biscuits'. Lars thought a nice, moist biscuit would hit the spot about now. Reaching in he grabbed one. However, instead of pleasuring his pallet with a moist treat, his gullet received a tasteless, hardened mass of dough. The uneducated would soon learn that the true value of the biscuit was its use as a weapon, either in folly or intent. As Tom's stomach was still not speaking favorably to the rest of his body, Tom declined Lar's offer and sat amused as Lars bit into the solidified mass, nearly breaking a tooth.

"Aye . . . we be in trouble, mate. If on Day 1 these biscuits have no taste, think how additionally inedible they will be by day 66," lamented Lars.

"Sixty-six? Did you say sixty-six?" asked Tom with exaggerated emphasis. "I thought ye had said, this be a month-long trip."

"Months . . . not month," replied Lars, emphasizing the 's'.

"By all that is holy! What will we do for months to pass the time?" asked Tom in a still unbelieving manner.

"Plan me fellow governour . . . plan."

"Months of planning?" asked Tom, continuing in a surprised and nearing shocked tone.

"Thought we had discussed this? I have charged ye governours with creating our new world. Ye shall not create the community of another . . . nor a mindless and uninspired transference of an existing shire out of our past. I have charged ye with creating our new world. What will we be eating? Where will we be worshipping? Where will we be living? What tasks will need to be done? How will the order be restored if chaos erupts? These are all questions which will need to be answered. . . hopefully nearly unanimously . . . by you, Squint, Mon, and the other governours. These will be your tasks for the coming months. I hope you have enough time . . . for the first day is nearly over," commented Lars in a matter-of-fact, unceremonious manner. With that clarification, Lars rose, departing the galley.

Upon Lars' departure, Tom suddenly realized that he was exhausted. Looking about, he foresaw no immediate need for his services and therefore deemed plodding along with little sleep a disservice to his well-being. The bunkroom was sparsely populated with but 4 of the crew who would be working all night partaking of sleep. Their snoring filled the cavernous room. Before Tom nodded off, he wondered how could endure this cacophony for the next 66 days. Pondering this number, Tom dropped off to sleep.

Transitioning from sleep to reality, Tom wondered about the source of a ringing bell. The tolling bell in his dream slowly became the reality of a ringing dinner bell on Figs. Groggily rising, Tom swung his feet onto the teetering floor and almost fell as he continued to refine the skill of standing on a moving floor. Crossing the room required Tom to concentrate on the act of walking . . . a task that he had not needed to concentrate on since toddlerhood. As Tom slowly made it to the doorway and entered the deck area, the captain immediately came around the corner.

"Aye Topper . . . ready for yer first meal onboard? Follow yonder line and we shall get some warmth into that body," replied McGuilocutty pointing to the line forming outside the galley.

Feeling better after some sleep, Tom realized that he truly was hungry. His departure at dawn seemed like days ago and not the 14 hours it had been. As Tom approached the line, he saw Lars and Barns ahead. Already seated on the deck eating a plate of steaming food were a few of the crew. Not sure if there was enjoyment, but the food appeared indeed hot and, at the moment, edible. Tom realized being outside all day and being outside all day on the water were distinctly different. A chill had remained all day on his body and he welcomed the warm food. Walking past the shrouds, Tom asked, "what be on the menu, mates?"

"Aye, bacon and beans . . . warm they are and dare I say much better than the biscuit they be served with."

"Thank ye, I look forward to shortly sampling them meself," responded Tom in the same friendly manner which had brought him employment at the Cantery.

A few more minutes and Tom entered the galley. A galley that was now occupied by a cook and two sailors providing food, plates, and rudimentary utensils.

"Grab a plate, spoon, and fork . . . bring back yer plate, spoon, and fork and you get some wine . . . don't . . . you won't . . . and I remember yer name. If ye forget . . . food may not be in yer future," repeated the ship's mate, looking each in the eye as he handed them their wares.

Proceeding down the line, Tom and the others received a heaping ladle of beans and bacon, accompanied by a biscuit. Looking at Tom, the provider commented seriously, "Watch yer teeth on the biscuit . . . you could lose a few."

Provided with a hot meal, Tom took his plate and headed to the deck in search of Lars and Barns. Surveying the deck, Tom quickly located his fellow governours. "Mind if I join ye?" inquired Tom.

"Please do," responded Lars. "As ye can see, Barns is ready for another ladle, so I welcome the company while he barters for more sustenance."

"I trust the cook wish not wrestle me, so I be certain that more bacon will be in me future!" Barns confidently stated as he headed toward the back of the line for more.

"Have you heard from Mon?" asked Lars.

"No . . . haven't seen him since our meeting earlier."

"Seems the sea is not agreeing with him. His illness came on suddenly and he hasn't had the energy to leave his bunk for the last few hours. Poor lad . . . I hope this isn't more than he be capable of," Lars lamented.

"We can ask the Puritans to pray for him," said Tom in a dispositioning manner — an appropriate skill for a future governour.

"How did you spend yer last few hours?" asked Lars.

"Napping," Tom replied matter-of-factly.

Laughing, Lars commented, "Problem-solving and daylight naps . . . I knew ye was governour material."

As Lars and Tom shared a laugh, Peti walked past and inquired, "A word, Lars?"

"Certainly . . . excuse me Tom, enjoy yer evening, we shall chat in the morning." Upon rendering the day's farewell, Lars disappeared with Peti, their conversation fading as they distanced themselves from Tom.

Tom spent the next minutes in observation, and as the daylight dwindled, found himself fixating on the distant rising moon and the shadows being cast upon the caps of the ocean.

"A beautiful sight it be," spoke a familiar feminine voice. Turning, Tom saw Rachael.

"Mind if I join ye . . . unless you were soon to return yer cutlery for yer wine," laughed Rachael, reiterating the crewman's warning about returning the knives and forks.

"Please . . ." motioned Tom for Rachael to sit.

In a doe-like manner, Rachael gently folded her skirt-hidden legs and lowered herself to the deck, using a secured box as her seat.

Attempting to start a conversation, Rachael asked, "How was yer meal?"

"Hot . . . filled the emptiness in me stomach," responded Tom.

Hesitantly, Rachael proceeded, "You did not tell me if it was good. A sack of dirt would fill a stomach, but not be good," came the reply, spoke in a coy manner.

Snickering, Tom countered, "Quite the direct question . . . I like that. Well, Miss, it would not hold a patch to me Aunt Polly's cooking . . . but considering neither me Aunt nor Lancelot of Liege prepared the pot, I shall have to be satisfied until another displaces the cook."

"Lancelot of Liege . . . I am impressed monsieur. I heard another discussing his culinary skills a few months back . . . have you met him?" inquired Rachael in an increasingly giddy manner.

"No . . . not I . . . but I assumed one of your class and upbringing would understand the reference."

Blushing, Rachael responded, "Ye have me wrong . . . I and my family are simple folk working to escape persecution. The Crowne wishes us to worship in a manner which we deem inappropriate."

"Seems the Crowne views me alcohol consumption as inappropriate . . . so I too know persecution," offered Tom, realizing that the two were not the same, but curious for the reaction.

Stifling a giggle, Rachael responded, "Me Uncle Martin . . . he understands that type of persecution."

Returning to a serious conversation, Rachael began, "Did the Crowne really try to limit yer drinking . . . seems as if they would have more important items to . . . err . . . control."

"Spent the night in jail . . . because of the Crowne."

"Really? Seems extreme!" Rachael commented incredulously.

"Thought I the same," responded Tom, " . . .'cept that be where I met Lars . . . so a good night it was. If not for Lars . . . I wouldn't be here."

"And not be a governour," added Rachael, "Did ye say Lars was also a governour?"

Before Tom could answer, an out-of-breath voice quickly approached.

"Rachael dear . . . there ye be," said a man Tom recognized from earlier as Rachael's uncle. "Tis almost dusk . . . time for evening prayer . . . come along."

Rising from the deck, Rachael looked at Tom. "I must go . . . I do hope to continue our conversation tomorrow."

"Certainly . . . rest easy," responded Tom in his most polite voice.

With that, Rachael rose, leaving Tom once again alone on the deck. His thoughts contemplating all that had transpired on the first day of his new life.

First Weeks

Arising from a night's sleep fraught with dreams . . . some real . . . some imagined, Tom opened his eyes to the snores of a room of bunkmates. The din of men snoring was not a dream. It took but a minute for Tom to remember that he truly had boarded this ship just over 24 hours ago and that he and nearly one hundred others were now slowly crossing the great expanse of water on a journey — a journey which a few days ago had no grounding in certainty. As Tom slowly rose from the bunk, he assessed the surroundings which would be a part of his daily existence. The most obvious change was that the earth was constantly rocking. Aside from a drunken stagger, Tom had never experienced the perpetual movement of that which he strode. Following the constant rocking was the equally constant noise. If not noise from the snoring, it was creaks and splashes, intermingled with unplanned crashes and the ever-present cursing. Aside from the Cantery, Tom's life was fairly devoid of constant clatter and chatter. When working on roofs outside the Crossing, Tom got to experience quiet. A quiet rhythmically pierced by a hammer hitting a nail, but still a quiet void of a human voice.

The new existence which troubled Tom at the moment, and pierced his consciousness in a haunting manner, was the spectre of uncertainty. Previously, Tom had known thatching from 7:30 to 5 and eatin' from 6 to 6:30. After eating, Tom would drink and work at the Cantery from 8 to 1100. Tom's day would end and begin with sleep from midnight to 7 am. Repeat. During these first days, Tom was learning and anticipating his reality. Outside of eating and sleeping, a reality that would include none of his former known life and daily routines.

Moving from bunk to deck, Tom prepared to experience his first full day at sea and the beginnings of weeks of the same. Even at this early hour, the deck served as a playground for the young. Running about and tossing a ball kept a small group of children occupied. Had these children been up all night? These were Tom's current thoughts as he realized that the current hour was not much past the waking hour for those in Plymouth.

Walking from compartment to compartment — a term he had just learned — Tom proceeded in an almost sentry-like manner assessing the who's and what's of ship life. Even at this early hour, crew and officers were studying maps, assessing the western skies, cleaning the ropes, and preparing for events both expected and unexpected. At this hour, 53 Puritans were behind closed doors proclaiming praise to God for the beautiful day of life. My fellow governours, minus one, were scattered throughout the ship making assessments and plans, preparing for a daily discussion to occur post noon. The one, Mon, remained in his bunk, unmoved since midday yesterday.

As Tom walked past the galley, he heard a clattering of pots and ventured in. Tucked inside was the same middle-aged man who yesterday was serving the bacon. Thin as a pole, sporting a white hat spotted with grease and other splatterings, it was to him that Tom spoke.

"Yo mate . . . dost ye serve breakfast?" inquired a curious Tom.

"Depends. If ye have a hankering for sardines and biscuits . . . there be food for ye every day. If not . . . I got wine to get ye through till noon's meal."

"Not sure if I have ever had a sardine . . ." offered Tom in a slow, cautious tone.

"No time like the present," offered the cook, as he handed Tom a plate with a biscuit and a few smallish fish.

"Are they supposed to smell like this?" asked a surprised Tom at the olfactory assault.

"No better way to wake the senses," chuckled the cook.

Exhibiting culinary bravery, Tom bit into the biscuit, ensuring that 2 of the fish were part of the bite. Eyes wide, and several coughs ensuing, Tom looked about for some liquid to quench the overly salty taste of his first sardine.

Laughing almost hysterically, the cook offered Tom a cup of mead to soften the blow and reduce the unfamiliar taste.

Still coughing – but recovering – Tom looked up. "Not awful . . . not the food of legends . . . but not the worst."

"There be an endorsement," the cook replied while laughing at Tom's less than hearty response. "By the way, me name is Horatio . . . but everyone calls me Carp . . . they say I'll eat anything, which is why I eat me own cooking."

"Well, Carp, you don't look overfed to me."

"Something to do with me innards and the sloshy stuff inside me. I'm told I could eat a tray of pigeon pies and not gain a single pound. A gift and a curse, I say."

"Me name be Tom, formally Thomas J Smythe. I be one of the governours."

"Governour? . . . Didn't I see you climb the rigging . . . never seen a governour doing actual work?" questioned a surprised Carp.

"Long story mate . . . short of it is, Cap allowed me to journey West if I served as his topper."

"Cap commands all, so if that be what Cap wants, that be what will happen." Carp paused a moment before continuing. "Cap likes them sardines . . . so likely you'll see him here a few mornings."

"What be on the menu for noon's offering?" inquired Tom.

Carp snickered, "Another few days and you won't be askin' about eatin', it will more . . . 'what did I eat that makes me feel like crap?'"

"Surely you jest?" replied a surprised Tom.

"Ah no . . . Carp's Crap . . . that be what they call what I serve ya."

"If I hear 'em, I'll challenge them speaking those words to do better," said Tom in a defending tone.

"Kind you be . . . and appreciated it is. Come by tomorrow and I may have a spot of honey or marmalade for ye at this early hour. Seems the sweeter the food, the shorter it lasts . . . have to hide it so we have some at voyage's end."

"Well Carp, I do thank ye . . . me innards thank ye . . . and I shall see you later today for a fuller meal." With an extended hand, Tom thanked Carp and proceeded back to the deck, the salty taste of the sardines still on his pallet.

"Aye topper . . ." was the greeting Tom received as he exited the galley. The voice was none other than Captain McGuilocutty.

"Aye Cap . . ." responded Tom in a respectful tone.

"Need ye to climb to the top and inspect where the rigging be tied to the spar. A loose rope and we lose control. Are ye up to it?"

"Aye, Aye Sir." With the confidence brought on by a new day, Tom approached the rigging, similarly as he had done the day prior. This time, however, he fixed his eye on the target and proceeded to climb the rigging, ascending toward the crow's nest while fixating on the spar. Once his ascent was complete, he looked down from atop the spar awaiting his next instruction.

"Give a little tug to each rope ring and ensure the knot be solid," instructed Cap.

One by one, Tom confirmed the tautness of the connections. Upon completion of the last check, Tom looked downward to Cap for instructions.

"Good job lad . . . come on down."

With the agility of a spider monkey, Tom agilely descended the rigging in the same expeditious manner he had ascended. Returning to the deck, Tom received a congratulatory welcome.

"Fine job lad . . . a far better job than yer first experience."

"Thanks, Cap . . . let me know when me services are needed again."

"Hopefully not till the same time tomorrow. If we need ye before, that can only mean problems and problems at sea are not welcome." Upon the completion of their discourse, Cap departed to his other duties, and Tom contemplated how to spend his next hour. The contemplation was not long, for not a minute later, the harmonious strains of Rachael's voice met Tom's ear.

"Mornin' governour . . . did ye sleep well?" inquired Rachel.

"Quite well . . . thank ye. Morning service complete? I heard the singing from yer quarters."

"Been complete for a short while, enough time to see you climbing the sails . . .may I ask a question?"

"Certainly."

"I be a bit confused why a governour has crew member tasks?"

"A long story it is. I shall be glad to explain if you have time."

"I shall listen on one condition."

"And that being?" inquired Tom with immediate interest.

"That ye call me by me given name . . . Rachael."

"Accepted Miss . . . er . . . Rachael."

"Rachael will be fine, you can drop the 'er'," responded Rachael with a spirited schoolgirl titter.

"Well . . . Rachael . . . I be both governour and crew . . . specifically, the topper for this voyage. Know ye the tasks of a topper?"

"Well, Sir, I cannot say for sure, but I would imagine it involves climbing to the top . . . at least that is what I saw your task being."

"And that is exactly how I explained the duties of the topper to the captain . . . Do you know what he said?"

"Pray tell . . ."

"He laughed . . . said I was right . . . but that means not that I knew the job."

"But how is it you became the topper?"

"Well, Miss."

"Rachael."

"Well, Rachael . . . I am embarrassed to say that I boarded Figs with not enough money for the passage. As luck would have it, the topper got consumption and the captain offered me the position. Wanting to escape the Crowne . . . just as you do . . . I agreed to serve as the topper."

"Well, that certainly explains that. Are not you afraid . . . that is quite high to climb?"

"It is, but my job back home . . . rather in England . . . was a thatcher. I spent all day on a ladder-climbing onto roofs."

"So . . . I'm really having a conversation with a thatcher?"

"No . . . you be having a conversation with an appointed governour who gained upper mobility experience ascending roofs as a thatcher," snickered Tom, appreciating Rachael's wit. Tom continued how he had met Lars and how during their evening of incarceration they had realized their commonalities. As Tom was beginning to tell of his job at the Cantery, their discussion was interrupted.

"Rachael . . . Rachael, do you have the mint? Grace's stomach ailment is not improving," asked a middle-aged gentleman with a lack of hair and a freckled face.

Sorry Mr. Lam," apologized Rachael, "I lost track of time with me conversation with Governour Tom."

"Aye . . . and a pleasure to meet ye," Mr. Lam replied, extending his hand.

"The pleasure be mine, Mr. Lam . . . Rachael, we can continue our conversation at a later time if ye wish?"

"Oh, I do wish . . . thank ye governour."

Rising from the deck, Rachael departed with Mr. Lam toward the surgeon's bunk, leaving Tom once again alone on the deck and realizing that the rocking had not stopped. Walking on the deck, Tom soon encountered several of the crew. With a bit of time to themselves, a group of 6 were practicing their dice skills while another produced melodic sounds from an accordion. Looking up from the dice game, one of the crew whom Tom had delayed on the plank spoke.

"Yo Raleigh . . . want to join?"

Realizing that it was he being spoken to, Tom responded, "I shall pass . . . no angels or pennies have I."

"What?" Surely you jest . . . a great explorer and lord like yourself. Thought ye could give me a loan if this ole seabag takes all me silver."

"Sorry mate . . ." replied Tom matter-of-factly while turning to continue his morning tour.

Walking toward the wheel, Tom again saw Captain McGuilocutty.

"Aye lad . . . did I not see you a tad earlier? You can't get far on this ship," joked McGuilocutty in an unusual show of mirth.

"Meant to ask ye earlier, what have you learned about the sailing ways? From yer climbing, I know you have a lot to learn . . . hoped that you have been learning about more parts of me ship."

"That I have Cap . . . spent some time watching the crew coiling the ropes, the same rope I attached to the jib. Watched the anchor being reeled in . . . from the crew's strain, that anchor must be heavy. Saw the barrels of 'prevosons' . . ."

"Provisions lad . . . provisions," corrected McGuilocutty.

"Ya, provisions . . . lots of em," replied Tom, attempting to say the word correctly, emphasizing the 'pro'.

"Well, I do detect a whiff of sardine so I know ya know where the food be," laughed Cap, "not sure if you can help me as a boatswain . . . that's me rope expert . . . but you be trying. Keep at it, and as ye stare at the sky, try not to fall overboard . . ." laughed McGuilocutty as he left Tom.

Tom heaved a sigh of relief, for in his view he had partially appeased the captain. Comforted by the assumption that Cap felt Tom was earning his passage, Tom concentrated on his next task. Having empty hours during daylight was not a familiar problem for Tom. Contemplating this quandary, Tom realized that thatching, seeing Aunt Polly, or visiting the Cantery were not options . . . not options for now . . . not options for any time in the foreseeable future. Continuing his stroll, Tom soon encountered Squint and Mouse.

"Aye Tom . . . care to offer your opinion on a topic?" inquired Mouse.

"Surely mates, what be the query?" Tom asked as he took a seat on a box labeled powder. A few minutes into the conversation, Tom's mind wandered to a thought, hoping that the box upon which he was sitting was not of an explosive nature. His choice of seating did not need to cause a large hole in the deck, sending his being and many others to an untimely demise.

Before that mental derailment, Mouse asked, "Storage room for food or the church? Which shall we build first? Both contribute to the happiness of the colony, but which is more important?" Tom immediately knew that there was no simple answer.

"Good question," began Tom as he mentally began assessing the two options. His answer began with, "If there be no food, there be no reason for a church . . .." He continued this line of thought by stating that if only one structure could be built, that one for storage would be the most sustaining option."

Tom could barely believe the words which were coming from his mouth. Words like absolute and sustaining were more likely to come from the likes of Sir Walter Raleigh and not thatcher Tom. Lars and his knack for eloquence must have had some subtle influence previously unrealized by Tom.

"Would a smaller version of both be a possibility?" inquired Tom, attempting his negotiation skills.

"Could," Mouse responded succinctly, "I was trying to be complete in our tasks and not do many partials. As you well know, partials will require re-work at a future time. Material conservation . . . I believe that be the term the educated would use."

For the next hour, Mouse and Tom discussed the facts. During this time, the two attempted to address an almost infinite number of questions. Mouse would ask, how would the governours address the happiness of the Puritans? Tom would counter with what was real religious freedom? Mouse would ask how the governours would ensure that the Puritan's stomachs were filled. Tom would ask what they would store? Together, they would ask each other what they would need and how much space they needed for these needs? The indecisive thoughts — numerous, the definitive conclusions — non-existent.

As they recited the facts another time . . . after the other another times . . . the food bell signifying the noon meal rang. Finally, a concurrence. The interruption was welcome.

"Perhaps we shall revisit this discussion in a few hours?" offered Tom. Taking a much-needed break, the group made their way to the galley. The noon meal was beans and bacon. A different type of bean, but the same bacon. To endear himself with the passengers, Carp had placed a touch of marmalade on the biscuits — appeasement for those with a sweet tooth.

As Tom proceeded through the line and took his plate, he greeted Carp. "Thank ye for this food, me friend and mate."

"Hope ye enjoy!" responded Carp, glowing a bit at the positive interaction.

The noon meal passed and aside from the planned discussion with Mouse and Squint, Tom had no plans for the next 6 hours of his life.

Then, in a pleasantly unplanned moment, the giddy voice of Rachael wafted pleasantly to his ear.

"Governour . . . we meet again."

Turning, Tom saw Rachael approaching. "Ahoy, Miss Rachael, I trust your morning went well. Are ye fully settled and preparing for the next days of your journey?"

"Days . . . don't you mean weeks?"

"That I guess I do . . ." replied Tom hesitantly and with a heavy heart. "What think ye of our ship?" Tom asked, changing the topic.

"Quite the extraordinary vessel. I will be learning for quite some time. This is my first time on a ship . . . I still cannot believe it."

"I must confess, I thought the crew was making jokes when I heard we would be on the water for 2 months . . . I guess they be telling the truth," replied Tom in a markedly somber tone, unexpectedly returning to the melancholy.

"Aye, that will be a long time. I have no feeling what that will be like. I have an aunt who made the journey 2 years past. Unfortunately, I have not heard from her to find out her thoughts on the voyage over."

"Who be your aunt?"

"Auntie Jane . . . Jane Pierce," she and I believe one hundred others sailed with Governour

John White to establish a new colony. Not sure of her success . . . but I hope to see her soon."

"I have heard of Governour White . . . one of my fellow governours is the nephew of Richard Grenville. I believe they may have sailed together. Perhaps he has heard of your aunt."

"I would cherish an invite to meet your fellow governour."

"I am sure that can happen," Tom replied in the affirmative, feeling like a leader and planner and not a follower.

"How many governours are there?" queried Rachael with increasing interest in who would be leading in their new home.

"We have six. I was recruited by me mate Lars . . . I spoke of him earlier today. He felt I lived by the code of Sir Walter Raleigh and would make a fine governour."

"I am being protected by Sir Walter Raleigh," giggled an awe-struck Rachael. "I do feel much better about our journey, knowing you will protect us."

"You spoke of yer journey earlier . . . care ye to elaborate?" Tom asked, almost feeling as if he were prying.

"I be happy to provide ye some background. We be separatists, literally members of the Puritan community who have separated from the Church of England. The Crowne has no interest in allowing us to worship in our way, as it is not the Anglican way. Therefore, I and a portion of our congregation elected to follow God's will and go West to worship our way . . . to farm our way . . . to spend our money our way." Like Tom, Rachael was internally pleased with her discourse. She had remembered the teachings of her elders. She only hoped that she had accurately portrayed the Puritan position. In closing, Rachael offered, ". . . and that is how we came to be on Figs . . . our ark."

"Does that mean Cap would be Noah?" snickered Tom, in an attempt to show his rudimentary knowledge of biblical topics.

"That he could be. Never really thought of it that way . . . but I suppose ye could be right. Course, that would mean we be animals. Pausing a moment, Rachael quizzically asked, "What animal would you be?" asked Rachael quizzically.

Waiting a moment in contemplation, Tom finally arrived at his answer. "An eagle. I am the eagle . . . perched high in my nest, protecting all from what be beyond the horizon. And you, Miss Rachael . . . may I guess . . . a toad?"

Giggling, "Certainly not! . . . I shall be a giraffe. A giraffe walking amongst all with a view towards the heavens."

"Well, that be interesting . . . perchance on another day, we shall assign animals to all the crew and passengers. We shall revisit that activity in future weeks," commented Tom, realizing that there most surely would be boredom in the future days and weeks.

"A plan we have . . . and with that, I should check on me family. Till later governour . . . er . . . Mr. Eagle."

"And to ye, a fond farewell, Ms. Giraffe," responded Tom with a whimsical smirk. As the two parted, Tom began again to contemplate his current reality, knowing a bit more about those he was to govern and protect.

As the days continued, the number of passengers exhibiting gingerly movements and shaky legs decreased. Another few days and they would be indistinguishable from the most seasoned. Watching them grow their sea legs, Tom wondered what lies were told, what truths withheld, causing these 53 to venture from the warm blanket of England to the uncertainty of the West.

Contemplating these thoughts, Tom had to be honest with himself that he too, had no more knowledge than the masses aboard. He had no actual experience or knowledge of what he would encounter. It was during this departure from the present that a rush of salty air returned Tom to reality. The next several hours and the rest of the day were the same as the first. Tom was quickly realizing that boredom would be the primary part of each day. This would be Tom's reality.

Unfortunately, the reality of another was becoming quite unpleasant. This increasingly real reality was the one on Figs who was oblivious to the newness being experienced by the masses — the reality of Governour Mon lying in his bunk. There Mon lay in much the same position he had assumed at the beginning of the voyage. Quietly moaning to himself, Mon had not been well. Today marked the beginning of another day that would challenge Mon's health; finding him again consuming no calories and minuscule amounts of liquid. Unable to provide much comfort or help, Tom uncharacteristically said a brief prayer for his fellow governor.

As this day came and went, the next five were markedly similar. As this first week went by, the next weeks also were similar. On each day, there were discussions. Discussions that lead to more discussions; all reaching the same conclusion - inconclusion. When not discussing their future, there were discussions on the poor sleeping conditions and the increasingly poor food. This lack of settlement — this departure from the norm of each — brought festering hostility and the beginnings of dissent.

This brewing disaster affected all, whether passenger or governour. The governours were beginning to feel the effects of their indecisiveness. Underlying was the concern about Mon and his continued decline.   Mon's recovery was looking quite bleak. His body was shutting down, recovery hampered by the rations lacking in nutrition and the constant movement of the ship. His lack of consumption had resulted in total weakness of his body and the beginnings of failure of the senses. Aside from some home remedies, the surgeon could help none. Some discussions of the governours were moved to Mon's bunk to allow his input and contribution; however, this had failed and Mon lay nearly comatose for most of the daily hours. As the days and weeks became nearly a month, Mon remained in his bunk, lacking color and weakening by the day. Walking was no longer possible, and even breathing became a chore.

The Puritans continued their prayers for Mon's recovery, but it appeared that their intercessions were lost in transit. For Tom, despite the negative of Mon's condition, Rachael became an equal positive. Each day now held a bright spot in the form of daily visits between Rachael and Tom. For one who had never been the glimmer of any ladies' eye, Tom and Rachael were becoming a noticeable couple. At this very moment, on their 33rd day, Rachael was playfully pulling at Tom's hair and trying to convince him that the cook's cleave was just what those stray hairs needed. Pulling at his hair and looking into his eyes, Rachael stood for a few seconds, taking in the surreal moment. Her mind began a "what if" scenario, causing her face to feel flushed. Attributing the sensations to the excitement of the hour, she turned and ascended the stairs to the deck. No longer just a deck, but in her mind, a deck of promise, a deck of dreams.

Unfortunately for others, the deck was a common location of disruption. Disruption arising from the displaced lives of the many materializing now as anger and petty squalls. Tempers flared, prayers were abandoned and at times the most seasoned and seaworthy would snap as if they were a swabbie on their first tour. As the mood of the ship continued to darken, more foreboding darkness became an approaching reality. In the western skies, growing darkness loomed, spikes of lightning visible to all. As the waves rose, and the rocking increased fourfold, the tiny Figs proceeded into the storm. A storm that would try the souls of all aboard. Gone were the days of merely moving westward, now were the days of painful escape. It was as if the Crowne were seeking their desperate pleas for return, and any reluctance to abandon their folly would be met with their planned demise.

The Storm

The storm had been raging all the previous day, and there was no sign of its weakening. Tom had never seen a wall of water taller than a house. Yet, many times over the last 24 hours, that is the sight that greeted his incredulous eyes. Now, as in the previous hours, the ocean had again taken on the attributes of a prized fighter. Rising from its normal prone state, the fighter had, after several attempts, stood and then with vengeful wrath began pummeling all in its path. The mighty Figs buoyantly held its own against every vengeful move of the raging storm. Water sprayed her with an incredible force. Winds rocked her, attempting to capsize her frame. Deafening thunder cracked repeatedly, reminding all aboard of their fateful foe's presence. This was the experience for those aboard their carrier. For most, the sensation was greater, grander, and far more menacing than any previous experience. Amidst the toppling, rocking, and uncontrollable lurching, many onboard feared the end was near. Many were disposing of their dream and fervently praying for God to have mercy on their souls in the next life. Amongst this turmoil, the call came.

"Tom . . . Tom . . . we need ye! . . . A rope is failing on the main spar . . . Cap needs ye now!"

This was the greeting Tom received from his near slumber as his tired body fought for a few moments of respite. As Tom's brain worked to convince his body this was a dream, the reality of the shouts came louder, followed by the all too real shaking of his body.

"Up lad, no time for sleep . . . the ship needs ya," beckoned a crewman tasked with rousing the topper.

Tom rolled over, looking up with glazed eyes, attempting to return to slumber.

"Don't make me knock you from that bunk . . . I surely know that will rouse you."

"A . . . Alright . . . I'm almost awake . . . what do you need from me . . . sounds miserable out there . . .!" Tom uttered as his senses became more attuned to the howling winds and crashing waves.

"The jib . . . Cap wants you to secure a loosed line . . . he wants is NOW!" bellowed the crewman, losing patience.

Sensing the urgency and realizing that Cap may end his journey West prematurely, Tom bolted up, grabbed a woolen coat from a nearby hook, and prepared to meet the storm. As Tom opened the door to the deck, a door which took considerable strength to open due to the gale forces being exerted from the outside; Tom was immediately immersed in a bone-chilling, spirit extinguishing, wall of water. An assault, intent on driving its raindrops through every pore on any who dared to escape the confines of the lower levels. Acclamation was unattainable. Ignoring the pain . . . impossible. Yet, a few yards from Tom stood a sole figure, commanding amidst the chaos.

"Yo Topper . . . secure the rigging below me crow's nest," yelled Captain McGuilocutty in a commanding voice which somehow remained audible over the raging torrents.

Looking up, Tom spied an unsecured rope. He estimated that the line no longer connected to the mast was some 90 feet above the deck. On a clear day, the ascent would have been instinctual. Hand on the ladder, other hand holding load . . . scurry up the ladder . . . begin work. Not so in the current storm. The ladder was a swaying web of rope. The destination . . . a rocking target. The whole was a slippery assemblage intent on embarrassing, or worse, any who dared the climb.

Tom saw his choices as few. He could refuse to climb, placing personal safety ahead of the good of the crew and passengers. Tom was certain that choosing to refuse to climb would not end well — at least for him. At best, he would spend some days in irons for failure to follow an order by the captain, at worst . . . walking the plank. His other choice — following the command and ascending to the top of the jib. Success would distinguish Tom as a genuine leader, one who forgoes all for the good of his charges. Of course, failure from that height may cause permanent injury or death. Looking at success in this way gave Tom little chance of success. Yet, knowing what he had to do, Tom turned toward the captain and asked through the raging storm about his task, hoping that he had misunderstood.

"Up yonder?" Tom asked Cap, pointing toward the jib rope flapping untethered in the gale. "Is that me task?"

"That it be," yelled Cap into the wind as his vocals challenged the storm. "The rope needs fastened . . . leave 'er be and we can't control the sails." Cap continued his instruction with a command as he challenged the discord. "Head up there lad . . . and may yer god be with ye."

Pausing only for a moment to confirm his direction through the blinding wind and rain, Tom staggered forward and latched onto the lattice of rope. Needles. That was the initial intense feeling as Tom's bare hands clung to the rope as he began the ascent. The weight of his body, rocked by the wind, pulled against his fingers and palms. Tom wondered again if this was a realistic and awful dream.

"Climb boy, climb . . . we need that line secured," yelled a crewman, further making Tom realize that dream this was not.

Ascending five rungs with seemingly 100 to go, Tom's mind wandered to a warmer locale. It was at that moment that Tom sensed a sensation. The sensation was that of freefall. Brief as it was, it was still a fall followed by a painful landing on his back. Tom's brief mental eclipse away from the task had once again resulted in a painful reminder to focus.

"Back at it, boy . . . no time for lollygagging . . . back to them ropes," shouted Sark who had joined those assembled.

Performing a brief bodily check, Tom confirmed he was still alive. Pulling himself to his knees, Tom slowly rose to a standing position. Soaked. There was no need for Tom to avoid the rain with cap or cloak; as there was not a dry inch on his being. Shaking his head to clear out the doubts, Tom looked again at his foe. His formidable enemy stood before him with its broad ropey arms, deep powerful breath, and cackling laughter. Laughter made louder as the gusts tore through the rooms and windows on the upper deck. Taking this in, Tom took a deliberate step toward the ropes for another attempt.

"You can do this lad . . ." encouraged McGuilocutty, with a slight hint of empathy in his voice.

Looking up, Tom once again assessed the situation and before creating a final plan — a plan to retreat — he began his second ascent.

Rung by rung, Tom made his ascent. Keeping his head up, Tom kept his eye on the crow's nest and the flapping rope. Rung by rung, Tom rose. Each step conquered placed Tom closer to his goal. Second by second, the minutes ticked by as Tom approached his goal. After several minutes, Tom was within 2 cubits of reaching the rope. During those minutes, the winds had increased, and the rain became a, if possible, more continuous sheet. The noise. The noise of the foe would have woken Chaucer from his very grave. It was against these powers of nature that Tom persevered, keeping his eye on the prize.

Arriving at the crow's nest, Tom hesitated for a brief minute while he quickly determined how to reach the rope while supporting his weight on the shifting and slippery ladder — a ladder that lacked rigidity. Sensing an action had to occur, Tom tightened his legs and feet into a knotty area and, in a single motion, reached out for the wayward rope. Success. The rope now needed securing. Viewing a pulley with no accompanying rope, Tom surmised that it be the home of the wayward line. Looking down to the deck for guidance, Tom pointed toward the pulley and awaited an answer.

"Ya lad . . . that be it . . . wrap the rope and tie a boatswain if ye can. If not, any knot will do for now." Of course, with the storm and the accompanying celestial explosions, Tom only heard 'ya . . . wrap . . . knot'.

Hope that was 'knot' and not 'not', thought Tom as he prepared to wrap the rope around the pulley. Precariously holding the rope in one hand, the crow's nest rim with the other, and his body secure to the ropes with knees and feet, Tom attempted to re-secure the wayward line.

During the next few seconds, Tom repeatedly reminded himself that if all was dry and sunny, the task would have been easier. However, with all wet, windy and far from quiet, Tom became more exhausted. His body depleted of energy by the minute. This simplistic task took three tries before success. Upon threading the rope, Tom continued to secure the rope with the only knot he knew — a bowline. The completion of the knot was Tom's penultimate measure of success. Completion of the knot would need to be followed by Tom descending the webbed shroud and placing his feet on the deck. Again, foot by foot, Tom lowered his body towards the deck. Fifteen feet, 12 feet, 10. Tom slowly descended. As he neared the deck at 3 feet above his goal, Tom's foot reached for a rung — a rung which was not there. His foot frantically clawed the air for a place to rest. Finding none, Tom's body plummeted the final few feet to the deck. Devoid of energy, Tom's wet crumpled body lay for only a minute before he was approached by a caring lass with a warmed, becoming wet, blanket. Rachael had been on the deck fascinated by the storm when she realized it was Tom making the careful descent on the webbing. Fixated on Tom, her eyes widened when she realized what was about to happen. As Tom's body fell, she gasped in horror, rushing toward him to offer comfort and renewal. Wrapping Tom in the blanket, she gazed at him, looking into his spent eyes; providing a look that Tom had never experienced from one of his age. Her soft hands gingerly rubbed his aching arms, striving to warm his chilled body.

"You poor man. Thank ye . . . thank ye for saving us," Rachael spoke to Tom in a slow and nurturing voice. "Stay still. I will help you move in a minute," Rachael assured Tom, amidst the rain pelting their crouched bodies.

Momentarily oblivious to the storm, Tom rested upon the solid deck, seeking solace in the dampening blanket and the eyes of one expressing genuine concern. After one or two minutes, a duration which seemed much longer, Tom rose to test his sodden muscles. Recovering enough to support his weight, Tom stood and began the slow walk into the dry shelter. Rachael walked with him step by step, ensuring that his frame would not take another topple before reaching his bunk. As Tom passed the captain, he extended a hand to Tom's shoulder, offering a single phrase of appreciation. "Ye has done well, topper."

Returning to his bunk, a bunk that was much warmer an hour earlier, Tom eased his body onto the familiar board and reached to cover himself with the well-used cloth which served as his blanket. Rachael offered a more substantial blanket and proceeded to wrap his chilled and wrought body with it. "This should help. Sleep well, me governour," and with those words and a parting peck to Tom's check, Tom slowly returned to the slumber he had known.

For the rest of the night, the rocking of the ship continued. When day broke, the skies remained black as night, devoid of all light. Amidst rousing, Tom was in the process of determining whether the events of the evening were real or the result of a magnificent storm-influenced dream. Innumerable pains throughout his body and the soaked blanket led him to believe that the ascent and subsequent falling were a reality. But what of Rachael? Was that too imagined? The memories were so vivid, the experience so real. A reality that was far more pleasant than the memories of the stormy ascent.

The next few minutes found Tom slowly preparing to exit his bunk. The usually simple task was more difficult because of his recent bruising and the almost constant rocking induced by the still-raging storm. Further annoying his bodily trauma was the cold. At this moment, dryness remained elusive to Tom. Instead of being refreshed from the hours of sleep, Tom's body continually reminded him of the previous night's challenges. Challenges that now brought pain and grimacing with each movement. Knowing he could not sleep his way to the western shores; Tom set his feet on the rocking floor and proceeded toward the door into the storm. A storm whose whistling wind and driving rain were still present and continued to challenge the resilient Figs.

Sticking his head out of his quarter, he saw Briant, a crew member he had spoken with earlier in the week. "Aye Bree, when will this storm break? Any word from Cap on its end . . .?"

"Not a one . . . if I were figuring, I would say we should be clear by noon. We be rocking for nearly 40 hours. This be one large storm. Biggest I've seen in me ten years at sea . . . saw what ye did with the jib . . . damn impressive. Not sure I could have done that. The crew is indebted fer none of us wanted to make that climb . . . Thank ye."

"Not sure I want to make that climb again meself. Climb I did back in England, so glad me skills could be used."

At that very moment, Tom realized how empty his stomach was. Knowing the rain would not magically stop, Tom decided to make a run toward the galley. Pushing open the galley door, Tom beheld a sight distinctly different from the one viewed a few days prior. Barrels lying on their side, boxes unstacked, oily matter lying on the floor. In a corner, Carp and the cooper were bending bands to fix a cracked barrel.

"Aye Tom," responded Carp when he saw the sodden Tom enter. "Storm has no respect for man or meal. Lost about half a barrel of oil and the same of butter."

Unsure of what that meant, Tom asked, "How bad is that?"

"Well . . . ye won't starve . . . but you may be eatin' dry biscuits for an extra week or two. That oil and butter make yer food edible . . . if that be possible."

"Oh . . ." responded Tom, his stomach rumbling in displeasure at having to eat dry, tasteless biscuits longer than necessary. "May I have a bit of food? I be famished. Climbing that jib took a lot more energy than I was planning."

"Tough work it was . . . but I and many others are glad ye made the climb. If you can't control the sails, you can't control where you be headin' . . . For all ya know, we may be goin' back to England . . . Can I offer you a bit of dried pork and a bit of mead?"

"A bit early for mead . . . but considerin' me plight, I accept yer offer," replied Tom.

Carp rose, reached into a box, and pulled out a few pieces of pork. Walking to Tom, he almost lost it all as he slipped on the oil. Catching himself, he handed the scraps to Tom. "Here ya be lad, let me get a cup of mead." A minute later, Tom was rocking in the suspended net which served as a chair, enjoying his sustenance.

A few minutes into his respite, another crew member broke into the doors, "Storm is endin'. Cap told me to tell ya that we be feedin' the masses at midday." With that, the sailor returned to the weakening storm outside.

"Well, I know how I'm spendin' me next few hours," replied Carp. "Ya, able to fix that barrel by yerself?" inquired Carp to the cooper.

"Should be, ya better start yer cookin', lots of hungry folks, since it was too rough to feed em for the last few meals. I be surprised they haven't started eatin' their boots."

"That be sure," replied a distracted Carp as he began organizing his wares for a meal of fish and cheese.

"How long we been out here Carp?"

Looking at a food-stained, dog-eared, placard on the wall, Carp commented, "Day 36 says me calendar . . . why ye ask? Bored are ye?"

"Just askin' . . . our food will last?" asked Tom with a slightly concerned tone.

"About out of the tasty fare . . . got biscuits for another month . . . would have been able to make fresh biscuits, but one crate of flour was really feathers. Call me a fool for thinkin' a crate marked 'f' delivered to the kitchen would be flour. I know none of you is hungry enough to eat a feather," joked Carp, making the best of his food situation.

"If we miss another meal, I may be tempted," joked Tom as he headed out into the rain. On the other side of the door stood Mouse, preparing to enter the galley.

"Aye Tom . . . been looking for ye . . . can we talk more about priorities when we land? Not sure we finished that topic two days past."

"A necessary topic, that be. Any of me fellow governours have time?"

"Let me gather the lot, and we can meet in the Poophouse in half a turn of the hourglass."

"I be there," responded Tom, and with that, Tom approached the rail. As he gazed westward, the rain continued to fall, but with much lesser intensity than the previous hours.

The rain caused an uneasiness in Tom's being. Each raindrop representing an unmet obligation, which if left incomplete would eventually cause the tumbler of Tom's psyche to overturn and lay waste for all to see. This was Tom's hidden fear that his fellow governours would learn that he lacked the experience and skill which was expected of the position with which he was charged. It was during this bout of self-doubt that Tom spied Lars approaching.

"Aye mate . . . have a few minutes for a friend?" inquired Tom, hoping for an affirmative response.

"For me fellow governour . . . always," responded Lars in his always confident demure. "What be yer thought?"

"That be the word I wished to discuss . . . thought," Tom began in hesitation. "My thoughts are increasingly ones of doubt. You may have confidence in me, but I have not the same. I fear I may misspeak, leading others to follow because they believe I have talents that I have not." Looking into Lar's eyes, Tom inquired, "Are these the words of a loon?"

Lars broke a smile, amused at Tom's uncertainty. "Tom, me mate, me pal, me fellow governour . . . thee be not a loon or any other mentally deficient fowl. You were chosen because you can achieve. Didst thou not secure nearly a year of wages in 10 weeks? Didst thou not secure passage with a lack of the agreed shillings? Hast though not become a member of the crew and not regarded as a maker of folly? Nay me pal, you are rightfully named and chosen to be a governour."

Taking in Lar's words, Tom had trouble speaking as he was still struck by Lar's unfathomable trust in his ability.

Not needing a response, Lars challenged Tom. "Me lad, go and govern!" Turning, Lars departed in the direction of the galley.

Strengthened by Lar's confidence, Tom looked back seeing the blackened sky and relentless lightning strikes signifying the inferno all aboard Figs had survived. For now, there was still much to decide, as God willing, cries of a land sighting may be only a few weeks away. With that thought in mind, Tom proceeded to meet his fellow governours.

Regrets & Conflicts

As planned, five of the six governours sat around a table in a room normally reserved for map reading and course-plotting. Missing was Mon, his empty seat a reminder of the price paid by some in the pursuit of their goals. Lying in his bunk, grasping for another day, Mon was no longer an active contributor. No more would his insights and wit be a part of the planning conversations. At that moment, Lars came through the doors, his exciting demeanor changing when confronted by the somber mood of the assembled.

As Lars looked for answers in the eyes of the governours, Peti spoke up.

"We were discussing Mon."

Sadness graced Lars' face as he spoke. "A sad turn of events, that be sure . . . yet one which must not deter our course. Mon wants us to succeed. If ye have a god . . . I ask that you seek his recovery from a higher authority. Unfortunately for us, we must persevere. Persevere we must, lest the entirety of our cause be lost. We must continue . . . continue in the spirit of Sir Walter Raleigh. Remember me governours that upon landing, there be no certainty that all aboard will survive another month. They be weakened in spirit and body. We must prepare to lead during adversity and to remain steadfast toward our goals." Pausing, Lars asked tentatively, "I trust you are still with me?"

In an almost immediate reply, Barnes responded, "I be with ye . . ." Slowly, each responded the same around the table.

"Good . . . glad we can agree on this. I was a wee bit concerned after our last meeting that we could not agree on a single item . . . even the color of the sky," Lars sarcastically commented to his fellow governours. "Today I wanted to establish priorities. What do you think needs completed in the first two weeks?"

Thinking for a few moments, the answers came. "Shelter." "Food storage." "Leadership".

"All good thoughts . . . care ye to explain?" asked Lars, directing the question to Mouse. Proceeding succinctly and creatively, Mouse explained further about shelter.

"A wet soul is a depressed soul. A depressed soul becomes an angry soul. An angry soul, in time, cannot be quelled . . . and after a time . . . becomes rebellious beyond control."

"Aye, but can't we make the same argument about food? Of the food we catch and find, we must begin immediately with storage and rationing until an abundance be confirmed," began Squint. "Even on these 40 odd days at sea, have we not seen the value of proper storage? Without it, all the effort and time spent on finding and gathering food is but wasted with a single violent storm."

"I see yer point, my esteemed friend; however, I believe we will know almost immediately the status of food. If I may be so bold, I say that the priority of food or shelter will solve itself."

"I also believe that to be true," began Barnes, "as both involve building, cannot we do both?"

Chuckling, Lars couldn't contain his comment. "Ah compromise . . . the sinew which connects all disparate ideas." For the next hour, the governours discussed shelter or storage. Once again, as in the past, the leadership discussion raised its ugly and opinionated head.

At a break in the conversation, Tom looked at the group commenting. "Well Sirs, that discussion took the wind out of me. Your words were as vigorous as the last day's storm. I need an hour in me bunk."

"It doth seem that agreement amongst us is a rarity," began Squint. "I heartily trust that escape from the Crowne be our sole common ground. Me goal be that when we land, we can at least commonly decide whether to remain on this, our floating familiar home or to take a chance and venture into the wilds of the unknown. An unfortunate choice would be to travel these thousands of miles, only to decide we had analyzed the least chosen option."

With that final thought, the group dispersed with a promise to meet later in the week to make a common decision.

Weighing still on his mind, this frequent division often became Rachael and Tom's discussion topic for their daily meetings. The meeting was characterized a bit differently by both. Rachael had portrayed their daily meetings as prayer time with a governour. This was her connived rationale, which she knew would pass the scrutiny of her religious elders. A regular meeting between a young single woman and a community — shall we say — leader would be fraught with scandal without the presence of another. However, under the confines of prayer, a smaller gathering of two was reasonable and drew little criticism.

To Tom's fellow governours, the meetings were becoming a distraction and a possible unwelcome influence. Tom's comments often introduced sentiments quite foreign to those he had made earlier on the voyage. There were times when Lars did not recognize the words emitting from Tom's mouth. Were these the influence of Rachael? Lars' analysis often would yield a resounding . . . yes.

In today's discussion with Rachael, Tom began. "The division amongst the governours is constant. Polite but constant. Squint voiced earlier that it be a shame if our travels so far had been an error and we should never have left the shores of Plymouth. I trust with all my being that his sentiment be not true."

"Who could believe such a thought? . . . although it sounds as if the governours lack trust," voiced Rachael to the assertion by Squint that the trip may have been a mistake.

"Trust can be a fickle maidservant . . . especially when you are the creator of that trust," waxed Tom almost philosophically. "If I am the one creating, I have a higher duty to ensure that my decision is right and that the decision be worthy of trust. This be the very reason some decisions are difficult to make."

"And that, my dear, is why you be the governour, and I, the one who trusts," replied

Rachael as she stared into Tom's eyes. The eyes of the one to whom she was smitten.

Staring back, Tom recited with a smirk, ". . . and to that I say . . . for those that trust what fools these mortals be!"

Shocked at the clarity and conciseness of the statement, Rachael replied in awe, "Tom . . . that is quite good. I like not being called a fool, but the words . . . me governour . . . are quite memorable. Oration . . . that be ye's art."

Laughing Tom replied, "that be one I shan't take credit for. A chap at the Cantery uttered those words a few months back and I have never forgotten them."

"Well, this fool will follow and trust whatever me governour commands," Rachael coyly stated as she edged closer to Tom and presented her lips for a kiss.

Tom reciprocated and after a few lingering smooches, the pair moved further apart dully understanding that if any of Rachael's congregation saw the act of intimacy, these meetings would come to a swift end.

The next quarter-hour's discussion gravitated toward how the division was growing and concurrence seemed further apart, approaching impossible. Tom hoped that the regret which had now seen the light of day was a single event . . . but only time would tell.

Rachael offered her perspective and the assurance of prayer. Receiving this, Tom sneaked another peck from Rachael's soft lips, and the two separated, heading toward opposing sides of the ship, counting the moments till they could reunite.

Unfortunately for the assembly, the topics of dissension and remorse entered the next several conversations of the governours. Even more troubling was a report by Rachael that some within her group were heard cursing their decision to leave England. The days and weeks were weighing on their souls and spirits. A situation only remedied by purposeful dialect or the end of the journey. The latter being wishful; the former, a tactic of avoidance.

In addressing the dissension of opinions, the governours repeatedly proved that they could not agree. Earlier in the voyage, Lars felt confident that if one of their protectorates had a wayward thought, that the fellow governours could constrain that thought and assimilate it to the greater good of the group. At week six, that sentiment ceased to exist. Today's meeting evidenced that each proposed conclusion resulted in . . . shall we say once again . . . inconclusion.

It was these discussions that ensued for the coming weeks. In hindsight, from the voyage's beginning, individual topics should have been discussed and resolved, one each week. Instead of the pottage of ideas that were reheated weekly addressing only the most prominent and their effect on the conclusion. Intermixed amongst the discussions and relations was the underlying sadness and regret caused by Mon's diminishing health. Adding to this sadness was the ever-growing frustration. A frustration that grew as day 42 became 45 and 45 became 50. These distractions added to the normal distress of a long journey . . . a journey becoming an even greater trial by the day.

Will this never end? This poignant thought increased in its recurrence. That for which he had waited months, he now wished to be complete. In simplistic terms — Tom had had enough. This dream . . . nay, this opportunity . . . was now mentally challenging and becoming unwoven. Tom had to remind himself daily that this voyage, these meetings of others . . . even this uncertainty . . . were the ingredients of success he would cherish in future years. When this cherishment would begin and the frustration end was the question? This was the mental distraction of the moment . . . a moment which was broken by an ever-loudening voice.

"Tom . . . Tom . . . have ye thought more about a leadership plan?" inquired Barnes.

The leadership plan had been an item of particular interest to Tom. He and Rachael had spent a long evening discussing how the leadership of their congregation could become part of the community's new leadership. Tom had argued that the governours would govern and the Puritans could participate — ceding final approval to the governours. Rachael had argued that the congregation's leadership had been in that position for, in some cases, longer than Tom had been alive. She argued that the group of governours could learn from their wisdom. In a final effort to persuade, Rachael even brought to Tom's attention that the Puritan leadership was taking guidance from one not from the Crowne and not of this earth. Tom had gently chastised her, reminding her that for all church matters her leaders would lead; however, the governours would lead the greater community. His opinion was not taken well. Before a discussion with Barnes could occur on this potential impasse, the ever-present topic of their friend and comrade began.

"Aye Good Morrow Barnes, any improvement with Mon?"

"Sorry to say there is not, I fear he is not long for this place," responded Barnes with a tear as he uttered these disheartening words.

"Were we all back in Plymouth, we would all have our health," began Tom in a sobbing tone full of regret. "If this trip had never begun, Mon would be about, full of vim and vigor, and able to be cherished by his mum. And now, it appears he will pass at sea, and his poor mum may never know what became of him. Why . . . why did this have to be!"

"Can't blame yourself or this venture," responded Barnes. Who is to say whether Mon would have caught the plague or another of the wicked diseases quietly infecting our borough? Who is to say what job Mon would have gotten next and whether he would return safely home each night from it? Ye cannot blame yerself, Tom."

"I can, and I know what I must do," said Tom as he turned and departed Barnes' company.

With a conviction previously unknown, Tom walked to the lower deck and, oblivious to all in his path, entered Mon's room. The room reeked of the sick, and a deadly gloom enveloped the very air. Lying in his bunk with a bit of uneaten food lying nearby; Mon lay near motionless.

Tom approached his friend, his fellow governour, and looked longingly into his eyes, eyes which were half-closed and barely able to perceive the surroundings.

"Mon . . . Mon . . . it is I, Tom."

Mon's lips quivered imperceptibly and his eyes blinked in subtle recognition.

"I just wanted to say I'm sorry. If it were not for the plan of Lars and meself, you would be out of that bunk and frolicking about the countryside. We did this to you. We are to blame! Forgive me. Please forgive me . . ."

Mon remained motionless, but his fingers moved less than an inch to touch Tom's skin. His fingers were chilled and there was no color remaining. His eyes enlarged for a mere moment and a stroke of his finger was his remaining act of this earth. Tom took the act to be final forgiveness and, upon receipt, he bowed his head, tears streaming from his eyes. A final moment of silence. The last to be shared with his friend.

Upon gathering energy, Tom slowly covered Mon with a blanket. He then rose and departed the room, advising his fellow governours and the captain of Mon's passing.

Later in the day, there was a ship's funeral where the earthly body of Mon returned to the sea. An emotional experience for all on board and one which brought a common sentiment . . . a sense of loss. As if the heavens sensed the loss of Mons, their response was a heavy overcast of the foreseeable skies, dampening further the spirit of those aboard Figs.

This overcast lasted for a full three days. On the third day, Tom awoke and immediately realized that he and the remaining governours were failing. They were failing themselves; they were failing their protectorate. The death of Mon led Tom down a path ventured seldom by thatcher Tom. Life is a continuum, thought Tom. It begins, it ends, it renews, and begins again. The death of Mon was a cause for sorrow, for it marked the end of his life — the end of his journey. However, the fact remained that 53 Puritans were resident on Figs. Each of these 53 renewing their life with each moment and each mile. These passengers of Figs were the ones. The ones awaiting their life's renewal and their new beginnings. It was Tom and his fellow governours charge to ensure their success and further their lives. Abandonment of this charge . . . this oath . . . this duty . . . would surely doom the renewal of their lives, increasing the loss already experienced. This insurmountable failure greeted Tom as he arose. Fortunate for all . . . Tom woke invigorated and ready to face the challenges of the day.

Tom's first thoughts were of the discussion from yesterday with Rachael. Racking his brain, Tom wondered whether Rachael's feelings were being influenced by their surroundings. Yea, it was bad enough to be cramped in this ship for the past 50 days. However, these days were combined with bouts of miserable, soul-drenching weather. In the case of this very day, a deeply overcast sky, one in which the cheeriest of personalities were becoming or had become blighted.

Armed with this sentiment and the words of Rachael, Tom began his day by visiting each governour and entreating them to join him on this very day. A day to be remembered as the first day of success. Tom's spirit was contagious, and later that morning the five gathered again. Tom took over the meeting and reminded those present that they each had been selected for their unique gifts and abilities. Barnes for his insights and experience with the protection and safety of others. Squint was a renowned leader in the world of analysis. Lars, a plan executioner, honing his strengths in the manner of Sir Walter Raleigh. Mouse, an acclaimed inventor, and Peti an artisan in the skills of politicking and concurrence achievement. The group was led by Lars. The group had lost their survival expert. Mon had the skills to ensure that whatever happened, they would survive to see another day. It seemed ironic that Mon could manage the survival of all except himself.

Assembling the group and beginning anew was Tom's task du jour. Employing his skill in the art of creative achievement, Tom challenged his fellow governours. Tom reminded them that the manner was unknown and the path potentially rocky; however, with creativity and strength, they would succeed.

Immediately resurrecting the previous meeting's topic, Tom forced a majority vote. Squint and Lars would examine the manifest of building materials in the hold of Figs. The exact quantities of material needed for a rudimentary shelter and food storage area would be determined and a list created identifying materials needed for expansion. The final report would state at which week expansion would begin and when the shelter and food storage facility would be complete.

This was a plan. A plan which could be implemented. A plan which, while not complete, would provide guidance. The governours were moving forward. The next topic was the tabled topic of leadership. What would a leadership council look like, who would be a member, what were the requirements for membership, and who would govern whom?

Relying on the talents of Barnes and Peti, a politically appropriate and workable plan was devised. As representation is critical in executing lasting and non-rebellious rule; who would make the rules was heavily debated. It was determined that the governours would break into councils. Each council would have two governours and one member of the Puritan community. Appeal rights were allowed by any member of council leadership. The hardest decision was, in fact, the most democratic and the furthest from the Crowne. Sitting over the councils was an appeals board. A two-member group with access to a court. The representative body would elect the two individuals who sat on the appeals court. There would be a governour board member and a Puritan board member. This decision gave unparalleled authority to the governed. A decision that Tom could not wait to share with Rachael.

As certain as the lands of the West were approaching, the hierarchy of the new land was also being constructed and solidified. These decisions and their impact began to wear on the governours. While necessary and largely delayed during the majority of the journey, the concentration and distraction of Mon's health had not helped the execution schedule. One could say that the accelerated success of gubernatorial planning could identify Mon's demise as the catalyst. As the days grew hotter and the end of July neared, the governours agreed to continue on day after morrow with the most difficult of topics, one being the reason they were on Figs — the separation of Church or Crowne from individual freedoms.

As the discussion and days continued, one could see a visible toll on the governours — tolls on their mental capacities and personal friendships. Earlier on the journey, these barrels of hope were abundant, but as the planning became more difficult, the barrels eroded. And then it happened, just when the hope of Elpis had almost drained . . . her cornucopia an empty shell . . . a sound was heard. A barely audible yell.

A yell, barely perceptible, but yet a yell. As the ears of those on Figs strained, the yell was repeated. A single syllable word was the totality of the yell. However, that single, simplistic word possessed the power of the ages, for those captive within Figs had been awaiting this very word. As the governours strained to hear through the confusion, they heard more clearly the source of elation. A crewman was repeatedly hollering the word . . . 'bird'.

Terra Firma

'Could this be real?' 'Are me eyes the subject of the vilest of deceit?' These were the thoughts of Tom and the others who saw these harbingers of hope. For those who did not initially see the winged beacons, they soon learned of the sighting from the adrenalized words traveling throughout the entirety of Figs.

"A bird . . . a bird was just seen."

"A flock of birds?"

"Birds . . . heading toward land."

These were the excited words conveyed in all or part. Within 10 minutes Puritans, crew, and governours, whether above or below deck, were craning to see the subject of excitation. The reward was soon in coming, for approaching from the West came a pair of blackened specks making their way closer to the ship. Closer to the ship they came, before making a majestic arc toward their origin.

This was a fabulous sign to all on board. A bird continuing West may be on a journey of migration, while a bird returning whence it came was most probably returning to food and nesting.

In the spirit of a triumphant march, the whole of the ship took on a sense of power. For now, after 57 days onboard there returned the same spirit and elation present at their journey's initiation. The same joyous bursts which emitted as Figs pulled from Plymouth harbor returned as the perceived end of the journey neared.

Well . . . possibly neared. Aside from the hysteria of the masses, there remained a few on the ship — the hardened naysayers — who believed there to be land only when they spied ground, not aerial beings. Looking out in all directions, these naysayers, these harbingers of hopelessness, would soon remind those listening that there was at least a league of water below the Figs. Until they saw a tree in the looking glass; there remained a nautical journey to finish. For the rest of those aboard Figs, the festivities and frivolity reminiscent of Christmas's past continued for hours. Slowly, with each passing hour and those thereafter, the sentinels diminished to but a few.

The initial sighting fueled the group. For the rest of the day, all aboard made frenzied final plans. Plans only interrupted by periodic checks on whether a visual confirmation of land had occurred. At the time of the daily meal, the sighting of land remained elusive.

Being unaccustomed to smiling faces, especially this late in the journey, Carp marveled that these same grumblers were behavin' as if they were at a cocktail party for the Queen herself. Politeness and smiles, giddiness and jesting. These were the actions Carp observed, as the group devoured the same gruel they had partaken of the last three days. Today, however, there was not a single cruel word and Carp even got a few 'thank ye's'. Carp's only explanation was that some part of the meal had fermented and those showing gratitude were partially inebriated.

During the meal and after, the Puritans spoke of freedoms just a few days removed, while the governours sat in renewed fear. Were the plans completed not 24 hours prior adequate? The governours believed that plans were needed. Plans for a new order, a new land, yea, a new hope. The question — would the plans work? Any glaring oversights could make the newly crafted rules un-executable. If the errors were too ominous, anarchy and rebellion could ensue by the same who longed for a reduction in rules and regulations. If we were to sight land tomorrow, would our plans succeed? The sentiment was a resounding — maybe. With this renewed fear, the governours retired early, either in avoidance of reality or hoping osmosis would once again complete the unfinished work, passing the content from the nether world into their brains.

Fully aware of the damage another disappointment could inflict on his tender passengers, Captain McGuilocutty chose the next morning to speak to the crew and passengers. Calling all together, he began.

"Rumour has it there was a bird sighting." To which excited affirmations by many began. The captain continued. "I do not mean to dampen ye's enthusiasm, but a bird over sea doth not mean land is to be seen within the hour, within the day, or within the week. Nay, some birds can travel over water for days or weeks. Land may not be till next week or the week after. What if that bird be wayward and headin' in the wrong direction? God willing that is not the case, but if so . . . let us all return to our duties," directed the captain to a group now mumbling with their newly dampened spirit. "There will be land . . . that I can assure you. The birds have confirmed the existence of land. However, as you have just found over these past 24 hours, birds do not mean that land is imminent. Yea . . . a land's presence will occur, but we know not the time, nor which land it be."

Stepping away, the captain himself hoped that land sighting would be soon. Journeys across this great ocean take a significant toll on the spirits of men and the sooner that land is seen, the sooner the recovery time can begin. An energized crew can take on all. A depressed and wanting crew can easily cause the destruction of the souls and psyche of the most well-intentioned crews.

The one group which had a bit of respite from the captain's words was the governours. While they had discussed the 'what would happen first' and 'how the governing structure would look', no discussion had occurred on the ruling document or the task leaders. If a discrepancy arose between planting corn or beans or storing pork or beef, who would decide? This was but one of the actual decisions which the governours had been charged with making. These were necessary both to appease all on board and ensure the colony's success.

For the next 3 days, whilst the rest of the ship feverishly surveyed the horizon; the governours met 3 times a day. The goal was to put into place ruling documents — documents they should have created over the previous 59 days.

Never had five gentlemen had such a range of emotion. With each topic, casual thoughts became unmovable edicts. Throughout the journey from conception to finality, each concept had taken on a life of its own. Working past dark on the first night, their candlelight-illuminated scowls and grimaces provided the visual embodiment of their task. It was not until Rachael timidly knocked on the door, advising the pentagogue that their screams and rants were disrupting others; a sign that their day should end. Before adjourning, the assembly made a resolute resolution to resume in the early morning.

Tom apologized again to Rachael, leaving the group to escort her to her cabin door. The whole while ensuring that his hand gingerly gripping hers beneath the shelter of his cloak. A last lingering look into each other's eyes was their last act for day 60.

The rise of the sun again brought no land. Frustration amongst the group was growing and yet amongst the unrest, there existed contemplation, presentation, mediation and . . . concurrence. Throughout the day and into the night, the governours debated, contested, and ultimately drafted the topics of priority and ownership.

With an eruption of glee, the christening of the Compaque d' Mer occurred at mid-morn on the fourth day after the sighting of the birds; the governours catalyst of creation. Fifty pages, scribed by the hands of the governours, identified the plans and futures of that which would be the new land. Identified within were the concepts related to law creation, adherence, and penalties. The group laid out subsequent sections addressing religious freedom, order of facilities, and structures within the new colony. Further addressed were economic plans to ensure the livelihood and success of the newly established settlement. Would history recognize that the governours substantially created this singular significant accomplishment in less than 72 hours?

Yet there was a single event that overshadowed this meritorious and historic document creation. A single, unexpected cry.

"Storms to the East, baton yerselves down."

While all aboard Figs were occupied with sighting the elusive land, a barrier to that sight was brewing. Bearing due west, the skies once again were blackening and the dampness in the air increasing. Those with eagle eyes could see the lightning bolts, which were now coming into view in the far regions of the sea.

Within an hour of Tom completing his tasks of governour, his shipboard duty was called upon.

"Yo, Tom... Mr. Topper... Cap needs the sails adjusted for the growing storm."

"Aye," replied Tom to the mate who had approached him. What was now almost a daily occurrence, Tom masterly ascended the webbing, surveyed the jib, and tested the lines. During his ascent, Rachael watched, standing silently in prayer for successful task completion and a return to the solidity of the deck for Tom.

After abiding by a few commands of Cap, Tom began his descent and soon was on the deck with Rachael by his side, providing a brief kiss to his cheek in a show of support.

The next several hours grew more inhuman as the strength of the storm increased. Future students of the event would determine that the storm came to a near standstill for nearly 6 hours. During this time the storm demanded respect while tossing the carrack to and fro. Throughout the assault, beams creaked, leaks sprung, and heavy boxes normally requiring 4 men to budge were tossed about as if made of straw.

Huddled in their cabin, the Puritans prayed unceasingly. Ever imploring that this trial would end and that land would soon make itself known.

Twice more during the storm, the captain would request Tom to ascend the rigging and tighten a loosed knot or wayward line. Tired, worn, and wet, Tom settled into his bunk after what he would hope to be the final ascent and in a departure from his norm — realized he was praying.

The prayer was simple and succinct. Some would question if it was intended to be a prayer; yet, it contained the essential elements of an ask. An ask directed at another whose powers were beyond those of mortal men. The words which Tom mentally directed to another — 'please let this end.'

With that, Tom's wrought body began its escape into the land of dreams. Tom awoke to a quieter and less turbulent sea. The rocking and thunderous booms of the previous hours were quiet. It appeared, at least initially, that the storm had passed. Donning a jacket, Tom approached the door to confirm whether the sight which greeted him would be a stormless sea. It was. A brief and quiet 'thank you' emitted from Tom's lips.

Approaching the deck railing, Tom beheld a blue sky, a gentle breeze, and not an inkling of the storm's residue. While taking this beauty and serenity in, the long-anticipated announcement happened. Staccato and sudden, the two simplistic words which would forever change Tom and his fellow passengers' lives. These words were broadcast by one Jonas Peletier, a junior seaman on his first voyage.

"Land HO!"

Those two wondrous, anticipated words were indeed the calm after the storm. Although calm would only refer to the weather and barometer, the words uttered created quite the opposite effect upon those who heard. Frenzied would have been the definition of note for all who heard the exclamation. Joined by the clanging of a bell and an immediate festive aura, the whole of the ship assembled on the port side and viewed a blur to the West. A shared spyglass confirmed a definite solid body of darkness rising from the horizon, distinguishing itself from the ever-present water.

The intensity of chatter nullified the clanging bell, and the whole of Figs resembled a party suitable for the conquering of a foreign army. Whether Puritan, governour or maiden, all were united in their joy. A spirit of unmistakable glee was present. The raucous sounds of euphoria resembling the uncorking of a bottle of fine champagne emanated through all of Figs. The final plans soon to be laid.

The provider of the forthcoming plan was appropriately the captain. Rising above the assembly as he had done just 3 days prior, he ascended the stairs and motioned for a bit of silence.

"As ye may have heard . . . we have sighted land." To which another thunderous applause arose, preventing further speech for several hundred sands of the hourglass. Upon a brief quelling of the excitement, the captain continued. "Our journey be not complete. Be warned that many a ship and her crew have perished within visual sight of their target. The storm of the previous day was yet another attempt at dissuading us from our goal. So, be warned . . . as the sea's depth diminishes, the chances increase for rocks and other submerged items which can permanently disable a vessel and plunge their passengers into the icy waters. While ye can see the land, none of the lot of you can swim that far in these deadly cold currents."

As the captain continued, the gravity of the situation tempered the enthusiasm. McGuilocutty continued that he would be spending the rest of the day preparing to breach the barrier islands. He explained that those before him had learned that a ring of islands, so deemed barrier islands, existed. A breakage in those islands suitable for a carrack would be sought, and he hoped that a breach could occur early in the next morn. The captain further explained that he could not calculate a final landing time until the second land sighting was made. He further explained that the beach they sought lay behind the barrier islands. However, that sighting could be as soon as tomorrow noon.

"Therefore, begin to assemble your possessions from the previous 60 days. Keep your daily items visible, but begin for a deboarding of your possessions in the coming days."

With that, McGuilocutty descended his platform to a rousing cacophony of cheers. Cheers from passengers now renewed in spirit, hope, strength, and conviction.

The next several hours brought the solidified landmasses of the West within sight of all on Figs.

Along with the sight of land came the coloration change of the water. The dark, grey, colorless void slowly was transforming to a more aqueous blue . . . a color of welcome . . . a hue of hope.

Closer the craft came to its desired goal. With every foot, anticipation rose. To the man, the demeanor of those on Figs was rising to a crest. The details of the shore were becoming clearer. An eye to the spyglass could, if lucky, spot a stray deer. A cement wharf with belching buildings this was not. Flora and fauna abounded, and the passengers of Figs were eagerly awaiting their immersion.

At three hours past sunrise, the break in the island was sighted and Figs set course for the narrow passage. Sailors on both sides kept their eagle eyes on the stern and bow to ensure no visible rocks would permanently moor their vessel before the voyage's end.

Slowly, Figs passed through the waters, a stick confirming the depth as they sailed through the channel. Clearing the channel took nearly an hour. On the other side of the channel lay a glistening bay, smaller than envisioned, yet deep enough for Figs but with marked fewer waves and disturbances.

McGuilocutty kept the glass to his eye, seeking the most appropriate spot to drop anchor and begin the next phase of his charge's existence. All the while, his passengers stacked trunks and satchels in corners and readied for transport to the shore.

Amongst the activity, McGuilocutty spied that which he had been seeking. Nearly a half mile ahead lay a broad expanse of open beach with a few shallow rocks forming the barrier. The dramatic coloration change told the seasoned captain that the depth change from shallow to keel deep was almost instantaneous. While a danger for a man walking on the sandy bed just off the shore, a welcome haven for a boat requiring 2 fathoms for water passage.

Closer and closer she came. 1000 feet, 800, 500, almost there. The mighty Figs dropped anchor within a quarter mile of the beach, the final leg of the journey reserved for the longboats to tender the passengers from ship to shore.

Landing

The time was nearly noon, the wind gentle. The anxiety of those on the longboat was reaching a fever pitch. Their journey was literally feet away from completion. Their worn bodies could attest to the grossly unfamiliar conditions of the previous 63 days. The feelings of near starvation, the recurring fear of death, the sights of sickness, and the near loss of colleagues and shipmates. Above all was the remembrance of the entombment at sea of Governour Mon, one who gave his all. It was these realities that had aged each and indelibly deteriorated their inner psyche and stamina. Yet, within their eyesight, feet from their grasp, was a new world — a new beginning. Perhaps this site itself, this view of the new world, was in its own way the mythical Fountain of Youth espoused by Ponce DeLeon. Could it be that the mere act of standing on solid ground would erase the trials and tribulations encountered on the journey? Would the perceived aging become mystically erased, and the body return to the naive state of 63 days past?

These were the thoughts and questions buried deep in the mental recesses of those about to land. Imperceptible would be the appropriate term, as the totality of their being was experiencing sheer joy. A joy that overshadowed any thoughtful analysis or cognitive evaluation of topics the likes of the Fountain of Youth. Nay, their journey was over. Sand and tree would replace water and wind. And for one moment, the world in all its glory stopped. The waves ceased, the birds quieted, the mental images of thousands of dreams replaced by reality. That one brief second occurred when the longboat hit the shoreline – a rocky reef some 50 yards from the sandy beach. This monumental meeting of the ocean with a land thousands of miles away signified the end of their journey. These brave souls who had stepped off the wharf in Plymouth, were about to step onto the rocks of their new home.

Standing, Peti was the first to set foot off the boat and trudge the final feet to the sandy welcoming mat. Attired in a manner that would make his father and uncle proud, Peti stepped from the boat and proceeded to slosh through the chilled water. With each step, his clothing took on weight as his boots, pants, and tunic received a thorough soaking. Minutes later, he traversed the final rock, placing the sole of his boot on the sandy beach. With this step; Peti became the first of the expedition to set foot on the firm ground of the western world.

For the next few minutes, the scene was repeated until all ten passengers of the first longboat stood on the beach – the beach of their new world. The reality that this scene would occur was at times, thought to be elusive; however, the long-awaited occurrence removed all previous doubts. Seeing that all were ashore, Peti raised his hand to the heavens and proclaimed loudly.

"All who can hear, know that the land ye stand upon has been named and forever will be named, the Province of Virginia. In ye travels short and long, refer to the lands ye see as the Province of Virginia, lest others may place false claims upon it. Welcome one. Welcome, all!" The proclamation complete, Peti took his sword and with a flourish which would make nobility proud, he stuck the blade into the pristine sand . . . a visible marker for all.

"Well done Peti!" affirmed Lars. "For all who ask, we have fulfilled our funders' request. With that confidence, Lars turned to begin his duties. Ensuring that none near could hear, Lars whispered to Peti. "Eh mate . . . thou dost know that few — if any — will act upon that which we have just proclaimed." Together, the two shared a brief snigger.

A moment later, a question was directed at Lars. "Sir, shall I return to the ship to bring others to shore," inquired Midshipmen Andrews, the ranking sailor on the longboat.

"Bring them forth," replied Peti, with an approving nod from Lars. Being ashore for less than 20 minutes, Andrews trekked back across the water to the waiting longboat. Upon boarding, he issued the command.

"Return to Figs," bellowed Andrews to the six rowers aboard. With that command, the longboat pushed off from its anchorage, heading just beyond the rocky barrier to the resting place of Figs.

Back on shore, Peti was conversing with Lars in an amazed tone. "Right ye were . . . we can start anew! I had me doubts. I was not sure I had the gumption of me uncle . . . seems I do."

"With a team of strong and willing . . . all is possible!" responded Lars in a strong commanding tone as he looked around and began to query those ashore.

"Daniels . . . Williams . . . care to do some exploring?" asked Lars, speaking to the two designated leaders of the Puritan community.

"Ready we are . . . what a beautiful land to explore," replied Daniels, still in awe.

"Sir?" inquired Williams, "may we first offer thanks to God for this bounty?"

"Me apologies . . . please," replied Lars, as he removed his hat and placed his hand upon his breast.

Looking to the heavens, Williams knelt upon the sand and began his solemn prayer. "O God in Heaven, we thank thee for our successful journey and praise ye for the land thee has delivered to us, your humble servants. Bless all whose feet grace this soil and the paths of those who have trod before. For you are all good and knowing. We, your faithful servants, thank ye for your merci and provisions. Bless us in the coming days and months. Amen."

"Amen . . . thank thee Williams . . . a beautiful prayer and the first of many in his new land," commented Lars in his most reverent tone. "And now, since this land has been properly claimed and blessed, let us see what our journey has wrought."

As Daniels and Williams set forth, they were stopped almost immediately. "Gents, one last detail . . . you will need another with a weapon. I trust we are alone, but one can never make such an assumption," commented Lars as he surveyed the crew on the beach. Two members of Fig's crew had been left ashore. It was to these that Lars spoke, "Endicott, have ye your sidearm?"

"Always. It be connected to me body no different from me arm."

"Can I ask ye to accompany Daniels and Williams on their brief journey inland?"

"Surely," replied Endicott.

"Good . . . remember 30 minutes out . . . 30 minutes back. No more. Look for a clearing for an encampment. I look forward to your report." These brief words were the commission Lars gave to the group.

Possessing their orders, Daniels, Williams, and Endicott journeyed across the sands and entered an area of shrubs that disappeared into a forest. Upon their disappearance into the woods, there remained seven — Lars, Peti, Sailor Sneed, and four Puritans. Lars knew only two of the Puritans by name — Nathan and Christof. Both were stalwart unmarried men ready to lead in the new land.

Lars turned to those on the beach. "Well, gents . . . the settlement plan states that our first task upon reaching the lands of the West is to begin the establishment of a camp. We shall see what Daniels, Williams, and Endicott find. I do hope that it be close. A bit of good luck would be welcome. Till we hear from them, we shall have at least 3 more trips from the longboat today. Some will remain on land this evening, others will return to Figs. Me ask of thee would be to survey the surrounding beach and see what is a short walk away. We shall convene in an hour to discuss the findings of the surveying party and your reactions. At hours' end, another longboat should be present."

Motivated by Lars' words, those assembled began walking to the North and others to the South. All taking in the glory of the new land and mentally preparing for the future. For those exploring the immediate beach, their arrival at their long-sought destination had been less than one hour prior. Since that landing, each sensation, each movement, brought a new and novel experience. The term virginal would seem appropriate.

And then, as if on cue, the panacea abruptly changed. Breaking the silence just over a nearby bluff, a barrage of gunshots broke the serenity. The shots caused all to stop in their tracks, unsure of what to think. The mind of all present raced between the sudden death of one of their party by one already on the land to an accidental discharge or an act of folly. Uncertainty was the common theme. Uncertainty followed by fear. The next several minutes were spent in silence as each ear craned for a sound. Each sought with all their being to hear a sound which would indicate either life of their compadres or indistinct voices, signifying a fear for which none were prepared.

The remainder of the hour passed with no repeat of a gunshot or other sound; instead, the air was filled with the sounds of nature. The singing of birds, and the scurrying of squirrels, were the sounds that greeted the ears of the party on the beach. A party anxiously awaiting the return of their own.

As the time for the return of Daniels, Williams, and Endicott passed, the concerns rose by the minute. At first, there was nervous conversation. The conversation soon became silence. Not just any silence, but a dreaded silence as the potential outcomes grew closer to manifestation. For some, the abysmal silence translated into pacing, as those on the beach continually agonized over what the shots were and whether there was cause for concern. The concern approached an almost unbearable level as the apex of frustration occurred 10 minutes past the one-hour mark. It was at that moment that a noise was heard.

At first, it was a faint, almost imperceptible buzz. As the moments progressed, the noise took on form. It was then that those assembled recognized the noise to be familiar voices — English-speaking voices. Voices that caused an immediate change in the mood. What had been fear became relief as the safety of the exploration party was nearly certain. In another 5 minutes, the brush surrounding the beach began to move and moments later, the three came forth from the opening.

Rushing to their side, Lars was the first to speak.

"Gents, we heard a volley of bullets, we . . ."

Interrupting Lars, Daniel broke in. "Ducks! . . . they be everywhere. As we walked through the woods, we came upon a pond, and as Sir Francis Drake be me, witness, two of the largest ducks ever seen by me presented themselves to me unbelieving eyes."

"Quick too! . . . escaped our barrage. No sooner than Endicott had them within his sight, they lofted and were gone," added Williams.

"Never seen ducks so large Sir," responded Endicott.

"Well, concerned we were . . . but glad all is well. We did not expect gunshots. Made us worry for your safety," explained Lars. Returning to the business at hand, he asked, "Did ye find a spot suitable for a camp?"

"That we did. A ten-minute walk in that direction . . ." pointed Williams. "An open area with trees surrounding and a stream not nearly a half mile further."

"The water be crisp and clean," added Endicott.

"That be more than I expected!" Lars jubilantly exclaimed.

✳ ✳ ✳

During the excitement of the hour, another excitement was occurring as the longboat returned to Figs. The entirety of those on Figs rushed to greet the returning crew.

"What did you see?" "Did you see anyone?" "Is there food?" "Is the beach rocky or sandy?" "Was the ground Christened?" These were the questions that peppered Andrews and his crew.

Their responses were a barrage of "aye . . . methinks . . . rocky . . . wherefore?" and "what be a proper Christening?"

The responses were well received and upon satisfying the curious, Andrews called for the second group to journey ashore. To those gathered, he relayed a message from Lars.

"Governour Lars says that there be three boats coming today and only two shall return. A group will spend the night in yer new home."

Winners of a game of chance for seats on the next longboat included a trio of burly Puritans. Men so large and haggard that members of their community feared that they may scare the very Savior they were preaching to.

After the brief jaunt from boat to shore, the longboard passengers bolted from the small boat to the spacious land. Their first act — expressing their jubilation by firing their guns in the air.

"You boys may wish to practice yer aiming. There be ducks in dem blinds. Follow the path and surely, you'll roust a few. Bring 'em back, and we be having duck fer dinner."

Anxiously, the trio ran toward the woods, the other inhabitants of the boat acclimating themselves in a much less obtrusive manner. Slowly and respectfully, they walked the final feet to the sand and then observed a minute of extended thanks for all the bounty entrusted to them.

As for the trio, they entered the woods and immediately took the stance of a hunter. Slow and methodical were their movements. Each with an exaggerated motion, all the while listening for sounds and chastising each other for the self-created sounds of distraction. After a few minutes' walk, they heard the familiar sound of the foretold ducks.

Each placing their eye on the sight, they began scanning the horizon, firing simultaneously. Stopping as the ducks rose into the air and then shooting again at the rising fowl.

From the beach, the barrage of bullets caused a small stream of smoke to rise from the forest where the discharged gunpowder met the cooler air. An eerie vortex rising upon the currents of the unfettered breeze. Such a phenomenon had not been experienced in industrial Plymouth for hundreds of years, and its existence today caused a brief pause as the hunters were temporarily blinded by the rising plumes.

Moments later, when full sight returned, the trio approached the blind and began gathering the still warm carcasses of the ducks. So many ducks were mortally wounded that some were left. An act which was not easily forgiven by another set of eyes and ears just outside the perceived perimeter of the gleeful and boisterous three.

While the gunfire scared the fowl and carnivores, the sound had attracted another. . . those indigenous to the land. Observing the three made them ill, for while still carrying the duck carcasses, they continued to shoot at that which flew. Killing the birds and leaving their heaving and still warm bodies to die in the sun, providing sport for a few, yet food for no one. These indigenous observers watched in horror as they revered life and believed in the killing of fish, fowl, or flighted only for sustenance or protection. The birds killed for sport could have fed several of their tribe for the coming weeks.

Looking at each other in disbelief and disgust, they uttered a single word, a word of gravity, a word of description, a word seldom used.

'Iroq.'

Killers.

Indigenous Ones

Their fathers and their fathers before and fathers prior had dwelt upon this land. Land shared with the bear and pig of the forest. Land shared with the great eagles of the air and the teeming fish of the water. For all time and memory, their ancestors occupied this idyllic land which provided for all their needs.

Elonoqui, the young brave, had asked his grandfather what he thought was a simple question. "How long have we been here?" This question had resulted in an explanation that was more involved than his 15-year-old mind could have imagined. On the verge of manhood, Elonoqui believed he should be more aware of his past. One way to be aware was to question the elders and more senior members of the tribe.

Elonoqui had never really considered the food chain of life. He had taken for granted what he ate, where he played, and who of the animal variety he was amongst. He had never considered that rich soil provided crops; that endless forests provided meat; or that flowing waters provided fish. Processing this further, his mind went to the care of these resources and those residents within.

"Grandfather? Will the pig, eagles, and fish always be here?"

"My boy, that is up to you. If you care for the land and the sea and sky, just as I and your father and your mother have cared for you; then these that the gods have provided will be here for your son and his son and sons thereafter. Respect for the land, sea, and air, ensures that all can enjoy it and that those who live within it will also share a long and prosperous life."

"But grandfather, just last night we ate the fish of the sea, and last week we ate the pig of the plain. Was that not an act of disrespecting their lives?"

Elonoqui's grandfather was filled with joy at the perception and questions of his grandson. His grandfather knew that a boy who understands these cycles of life will respect these cycles and ensure that all can enjoy their contents.

"Great question, my dear Elonoqui. We eat the fish of the sea and the pig of the land. We have eaten the bird of the air and the bear of the forest. What we have not done is hunt for sport. We have eaten all that we have caught or killed. Each fish, bear, or pig also bears young. If these creatures were not hunted, in time, there would be no room in the seas or lands. If we left the bear or pig to continue producing young and that young the same, there would be no room for our tribe or other animals. Respect for life is the key. Take the life of only what you need. Catch only the fish you intend to eat; kill only the deer you wish for the coming meals. Do you understand?"

"Yes grandfather, I do."

"Dear Elonoqui, please remember our story for years to come and share it with others, with your friends, and with those you may meet."

"I shall." And with that, Elonoqui departed his grandfather and began looking at the world around him entirely differently.

It was conversations such as these that were commonly held with members of the tribe approaching manhood. Whether initiated by the boy or offered as learning by the elder, it was hoped that all would embrace this learning. These teachings furthered the continuance of the tribal culture and helped to assure peace and harmony with those with whom the tribe interacted, whether human or natural.

The tribe of which Elonoqui was a part represented one of many who spread across this great expanse of land; an expanse of land with tribes and cultures dating back thousands of years. As these conversations occurred within tribes, it was hoped that as tribes discovered each other that they would remember the lessons learned and not kill or destroy with no purpose. Destruction for the purpose of destruction was not the tribal way, not for Elonoqui's tribe, not for any tribe. Locally, Elonoqui's tribe had few interactions with other tribes. There would be a periodic sighting across a body of water or the smoke of a distant ceremonial fire; however, respect for the lands of another had contributed to the peace Elonoqui had known.

For as long as he could remember, his life had been pleasant, wanting for naught. Living by the sea provided a near-endless supply of fish, crabs, and clams. Living in the forest provided an equally endless supply of fresh meat. The ground, if prepared properly, provided corn, bean, and fruits.

As a child, this fertile environment was his playground. Young Elonoqui would climb trees, gathering nuts and berries. Not realizing he was contributing to his tribe; he only knew this as fun.

How high could he climb became a game; a game he competing with the other youth. His prowess at climbing became known by all, and because of this gift, the tribe had a steady supply of nuts and berries, even when the lowest pickings offered only barren branches.

These activities were fun, whether nut gathering or tag, providing exercise and developing the skills of speed and maneuverability. Games involving quiet and sneaking would suit the boys well throughout their lives as unseen observation of others became necessary. All were necessary skills to be honed on the path to manhood.

As the young boy grew, games of glee and childhood ended, making way for the skills of a man. Hunting and fishing provided food beyond the nuts and berries of youth. Elonoqui could still remember his first hunting trip with his father and the other men. Sitting for hours in a tree, practicing the art of non-movement and fixing his eyes on the slightest movement in the forest ahead. More recent adventures involved arrows. Sharpened points were capable of piercing the skin and organs of the receiver. Care was required, for lack of care could result in a cut or a serious puncture to the skin. An accident with an arrow could lead to a loss of a limb and the loss of a brave's future. An adult male tribe member who could not hunt would become a burden on his tribe and one whose longevity would be in the hands of others. Therefore, care was taught and retaught when teaching the arts of hunting and other acts which could cause injury or death.

As the skills of a hunter increased, so too did the opportunities for camping. Elonoqui was about to embark on his first overnight adventure. The anticipation began weeks before the trip planning began. Elonoqui, two of his friends, and their fathers would journey to the far reaches of their tribal land. The trip would involve two nights in the forest and two full days of hiking. Training for this transitionary experience was weeks in the making, with many smaller hikes and repetitive practice at stealthily walking through the woods. The skills gained on this trip would be many, signifying yet another reason for the importance of this event.

The trip was now within a day, and final preparations were being made. Food was secured and bundled, arrows and knives were sharpened, bows maintained to peak efficiency. The fathers brought their bedrolls for comfort; the boys would build their sleeping surfaces. Provisions were limited by design, as all had to be carried out, and decisions on necessity were made with each addition. The boys found it humorous that Elonoqui's father viewed his pipe and tobacco as an absolute necessity. On the morning of the departure, the weather was misty, yet the souls of the boys were erupting with joy. As the boys bade their mothers farewell, they turned in a symbolic act of a new beginning, before joining their fathers for departure.

The morning hiking hours were devoid of speech. As they trod through familiar territory, their fathers had challenged them to listen and hear, to take in fully the unfamiliarity within this familiar setting. While the intent was high, the frivolity of youth began to show after a few hours. As each conversation began, the fathers had to warn of their purpose and admonish appropriately.

This cycle of observation, retreat to boyhood mirth, correction, and return to observation, continued till the noon hour, at which time the group stopped for the mid-day repast. Settling upon larger rocks, the discussion of the morning began. Who had noticed the beaver dam, the beehive, the paw print of the large bear? What did the lichen and moss tell of the area we had passed through? What were the species of tree and what could each be used for? Who had noticed the remnants of a fire and how long extinguished had it been? These were the questions and lessons discussed as the group ate berries and biscuits brought for nourishment.

With each discussion and with each question, the assembled boys began to break from the cocoon of childhood, shedding their childish thoughts, and slowly entering the world of the man. Their thoughts were beginning to change, their senses refining, their knowledge increasing. After a sufficient amount of discussion and querying, the group resumed their hike; the boys being far more observant than during the morning hours. Hours and many observations later, the group arrived at a clearing. The fathers feigned moving forward, while Elonoqui spoke up.

"Sirs, should we not begin preparing for the evening?"

Another father in the group responded appropriately. "Boy, is this because you are tired? A true son of the Moon would hike for hours more."

"No, Sir. I could hike for hours more, as I'm sure my friends could as well. Yet, you had earlier spoken that we would need to catch our dinner and prepare our shelter. A large clearing, as this appears to be, would be the perfect location for an evening's rest."

"Please expand on why this would be a good site for our rest?"

With this challenge, the fathers listened to each boy explain about the stream nearby, the stability of the tree branches above, the natural barriers to prevent flooding, and the abundance of berries on a nearby tree. The fathers were pleased and although it was known by them that this would be the resting place; they were glad their teaching had been retained, and the boys had a better answer than their own sore feet for choosing this location.

Reclining on a few rocks, the fathers prepared to be fed by their boys. The youths unpacked their fishing gear, heading toward the stream to catch the evening meal. As a result of a successful catch, the boys were able to provide their fathers with a meal of smoked fish and berries.

After the meal, teachings continued regarding fire preparation, smoke mitigation, and safety from the wild. Some topics were known, others were new. The final hours of the day were filled with stories of previous conquests by famous tribal leaders and what being a man really means. Before a final retreat into the familiar lands of slumber, all offered a prayer to the gods, reiterating the importance of reverence. As the first day ended, the boys headed to piles of leaves they had assembled which would serve as their bed;

the men unrolled the stuffed skins they had brought for rest. Throughout the hours of the evening, glowing embers warmed the area and protected the six.

At dawn, the boys were awoken by their fathers and dispatched to gather berries for the morning meal. While gone, the men partook of some cornbread they had brought, a treat for the elder, not the youth in training. Upon returning, the boys shared their berries with their fathers and the day's lessons began. Campsite etiquette was the morning teaching, addressing topics of reducing destruction to the environment and the importance of fully extinguishing fires. Upon completion of the lesson, the boys were charged with breaking down the camp and ensuring that a visitor in the coming days would not realize they had been present.

After the boys had appropriately camouflaged their existence and assembled their possessions, the fathers provided guidance on how to improve their efforts and ensure that, if they had been pursued, the tracker would overlook this area and search elsewhere for their presence. To prevent over-reaction, the fathers assured the boys that as long as they were not reckless in their treatment of other tribes, that pursuit would not be a matter to concern them. The fathers taught that the Indian culture was one of respect and a true Indian would never pursue one of another tribe unless a great disrespect had occurred.

Replenished, the group began their second day of hiking. The goal of this day was to reach the Great Stream — the acknowledged boundary of

Elonoqui's tribe. The day began quite similar to the first, with observations, relapses to youthful mirth, and teachings on their surroundings. Near noon, the group received a treat from above. Roosting in a tree high above the path, a Golden Eagle had chosen at the moment to make its presence known. The unfamiliar chirp of this majestic bird caused the entire group to halt and take in this wondrous rarity of nature.

Upon the eagle's flight, the group looked about and saw some larger placed stones, nature's provision for a mid-day meal. After a meal of berries, nuts, and fruits, their hike resumed for another hour until reaching the Great Stream.

Great, it was — nearly 300 yards in width. The stream was a near-raging river from the recent rains. Uncrossable without a canoe or raft, the boys and their fathers stared in awe at the power provided by the gods. This stream and its surrounding area were a provider of nourishment for the surrounding trees; a home to the fish; and sustenance for the creatures which graced the shores and surrounding area.

Seeing land beyond the stream, Elonqui asked, "why do we journey no further?"

"That is the land of the Croatoan. Just as we have claimed our land from this stream to the great sea, the Croatoan has claimed the land from the stream for many miles to the West. We must respect their land, just as they have respected ours."

This response appeared to make sense to the boys, and now another generation had been educated on ownership of the lands beyond the Great Stream. The Great Stream marked the end of their hike and the beginning of the return trip. For the rest of the day and the beginning of the next, the small group made their way East. Filled with memories of the previous days and nights, the small group made its way past increasingly familiar territory as they approached their home. The boys had been cautioned to stay quiet during the return, to reflect on what they had seen, and to ask the gods for guidance and insight. Their fathers had explained to be watchful, for, on an apparently normal day, the gods could communicate. Communication could be through a falling feather, a disfigured tree, or a rare creature of unusual coloration. It was these signs that the boys should be looking and listening for. Idle conversation amongst themselves could only prevent this godly experience from occurring. And so, for the next hours, the boys trudged forward in silence, carrying the materials they had brought back to their camp for a future adventure.

Upon returning to their camp. The boys were sequestered in the elder's hut for the final teaching. During this teaching, the boys were taught the new ways versus the old. The present bore challenges to which the elders and men of the tribe were not wholly familiar. The youth in the assembly would have to learn to work with those who were not Indian. In recent years, boats from foreign lands had been spotted. The elders of the tribe had watched from a distance and ensured the tribe would be safe. These viewings were not made known outside the circle of the elders; however, it was almost certain that from where these boats had come, others would follow. The elders cautioned that in the coming months or years, the boys may find themselves face to face with one of these visitors. This would be a challenge that no other member of the tribe had experienced. The readiness of the boys was the lesson conveyed on this very day in this very hut.

During the teaching, the boys sat quiet and wide-eyed. This intrusion into their life was not expected. They had not envisioned that becoming a man would involve situations of such gravity, for they thought being a man meant a better seat at the table and more food to eat. None of those assembled realized that the reality of the elder's words would be far closer and far more imminent than anyone in that hut could imagine.

The following month was deemed the month of manhood. A group of males two years older than Elonqui were preparing for their manhood ceremony. As dictated by generations past, the ceremony would occur on the day following the blue moon. That blue moon having occurred the previous night, the group found themselves hours into their ceremonial ritual. Walking through the woods, observing all, the group silently waited for a sign from the gods. A moment later, they heard their sign.

The sound of the sign caused all in the group to stop and to stare at each other with wide eyes, for none of them had expected a sign from the gods to be so vocal or so obvious. As the elders had taught, a sign from the gods is often subtle and must be discerned. The sign they were experiencing was not a gentle feather slowly guiding silently to earth, nor the warble of a rare bird staring intently at them from a branch. Nay, the sign was even more obvious than the bellow of a white wildebeest, providing a warning to those within its vocal range. No, this sound was the sound of voices. Voices of a human. Voices of one not of the Indian way.

Remembering the stories from recent years, the group quietly crawled to the edge of the woods and spied on the newcomers, observing their actions.

They now would see firsthand what others had believed to be.

Sightings

The storm of days past would certainly affect the tribe's Fall harvest. Those crashing winds and roaring rains had destroyed what months of nurturing had created. The squash and corn would suffer from the driving winds, tearing the tendrils and piercing the leaves of green. Throughout the previous days, the tribe had worked to repair the damages, staking the bent plants and trimming where the leaves were extensively damaged. During a break from gathering vines for tying, it occurred. An occurrence that would ultimately affect every member of the tribe, dare we say, every indigenous person of the tribal nation. The source of the warning was not one of the elders, but a single youth gathering vines.

At first, it was but a blur, but as the minutes passed, the blur did not pass and slowly took on solidity. It was then that the boy spotted the shape. Far off and quite indiscernible, the shape was beyond the barrier islands and easily could be a figment of one's imagination. Not much more than a square of brown occupying a space that should have been blue; the shape in its persistence caused the boy to run back to the village seeking an elder.

"Orowoc Sir . . . excuse me sir!" began the excited, out-of-breath boy as he approached the tribal elder.

"A moment of patience, boy . . ." commanded Orowoc as he completed placing tobacco into a bag, ensuring that none was wasted.

Finally, turning to the boy still panting from his run, Orowoc asked.

"Yes, boy. What do you wish from me?"

"The sea . . . the sea . . ."

"Yes . . . yes, is it still there? If not, we have a problem," joked Orowoc.

"The sea . . . it has a speck, Sir."

"A speck? What kind of speck?"

"A brown speck Sir . . . I first thought it to be a gigantic bird or perhaps a dream, but it is still there, and will not pass."

"Take me to this speck," uttered the Orowoc in quaint curiosity.

With that, Orowoc and the lad made the 15-minute journey to the opening in the forest where the expanse of the ocean could be viewed. Upon their arrival, Orowoc's fear was immediately realized, for in the distance was far more than a speck. In the elapsed time, the speck had become a brown block, a block with white sails. Still too small to make out in totality, it was clear that this approaching shape was made of this earth and, based upon previous instances, was inhabited by those, not of the Indian culture or values. However, one could hope for error. Perhaps the ship was manned by a heretofore unknown tribe; sailors who valued the Indian code and sought to preserve all that they touched.

A momentary utterance returned Orowoc to the present. "Sir, what are your thoughts? The speck looks much larger now," asked the boy of his elder.

"Yes, boy, a speck that is not, but rather a ship. A large ship which has brought its inhabitants on a very long journey."

"Shall we greet them?!" the boy asked excitedly.

"We must treat the ship's inhabitants with care. We shall discuss this immediately. Run ahead and gather the elders. Tell them I must speak to them immediately, but do not speak of the ship. Do you understand, boy?"

"Yes Orowoc, Sir . . . the elders will be waiting for you," replied the boy confirming a command by his elder. Armed with his mission, the boy stealthfully ran through the woods toward the camp.

Thoughts of fear and dread were his companions as the elder made his way back to the tribe. Walking at a much slower pace, the elder contemplated the sight he had just taken in with his very eyes. A sight that produced an internal battle; a battle of observation versus heuristics. As an elder, Orowoc had been taught and learned from experience that actions must only occur when definitive acts are observed. In the case of the ship, until its occupants' exit and their actions were observed, judgment — nay fear — must be reserved. Unfortunately, heuristics have taught that when ships bear visitors from many moons over the great ocean that their behaviors are barbarian and their actions destructive. These were the thoughts of the elder during his solitary walk back to camp.

The morning meal had just been completed and the tribal leader, Opechancanough, remained at his table. At the table's head sat Opechancanough accompanied by his fellow chiefs. A few minutes prior, one of the young boys from the tribe had requested that they stay seated and that the elders be gathered for a discussion of grave importance. As Orowoc returned to camp, he sensed that his calling of this meeting was bringing unrest to some within the tribe. Approaching the table, Orowoc spoke.

"Opechancanough and members all, I bring to your attention a situation which may challenge all that we are and represent." Indistinct muttering greeted Orowoc's opening statement. All eyes were on Orowoc for his next words.

"Minutes ago, my eyes set upon a wooden vessel. A vessel presumably from the East, a vessel similar to the four previous. As you recall, the three previous caused death and destruction to our way. Our warriors were taken our chief, murdered. Lest ye forget, I shall again recite the names of Manteo, Wanchese, and Wingina. Taken from us by Amadas, Barlowe, Raleigh, and Drake. Their feet upon our shore caused the disappearance and capture of our Croatian friend and brother, Manteo."

As those assembled digested this information, the muttering resumed and a noticeable uneasiness permeated the tribe. "This is the reality of today. This is the fear of tomorrow. How shall we address these visitors from the East?" asked Orowoc in an open question to his fellow elders.

Silence. Agonizing silence as the elders and chief contemplated an answer, an answer which would provide safety while embodying the ways of the tribe. Then, the words of a single tribe member were heard. The words came from a young man who only recently completed his ordeal and was for the first time joining the ranks of the men of the tribe. He was seated at the table as an exercise in learning. It was he who spoke.

"Obliqui. Obliqui heron ut!" Translated as Kill them. Kill them before they kill us.

Shudders emitted from the elders. They quaked at the thought of promoting violence and were equally shocked at this response from a member of the tribe who had fully learned the way of the Indian and the values of the tribe.

"No, we shall not kill them!" This edict was uttered by the elder who posed the query and seconded by Opechancanough. "They have done us no wrong. We shall watch and learn of their ways. This is a better solution, and one based on the teachings of our forefathers."

"Have we another solution?" asked the brazen young man, who wished death upon the visitors. "I have offered my opinion; you have offered yours. What is the desire of the tribe?"

Hearing no further response, a vote was taken. The decision? — to observe the arrivers. Plans were made, and the watching began.

Alyonsa and Onacheron, two tribe members who had just passed their 20th year of birth, volunteered to watch for the first day. They immediately headed from the encampment to the shore, checking on the progress of the ship. The ship was slowly making its way toward the shore, still several miles from the sandy beach. Observing the slow movement of the ship remained fascinating. Nearly two hours into their observation, a longboat was launched from the ship.

The longboat held six; one member of the landing party electing to stand the final yards of the landing. His heroic stance resulted in the loss of his balance and falling out of the boat as the boat struck solid earth. This celebratory dousing was met with grumbling in an obviously annoyed manner by he who was drenched. This same act was greeted by suppressed laughter by Alyonsa and Onacheron who had not seen an act so foolish in several moons.

Upon entry on the beach by the six, the desired task of keeping track of their movement was not difficult as those in the boat were quite loud. From their first footprints placed upon the sand, it was obvious that these men and women from across the sea were in almost every way opposite of the indigenous ways which the tribe had known since birth.

Upon their landing on the shore, those from across the sea proclaimed loudly their happiness. Alyonsa and Onacheron could not understand their words. However, their facial expressions and huge smiles, complete with an almost constant hugging each other, led Alyonsa and Onacheron to believe there was great joy in reaching the shore. Even the drenched one managed an immediate change of attitude and, for the moment, appeared to forget his wet attire and proceeded to jump about, providing harmonic and happy tones to the others' joyful outbursts.

The coming hours found talking, nearly incessant talking. Talking in small groups, talking individually, many talking at once. The sounds of nature were all but consumed by the talk of the visitors. At times, a few would disappear into the woods, only to return a short time later to the larger group. Even in the woods, a place of solace, a place of reflection, there was no respect afforded. Tramping of woods, breaking of branches, killing of plants, destruction of habitat. These were the gifts rendered by the new arrivals to the land of the Indian and their forefathers.

As the day progressed and the afternoon hours waned, some returned to the large ship, some began to establish a shelter, and still others explored their new world. As the wondrous world was unfolding before the visitor's eyes, their manners, means, and practices were studied and observed by Alyonsa and Onacheron. Not a single action was missed. They observed the groups who went into the woods. Groups gathered on the beach, were observed from the foliage. As the groups wandered and explored, they were viewed from a safe distance, providing the Puritans and governours, the misperception that they were alone on this new land.

Being quite observant and studious, Alyonsa and Onacheron, in a few hours, began to learn of the way of the visitor. They noted a few similarities in the ways of the visitor and the Indian way. Both rarely traveled alone. Both wore clothing of a comfortable variety and both became quieter when a sound was detected. However, there were far more differences between the visitors and those native to the land. The visitors were loud and abrupt. When walking through the forest, all knew of their arrival. The yells and boisterous chat caused birds to loft and small animals to scamper in fear. When walking on the beach, they routinely disturbed or destroyed items that had lain dormant for many a day. Rocks were tossed, branches kicked, and fauna ripped and discarded. The respect for the food chain was non-existent. Their observers knew not whether this was due to ignorance or a lack of concern for another, no matter how small or seemingly insignificant.

As Alyonsa and Onacheron continued to observe their new neighbors, they wished that they understood their language. Loud hooping or one-on-one discourses, complete with pointing fingers and scratching brows, were woefully incomplete when trying to understand fully those observed. Were these visitors as unfamiliar with forested and sandy land as they appeared?

As the groups proceeded with their individualistic tasks, another familiar sight was occurring. The winds were picking up; the temperature was dropping and the skies bore ominous clouds of black. A storm was approaching.

Looking towards the East and then panning to the West, the braves who were observing the newly arrived saw that the blackness of the sky was approaching rapidly from the West. In just a few minutes of focused observation, the ship which brought the visitors was beginning to rock more violently. The winds, which were previously still, had almost immediately taken on a force; a force sure to increase over the coming minutes. While the arrival of the storm was a certainty, its duration was still unknown. The storm of previous days had drowned the tribe's fields for nearly a full moon and half of the next day. Barely recovered from that damage,

Alyonsa and Onacheron hoped this one would not last nearly as long. Resting themselves against a solid stump with a dense canopy of leaves and boughs overhead, Alyonsa and Onacheron settled in for their next observation. How would these visitors brave their encounter with the god of thunder and lightning? How would they improvise shelter?

The ensuing observation almost resulted in the visitors being made aware of their observers. It took all their muscle and strength to contain the laughter erupting from their inner beings. The two braves had never seen such a comical sight. Upon the release of the torrential rains, the Puritans began running about as if they could outrun and outmaneuver the torrents from above. Having no cabin to retreat to, as had been the case for the previous 60 days, the Puritans headed for the brush, a move which caused Alyonsa and Onacheron to back further into the forest to avoid detection. Some felt it was their duty to protect what had been brought ashore. So, stand they did next to bags that had been placed on the sand. Some contents, which had survived the long and perilous journey, were now being reduced to a wet and useless version of itself. What had been preserved for thousands of miles, now was destroyed as a result of movement from the dry ship to the rain-drenched shore.

As the skies continued to empty themselves onto the land, the Puritans huddled beneath the leaves, not expecting the greenery's disposal of their watery load when the weight of the water exceeded their willowy strength. The governours on land attempted to maintain a decorum of leadership.

Standing stoically in the driving rain, shielded only by a wide-brimmed hat of one sort or another, Peti, Tom and Lars surveyed the situation at hand while their charges attempted to stay dry.

The storm lasted for 30 odd minutes. 30 minutes was long enough to soak and remove the spirit of enthusiasm and glee from the 20 who had made it to shore. As the last drops made their way to earth, the grumbling was renewed. That grumbling would increase, for after the rain came, the sun returned. A sun that provided scorching humidity was enhanced by the fresh watery layer. A comforting feeling it was not, challenging the spirit of all.

Sighted

The brief daytime storm in some ways had been almost as damaging as the huge storm days encountered before their landing. Whereas the rainfall was not as long in duration, its intensity echoed the deluge experienced at sea. While the passengers of Figs did not experience the full force of the storm, the driving rain ensured that all aboard experienced the misery of the torrent. On land, with no shelter save the foliage and treetop canopies, Lars, Tom, Peti, Barnes, and a host of Puritans who were caught on shore had no respite or escape from the rain. Never had a structure of any manner or means been so taken for granted. Back in England, storms were passed under the roof of a home or church. On the sea, protection was offered by Figs. Alas, in this new world — this desired world — this world where dreams were to come true, there was no shelter. On this, their first day and first hours, the group ashore had no place to provide shelter from the driving rain.

Where joy should have been a common sentiment, frustration and scowls were more the norms. Neither the governours nor the Puritans were enjoying their current drenched state. A mere few appreciated that being drenched on land had a few advantages over being drenched at sea. At sea, the waters were salty and after the drenching by rain, the drenched then subjected their bodies to an encasement by the salty layer of residue. Still, their wet and sodden state drove from their mind any logic that 'this could be worse'.

In a few hours, dark would descend upon the land. Aside from the crew, there were 30 on land and 29 remaining on Figs. Peti decided to spend the night in their new home. This act of enthusiasm and adventure was greeted appropriately, and 20 elected to remain on land for the rest of the day and evening. While Figs was but a mere quarter mile out, this minute distance — a distance still visible to all but the nearly blind — was a distinction between the world of the past and the world of tomorrow.

Before departing back to Figs for the evening, those onshore began to lay out their new reality. The earlier expedition, besides confirming the presence of ducks in the area, identified a rather large area with potential for a village. Lars, Tom, and Peti called together a few of the men in the immediate area and began to share the contents of the Compaque d' Mer regarding the first activities. It had been a consensus that the first items to be built were a large shelter, a large hut with many walls, and another shelter to serve as the church. The rationale had been that the large shelter would provide what its name stated, shelter from the elements. Until constructed, the group would be subject to rain, wind, and barrages of flying insects. Concurrently, there would be the beginnings of two other structures, a large hut subdivided for sleeping and another medium size shelter to serve as a worship area. Food, rest for the body, and rest for the soul. These three were identified in the Compaque d' Mer as priorities. The assembled group saw no reason to challenge this plan and found it good.

"Very good gents," Lars offered in a manner suited to a proclamation. "If I hear no dissent, we shall discuss our plan with others. Until then, this will be our plan for the immediate present. I shall need a lead and a crew for each."

Barnes immediately responded, "I shall lead the construction of the large shelter. Who shall join me?"

Two of the men assembled spoke up and also promised to bring more from Figs to begin this task in the morning.

"I and me mates be pleased to perform this task," responded Barnes.

"Aye, your enthusiasm is appreciated," added Lars. "And now for the initial lodging. If ye do not mind, I shall have Squint take on that task, as he has spent time in the construction trades. Who shall join my fellow governour?"

As with the shelter, two volunteered and offered to gather more from their assembly upon Figs.

"The final initial task shall be the temporary place of worship."

Before Lars had completed the sentence, Tom was volunteering for this work.

"Aye, Governour Lars, if ye doth not mind, I shall take on this task."

"Mind I do not, thank you Governour Tom, and who, may I ask, will assist you?"

"I shall secure a few men from Figs, but I shall also gather insight from Ms. Rachael on this matter."

"Aye, a plan I see, and one which may . . . shall we say . . . succeed," responded Lars whimsically.

"Well gents, you have your direction. May I suggest you begin contemplating where in the clearing on the other side of yonder trees yer structure will be. Create a more complete plan, confirm with the other leads your intentions, and provide me with details as they are confirmed. I, nor you, wish two structures to be within a cubit of each other." With that final word of affirmation, the group dismissed and began their planning.

Coming to the landing, each group assessed the space needed for their task, the potential hazards, and how their structure may interface with the others. However, an initial task and potential concern were immediately made known. Because of the rain, the entire area was a pool of water. The group had a choice: pick another area or modify this area.

While the group was making this decision, a new group of observers was finding humor similar to that found by Alyonsa and Onacheron. This superficially perfect site for an encampment also had the very real negative of standing water. The observers knew that upon each rain; the area gathered water and, when left alone, became a haven for mosquitoes and other annoyances of the human body. This was a reason that it remained undeveloped by the tribe.

As work progressed, it came as no surprise that the group of governours and Puritans in their ignorance were apparently moving forward with the decision to build. The observers still had to stifle a laugh, knowing the large tasks ahead of the group that those new to the land had not contemplated.

As the day waned, the group who had remained on the beach, choose to shelter on the cusp of the woods while in the near distance, Figs buoyed, tethered by her anchor. Aboard Figs remained a group that included the young, the timid, and the uncertain. Aside from the very young, each had left the persecution and lack of freedoms they had previously known. They had freely joined with others to begin anew, to leave behind the previous constraints, to become part of a world where they would lead and not follow. Yet, the expanse of sand and trees seemed more primitive than they had envisioned. They had not fully grasped that there would be no existing lodging, no place to secure food, no . . . anything. It appeared there were a few questions they had naively not asked or consciously not listened to. It was these who queried those who had returned to Figs.

"The woods are dense." "The sand, it be as crystal." "Aye, we saw no others." "Indeed, there be a large area to build for our lodging and worship needs." These were the comments made numerous times to the many who asked. Some grew more eager to begin, yet others were wondering why they had made this decision, realizing that it may be too late.

Ultimately, late it may not be. In the coming days, there began word of the return to England for Figs. When these words reached the ears of some naysayers and doubters, they weighed their alternatives. The alternatives were to stay in this unknown land now that they had braved the 60 days to cross the mighty ocean. The other would be to brave another 60 days of uncertainty but to return to a place of a known future. A future not perfect, not necessarily desirous, but known.

As the light became less, Figs had noticeably fewer diners for the evening meal, due to the group who had elected to spend the night in their new home. Dinner for them would be biscuits and dried corn; however, to them, it was a meal of freedom. Never had such bland fare tasted so good.

With the waning light, those ashore gathered to plan for the night. A circle was formed and 3 chosen to spend parts of the night awake. While there was no reason to believe there were others near, the possibility of man or beast remained. Each of the 3 would take a 4-hour shift. These 12 hours should provide safety until the rising sun began another day; a day designated as Day 1 of their new life.

Surprisingly tired despite the excitement, Tom curled up in a blanket and, using a pile of leaves for his head, fell asleep almost immediately with the foreign sounds of small animals and wind through the branches. Tom's dreams were of an entirely different variety than those superimposed over the swaying cabin and the ever-present feel and smell of salt. The wind and chirping provided a foreign solace leading up to just before dawn when he swore, he smelled Aunt Polly's coffee before opening his eyes. Ah, Aunt Polly, not a day went by that he did not think of her and wonder about her current state. He truly hoped that they would be reunited and celebrate Candlemas, as stated in his last invitation. As reality breached his brain, Tom again realized that his reunion with Polly may not be this Candlemas — but perhaps the one thereafter.

As Tom returned to the present, he realized that leaves were not the best sleeping aid for one's head; boots would have been a better choice. As Tom brought himself upright, he surveyed the surrounding area. A circle of travelers, except for a few empty blankets which were possessed by occupants who had risen earlier than Tom. Stretching into a standing position, Tom chose a brief walk into the woods to bring the circulation back to his legs. During the brief walk, he marveled at how wonderful it was to walk on solid ground.

Walking into the woods was an entirely different sensation. In some respects, Tom's senses were heightened due to the unusual quiet. A quiet that caused Tom to pause when he heard a grunt. Looking about, he saw nothing, but that sound did not sound as one originated from an animal. Standing still for what seemed like 10 minutes, but in reality, was closer to 3, Tom finally dismissed the sound and proceeded on his early morning hike.

Tom had been correct. The grunt was not from an animal, but rather from Theoclys, the brave observing the visitors. Last night had proven too comfortable, and Theoclys had nodded off for a moment; being awakened as Tom's footsteps approached within 5 yards of his observation spot. Tom's closeness of Tom had caused a bodily grunt to be emitted. A grunt which Theoclys strove to contain while ensuring the rest of his body remained compliant and quiet.

As daylight broke and the remainder of the new arrivals woke from their sleep, Theoclys's fellow tribe members joined him for the next hours of observation. Alderon was a seasoned warrior and one whom Theoclys had great respect. After a cursory nod, they returned to observing the ways of those who, it appears, would now be living nearby.

Shortly after Tom arose, the first boat of the day from Figs made its way to shore. One member of the landing party was Rachael. She started the preparation of a morning meal for those who had spent the night in their new home. Upon the boat reaching the shore, she and 5 other women of the congregation lifted the hems of their skirts to avoid their becoming drenched and made their way across the rocks onto the soft and welcoming sand. They bore a box of biscuits, some remaining honey, and a jug of pear cider.

Seeing Rachael brought additional life to Tom's soul. His offering to oversee the building of the shelter for worship would assure that he and Rachael would work closely together these coming weeks. Like the large shelter, construction would entail felling trees for the beams and gathering vines and straw for the roof and walls. The governours had estimated, with proper planning and labor, that the two shelters could be erected within a month. Tom planned to begin gathering the wood as early as this very day. In the storeroom of Figs, were several saws and tools which would be necessary to begin construction. Tom had requested that one longboat carry these tools to the shore and place them in an area where there was constant movement. As security had been a factor discussed in the Compaq de Mer, in the event there were others on the land, this would decrease the chance of their tools becoming gain for another. Further, the governours had realized the immediate peril their charges would be placed in without the proper tools.

Sitting down for a meal, Tom sat with Rachael and explained the plans for the day. Rachael sat and intently listened as if this were the first time she was hearing the details. Tom explained that a three-minute walk into the woods led to a large open area, an area which would easily house 10 structures. It was there that their new existence would begin. The first steps would begin today, which would be the rough outlines of where the three main structures would be located. There would be a large shelter to protect them from rain and wind. Accompanying this would be a smaller structure to serve as a place of worship. These two structures would be in place until more permanent structures were built. It thrilled Rachael that on the very first full day that the worship needs of the community were being addressed. This was the reason they had left England. If the Crowne had a part in identifying priorities, it was a certainty that building a place of worship would not occur for the first months, if not years.

As Tom talked, Rachael tried to stay connected; however, she kept finding herself getting distracted. His nose. Those freckles that had intensified from the days in the sun. That hair, wavy and thick. His voice, more angelic than the very choir she was a part of. It was there that she decided again that she must avoid distraction and, for now, abandon her personal gains for a future month. She had elected to come to the new land to support her family and her church. It should be only after their needs had been met that she should be allowed to appease her own wishes. Upon fighting with this internal demon, the words of Scripture addressing temptation seemed all the more real.

The coming days brought the beginnings of construction and further exploration. Exploring this forested land was a different type of exploration than finding an unfamiliar street in Plymouth or Leichester. Yea, no street nor worn path existed. Standing and dreaming, one could begin to imagine that the footpath they were beginning to tread from beach to inland would become frequented by more. How long would the evolution to a Plymouth or Ivywood take? Was there a desire for this type of industrialization, this desecration of the landscape? How long could society be confined and naivety — nay youthful dreams — be allowed to flourish?

For now, this land was a land of dreams and as there was none to stifle, the dreams could be elaborate and seemingly insurmountable, yet achievable. For Lars, Tom, Barnes, Peti, Mouse, and Squint, their role — their job, if you will — was to make the unsurmountable achievable. If indeed they fulfilled the dreams of their fellow passengers upon Figs, then success be theirs.

The first month

The next days marked beginnings.
Beginnings of life in the Puritans' new home in the
West and the beginnings of the voyage back to
England. Both had similar but different timetables.
Both had to make significant progress before the
beginning of the winter cold. Those staying in the
new land needed to have shelters built and all that
would be necessary to survive the winter. Those
returning needed to be back in England before the
winter winds and the treacherous travel known to
accompany the later months of the year. Fervency
was the word, and to an observer — chaos was
reigning.

It took the 59 Puritans and governours 3 full
days to unload their provisions. Provisions included
not only their belongings; but all they had brought to
establish a civilization. Tools, construction materials,
and hardware were all needed to cut trees, form trees,
and create structures, whether buildings or homes.

The area they were settling in had many trees.
A prayer answered for those with wishes to construct
an encampment that would serve as the beginnings of
their footprint. What the forests provided in trees;
the ground did not provide for planting. It became
immediately obvious that the ground would need
considerable work to produce a harvest of straw,
vegetables, and fruits. Members of the church were
in charge of this area. They soon found that they
needed to provide equal parts prayer and toil for even
a moniker of success. A successful harvest would

produce pumpkins, barley, oats, beans, and peas; an unsuccessful had to produce at least cabbage and wheat, along with a few vegetables. The plan for consumption, what would be ready to eat when, needed modification, as no one had expected the soil to be so 'non-English'. It was indeed an oversight to have not brought barrels of fine soil for the beginnings of the early gardens; worse yet, no one had thought to bring gardening tools. Therefore, no plow or tiller existed for the new crops.

While the challenges of the earth, including diversion of the water source flooding the area, were being evaluated and addressed; the gatherers of meat had an opposite problem. The human population was in the minority when numbered against the beasts of the ground. Squirrel, deer, pig, partridge. All were plentiful and sure to provide sustenance. It was these meats and the equal abundance of fish that not only would provide food for the encampment but also would replenish the coffers of Figs for the long return to England.

This sudden entrance into pre-industrialization in the form of food gathering and construction was an uncommon and unwelcome sight to the indigenous. While the Indians were born and lived respecting the land and all it supported; they now viewed these outsiders who, if left unfettered, could extinguish previous years of growth. Gluttonous was an appropriate term to describe the daily mortal wounding of trees. Wounds that would quell all future growth. Gluttony was also seen in the near-constant shooting of pheasant, pig, or partridge; shooting in quantities far over what could be consumed in a month's sitting. A final act of degradation of the tribe's land was the fishing of their streams for sport, not for feeding their bodies. Excessive killing or damaging without thought of future needs was a concept not embraced by the Indian way. As they had for all time and memory a plethora of goods provided by nature, there were seldom wants. The thought of diminished resources was a foreign and disturbing concept. It was these disturbances that required greater observation and understanding of these poachers, murderers, and defacers.

For nearly a week now, at the end of each day, the 59 from Figs would gather under the frame of two large structures which had been erected to provide safety and comfort from the weather. Protection was offered, though not to the extent provided by the walls of their cabin on Figs. The tradeoff was a quandary. For the Puritans, it was 59 bodies in a 75 by 20-foot single room for 60 days. Each in that room daydreaming of freedom from those walls. Now, they had the extensive earth to wander, but no walls at all. While on Figs, the Puritans contended with the daily assault by the heavy salty air, which prevented one from ever being truly clean. However, here, in their new home, the lack of walls brought on a new frustration. That of the biting variety. Mosquitos and flies, foreign at sea, were everywhere. Tolerance was for the few. The rest bore the mark of their weakness as they developed welts upon their body from the scratching in search of temporary relief.

With the frames complete and the roofs in progress, the Puritans and governours were seeing progress. While these structures were being completed, others planned the construction of a group of smaller buildings. These smaller structures would be for worship and for individual living arrangements amongst families or friends. Those constructing predicted that nearly 10 structures would be fully roofed and have walls by early November. These would be welcome protection against the expected cold. All present were thankful that they had landed in July and not in September.

For those staying, the plans were slowly coming to fruition. Speculation and discussion were slowly being converted to accuracy and fact. The Compaq de Mer had been ratified by a majority and now served as the governours' bible. The topics not addressed in the Compaq de Mer would be evaluated and dispositioned through the Council of Leaders. Through prayer, experience, or happenstance, the group's timing had been nearly ideal. While the days were initially hot, humid, and . . . miserable. Those annoyances and frustrations were slowly waning as August became early September, and preparations for the winter continued in earnest in the form of continued construction, food growth, and storage. The aspirations and dreams of those who had chosen to escape the Crowne were being fulfilled at this moment — the future looking brighter each day.

Aside from the Puritans and governours, there also existed the contingency of sailors commanded by McGuilocutty. The upcoming journey would be his second time to venture from the

West and return to England. He knew from the past the trip back would be with most of Figs empty. He also knew that the meats onboarded would have to be carefully watched for signs of spoilage. A sick crew could serve no one. If the meat and fish became inedible, there would be those sea biscuits. With a life of years and a taste of never, those tasteless morsels would have to sustain him and his crew for the final weeks of the journey.

While those who were staying built, McGuilocutty and his crew repaired. 63 days on the raging seas takes a lot from the most seaworthy of vessels. Figs in her advanced years was far from that. Many a time McGuilocutty swore he would retire the old crate if it made it back to England. That became his goal, his mantra, to return the formerly great Carrick Figs to her home and join the ranks of other esteemed retired vessels. However, a return to England required repairing several holes and reinforcing several cracks. It was during one of these repairs that the return to England became a question. The hold had always been wet; yet during one of the crack repairs, the water level was noticed to have risen to a level not previously seen. McGuilocutty called upon his sailors to use pails to bail the water. A laborious task it was, as the hold was three levels down. A chain of sailors and a day of work were necessary to remove the water from the hold. Unfortunately, and not entirely unexpected, the next day the water had returned. The exact location of the breach was determined; however; the cause was believed to be due to hitting a rock too violently. A blow that caused the wood of the ballast to splinter and crack due to age and rot. If not that, perhaps damage by a substantial weight sliding about during the violent storms. All were possible causes. None solved the problem. A leaking ballast would surely doom Figs to a watery grave within a few days of departure.

Additional investigation found the crack to be on the inside of the ship. As expected, there was a gash in the ballast. This find confirmed why the water came in so slowly. The crack at this time was not overly wide. A larger gash would have noticeably filled the lower level and caused the active sinking of Figs. As a seasoned sailor and captain, McGuilocutty knew what was needed, but was not sure if it existed on this land. Taking a party of two ashore, the captain began his day in search of an elusive tree. McGuilocutty knew that a few select trees produced a cottony fibrous growth around their roots. This soft and wispy wood-like substance could fill cracks as it expanded and mimicked the wood when exposed to water. This could salvage the journey and allow for the return of Figs to England.

The results of the first day of searching produced no success. McGuilocutty had spied several trees that he thought might bear the growth, but in the end, all failed. For two more days, the forests were surveyed and luck was not to be found. All this activity was quite confusing to the Indians. They decided they needed to increase their number of observers. Occurring at the same time were construction activities in the compound and material gathering in the surrounding area. Concurrently, there was food gathering and assorted searches throughout the forest. The members of the tribe realized quickly that their lives were now forever changed.

As McGuilocutty contemplated his forced retirement in this new land — a concept he did not relish — his hope began to wane. Daily, his crew removed the water from the hull, providing hope that Figs would once again make the journey across the great ocean. It was on day four that McGuilocutty began the exploration of a particularly marshy area. He spied several species whose roots were fully submerged, yet the tree grew strong and upright. Tasking one of his sailors with him, McGuilocutty charged the sailor with further exploring the roots. The results of the task provided success. McGuilocutty was soon presented with a fibrous white substance that had grown around the roots. McGuilocutty's lips formed a smile and a raucous "Hallelujah" resounded from his being. Success was his!

Returning to Figs with a large ball of the substance wrapped in a simplistic rag, McGuilocutty descended into the bowels of Figs and fixed his gaze upon the crack, now exposed after the recent dredging. Already beginning to breach water, McGuilocutty pressed his fibrous savior into the crack. An initial layer was made and beginning every few minutes, inspections for leakage. Seeing none, he returned on the hour. By day's end, there remained no breach of water, and the fibrous material may indeed have been the greatest gift of life ever provided to Figs.

McGuilocutty had a restless night of sleep. His night included a candle-lit trip to the lowest level, where he felt for water. None. A sigh of relief came and, with this assurance, he returned to bed for a more peaceful rest.

The next morning, McGuilocutty called the crew together. "Gents 'tis almost time to bid farewell to land and return to our home upon the water. I nor you wish to be a part of the wintery gales of the great Atlantic. Upon the arrival of those wintery swells, I wish to be in a warm room, surrounded by walls and heated by a roaring fire. That is my wish for the weather of November and December. I wish not to be thrashing about in the frozen sea, nor attempting survival with minimal walls and unknown weather. Therefore, gents, we sail at the end of this very week."

After several murmurs by the crew, they ultimately followed their captain's orders and prepared for departure in the coming days. The hull of Figs was loaded with freshly hewn lumber for any necessary repairs at sea. Rations were placed within the barrels of Carp's kitchen. Unfortunately, full replenishment of the candied fruits and other sugar-laden staples were not to be had. Fortunately, the trip would have many weeks of meat for cooking and consumption. This new land was bounteous from that perspective.

It was during this preparation that a husband and wife approached McGuilocutty. Ephram and his wife Carlisle had elected to make the trip from England to the new world. Like all on board, they had made the journey to be allowed to practice their desired religion. However, it was during the long and painful trip over that they began to question the reason for leaving that which, while restrictive, had been all they knew. The Crowne had provided protection, and protection was not necessarily promised in this land devoid of establishment and basic essentials. No housing, no walls, no warmth, no guarantee of sustenance beyond meat and berries. After careful prayer and conversation, Ephram and Carlisle decided to make the journey back. They knew of and willfully agreed to the pain of crossing, the hunger which would ensue, the lack of sleep, and the danger. It was agreed these potentially life-taking events were worth the risk to return to a life of certainty. While existence in England was not necessarily ideal, it was a certain existence.

McGuilocutty listened to their plea and appreciated their feelings. He conveyed the risk and the chance of not returning to England but ending their life in a watery grave. In the end, McGuilocutty consented, and Ephram and Carlisle became a part of the return crew. Carlisle would assist Carp with food preparation and serving. Ephram would perform the duties of a novice sailor. Their future had no bright shining star, but in the event of failure, they would fail together.

The next few days were filled with more activity than the prior ones. McGuilocutty and his crew finished final preparation for returning to England. The governours and Puritans continued their construction of housing and the house of worship. Gardens were tended and alternatives to hay and other insulations were sought. For their first winter, it appeared that leaves, an abundant yet deteriorating material, would provide a modicum of insulation. While harvesting was a term generally used with hays and grasses, in this case, the resource harvested would be — leaves. Amongst these survival tasks, the congregation of Puritans bid adieu to Ephram and Carlisle. Rachael took their decision to return harder than most, as she viewed Carlisle as an older sister and mentor. Whom would she share her deepest secrets? Who would provide her guidance as she navigated her relationship with Tom? Who would provide her the comfort that only a sister can? This would be lost and at the moment, irreplaceable.

As the days passed, the eve of Fig's departure was upon the group before they realized it. The last evening meal was a feast of fish and pork. The ladies had conjured up a nearly edible sweetened treat that would have to replace the loss of candied fruit. Many stories were told and, in the end, hugs were shared and tears were cast as the group that had lived together, experienced together, and worked together separated for probably forever.

Morning came, and for the last time, the longboat returned to Figs. Tom, Lars, Barnes, Peti, and Squint formed a line and saluted the departing craft. Rachael and others joined the early assembly, providing a tearful wave and a prayer for their successful journey.

The longboat pushed off and traversed in the direction against the current. Later that hour, the anchor was seen being pulled back into the ship and a long single note of departure was blown upon Fig's bugle. With that, the mighty Figs inched away from the rocks and over the coming minutes gathered not quite speed but shall we say advanced movement. The group onshore stood steadfast in solemn solidarity and respect for those who had embarked. In time, Figs became that very speck seen earlier by the indigenous and prepared to break the barrier islands and enter the full of the Atlantic.

Upon prayers for health, success, and guidance, the assembly returned to their camp while the crew of Figs made their way toward the rising sun.

Initial meeting

Uneasiness. The uneasiness that comes from a perception; however, in this case, the perception was reality. The perception that they were being watched was, in fact — a fact.

Governours Lars and Barnes were performing their daily stroll around the perimeter of the camp. Weeks earlier, the walk resembled more of a militaristic maneuver, complete with sharp turns and exaggerated steps. The charade was meant to elicit a total consciousness surrounding the current state of the forests and grounds with the intent of determining whether any changes had occurred since the previous inspection. As described in the Compaq de Mer, any perceived change no matter how minor, had to be evaluated to determine the source, from 'their party' or from 'another'. Changes from another would result in an elevated state of attention amongst the settlement until it could be determined whether the group should fear these others.

During one of these expeditions, the governours noted that a pile of leaves bore the slightest sign of smoke. A closer examination revealed a perfectly round pit made with nearby stones, hollowed out a few inches below the ground surface and then covered with leaves to hide the evidence. Were it not for the unusual chill in the air, the covering would never have been detected. However, today it was discovered within hours of its discontinued use. This pit, this fire, was a mere quarter of a mile from their camp. Stifling their voices, they were amazed that the sounds of their camp were audible at this distance. As they were certain none of their party were making fires so close to camp; this was the sign they were dreading. There were others. Were these others friendly, or were the Puritans and governours very lives in danger? That was the question, which would occupy every waking moment while the governours planned their next move.

Returning to the camp, Lars immediately called a meeting of those selected for the leadership council. The council's membership included the five governours, the Parson, and four from the assembly. Duties for this group, as described in the Compaq de Mer, included meeting to discuss priorities, identifying challenges, and — as related to the present matter — addressing concerns.

"Greetings all, thank ye for joining me in such a quick manner," began Lars.

"A surprise to be called, what be the reason for this convocation, governour?" asked the Parson.

Lars continued. "Me fellow members of the leadership council, we have an event which may be an issue."

The group looked back and forth at each other and awaited Lars' next word. Having been on this land for not quite 6 weeks, the group had not expected a major concern.

"We may not be alone . . ." Lars stated in a manner whose receipt was as dramatic as expected. Shock and wide eyes greeted these words, and there was a chilled silence as the group waited for Lars to continue.

"Meself and Governour Barnes were performing our daily inspection not quite an hour ago. We came upon what we believe to be the remnants of a fire. Were it not for the dampness in the air, the wisps of remaining smoke would have been undetected. Upon further discovery, Governour Barnes noted that the remaining sticks and the ground surrounding them were still warm to the touch."

"How far away was this fire?" inquired Brother Elphon of the assembly.

"Not quite a quarter of a mile . . . close enough that in silence ye can hear the talk of our camp."

Silence fell on the group; this invasion was unexpected and took a few minutes to process.

"A quarter mile. . . really?" asked the Pastor speaking incredulously, "that be too close for me liking. I do wonder if they are there now."

"That I cannot say with certainty . . . but I can say, we may be watched, and we need to begin working as if we are watched," responded Lars.

"Shall we tell the others?" asked another member of the assembly.

"I would suggest not, at least not immediately," offered Barnes.

Lars began. "I concur. No reason for scaring the others until we know that fear is the appropriate response. I suggest that we begin more frequent trips outside the camp. We may actually see our observers in the open."

"Dost thou think they be friendly?" asked the Parson.

"Well, we are not dead yet; so a massacre is not their first priority . . . at least that be me opinion," replied Tom in response to the question.

"Then it is settled. We shall not pass on this news, and we shall plan to explore in shorter intervals. Stay strong, me fellow leaders." With this word of encouragement, Lars dismissed the assembly.

As Tom was leaving the group, Rachael caught his eye.

"Good Morrow, governour."

"Good Morrow, Miss Rachael."

"A bit early for an assembly. Was that not the Leadership Council?"

"Ah, so it was," responded Tom in a bit of an evasive answer.

"Is there a problem?"

"Problem? Oh no . . . not a problem."

"I do believe me Great-Aunt Faniel would think differently. If she saw that assembly of yours meeting this early, she would surely believe ill was afoot. Are you going to call me great-aunt a liar, governour?"

"If we don't meet, there be no reason for the council's existence," Tom began, trying to put Rachael's mind on another track.

"Thomas Smythe, I dare say you are avoiding the question."

Quickly thinking, Tom responded, "Seems a few are feeling ill and didn't want to scare the others. One's mind can play tricks on them, and before you know it, the entire camp has a mostly mental epidemic. The council was discussing how to address this issue before it becomes real."

Taking it in, Rachael surveyed Tom's demeanor. "I am not sure I believe you Governour Smythe. I will have my eye on you," replied Rachael with a whimsical emphasis on the final words.

"God give ye a good day, Miss Rachael," Tom responded, attempting to provide no visual clues.

Believing he had initially escaped Rachael's inquiry, Tom proceeded to the far corner of the camp where he found Elphon.

"Are ye ready?" inquired Tom.

"That I be," responded Elphon. "Governour, do you think I shall need a weapon, a knife, a gun, at least a large stick?"

"No gun, we go in peace. I trust your muscles will suffice if needed. If those fail, be rest assured, your yells of terror shall serve as our weapon to save the others, "replied Tom, showing little comfort as those words left his lips.

"Aye . . . Aye Sir," replied an uncertain Elphon.

With these thoughts of uncertainty, the two left to the North and kept that direction for 5 minutes. Coming to another natural opening, they paused and listened. Both men looked around while standing firmly on the dirt path. While showing gentle use, the path did not disclose the tracks of recent feet or boots. The weather was idyllic; a gentle breeze making its way through the branches and boughs accompanied by traces of light breaking through the upper lofts and illuminating the earth below. It was in this perfection that an unnatural hue was detected. Just to the right of Elphon, Tom detected a swatch of color not of this earth. The hue was a pale brown containing a mixture of cream and a darker pigment. A few inches higher amongst the leaves, a blue which no leaf would exhibit.

Showing no emotion, Tom slowly turned to say in a matter-of-fact voice, "Elphon it is time to return."

Tom's heart beat at a rate rarely achieved as he made the first steps toward the camp. With each step, he carefully listened for the sound of others following. There were none.

Upon reaching a point within a few yards of the camp, Tom spoke to Elphon.

"I saw them . . . did ye?"

"You did?" asked Elphon with surprise.

"Yea, when we stopped, I saw a face and an eye . . . colors not of the forest, but of man."

"What shall we do?" inquired Elphon knowing that those who were viewing them were not far behind.

"We shall go back, not at this moment shall we return to the very lair whence we came, but soon," Tom stated in a definitive voice of leadership. "As we are still alive, those nearby do not wish us immediately dead; otherwise, they would have attacked while there were only the two of us. Therefore, we shall return."

That evening, Tom reported what he had seen to the Council. It was agreed that a presentation of a gift may help with what was sure to be an eventual meeting. As their viewers had already seen Tom and Elphon, the assembly agreed that they would be the bearers on this expedition, an expedition dubbed 'when we meet'.

Probably not by coincidence, as the council meeting ended, once again Rachael was present to approach Tom.

"Another sick Puritan?" asked Rachael with skepticism. "I asked casually and there are none among us who are sick, lest none of who will admit their malady. So, I must say I am not currently in a position to trust your responses, Governour Smythe."

"Ah dear Rachael, today was not to talk of the ill but to begin a discussion of the next construction phase for your house of worship. Your very lips have told me that one who worships and feels closer to their God is happier and more productive. With the approaching Fall, we will need a grandiose amount of productivity, and the completion of your house of worship is next in line."

Taken aback by the potentially accurate answer, Rachael knew not what to say. "Fall? Really . . . I dare say I had not thought of that."

"Aye, one can't be building while snow be a blowing, for now, we have only a frame, we need walls and roofs if we wish souls to be happy and proclaim joy!" Tom responded, internally happy that his diversion had been appropriate.

"A beautiful night it is," Tom began in his continued distraction. "Do you find the weather more pleasing here or back in Ivybridge?"

"Aye Tom, the weather here be so pristine and clean. The air be not fouled by the smoke of industry, the trees flourish and hide not the growth of towns and villages. It is so simple . . . so wonderful, so . . . godly."

"And not a remnant of the Crowe to tell us otherwise!" joked Tom to which he earned a smirk.

"Well, I shall go," responded Tom, "I wish to not cause speculation and rumour amongst your community. Wandering in this godly environment when light is falling cannot be appropriate for a woman of your standing."

"I accept your departure and your appreciation of my virtue," replied Rachael as she reached for a gentle touch of Tom's hand before returning to her shelter area.

The next day, Tom and Elphon began the execution of their plan. Before their walk, they gathered some berries and took a few of the remaining candied fruits. These they placed upon a small plate and then ventured for the 5 short minutes to the clearing.

Hesitating in the same place, they placed the plate on a nearby rock and quietly turned and slowly returned to their aspiring village, a village they had previously thought to be safe. This event continued the next day at approximately the same time; however, this time they bore large apples harvested from the trees along with a few more of the candied fruits. As they approached the clearing, they noted that the plate previously left was empty. Approaching the plate, they looked about, detecting none obviously in the nearby surroundings. Tom and Elphon placed their new gifts on the plate and slowly turned to return. A few moments later, Tom thought he detected a movement in the brush but chose to not look and focus on the return to their village.

Day three was to bring the same routine; however, earlier in the day, another routine was changed. As Barnes and Lars were performing their mid-morning walk, they spied a wood-hewn bowl sitting upon a rock, a mere 200 yards from the camp perimeter. Approaching the bowl, they saw slices of prepared fish with berries. It appeared that their indigenous friends were attempting to show similar gratitude, or so they hoped. Yea, Tom, and his fellow governours knew that even amongst the council, there would be a few doubters who would believe that this offering was in reality a manner of eliminating them. Poisoning their community would surely contribute to their demise. These would be the thoughts of some. They could only hope that saner minds would prevail, and a majority of the council would view the previous actions as positive and not threatening.

Upon a retelling of the prior events, the council decided that for the next offering, Tom and Elphon would stay a few minutes in the hopes of an actual meeting. A few hours later, Tom and Elphon gathered some cooked pheasant which had been fermenting all day in spices, and again the candied ginger sticks. Walking in fear, they approached the clearing.

Surveying the area, the presence of another was not immediately known; however, as this was the third day of exchange, Tom and Elphon were quite sure their diligent observers were present. Once again, the plate provided on the day prior lay empty. Approaching the plate, Tom placed the daily offering upon the delivery rock. Upon its delivery, Tom and Elphon backed to a respectful distance on the edge of the clearing. A distance that provided sight of both the plate and the surrounding area.

It was there they waited. One minute, two minutes. At minute four, a rustle of branches was observed in the brush nearest the plate. Within a few seconds, Tom and Elphon's lives changed forever, for slowly erupting from the brush came two men, tanned of skin and black of hair. Their arms were muscled, their eyes piercing. The hair on their head was long and adorned with colored trinkets. The garments they wore were of leather, as were the shoes on their feet. They too spent a few seconds staring at their guests, taking in the same details for reporting back to their tribe.

While watching Tom and Elphon, they reached out and gingerly took the plate, immediately removing the candied fruit and placing it in their mouth, a mouth which displayed an enormous smile upon receipt of the candy.

Tom and Elphon returned a large smile and then both bowed a deep bow and slowly turned to return to their camp. It was at that moment that the quiet was broken, as one of the members of the indigenous tribe uttered a word.

"Migwetc," while rubbing his belly.

Tom and Elphon returned the greeting. "Migwetc" as they too rubbed their bellies.

In response, the tribe members broadly smiled.

History had just been made, reflecting the first meeting of the indigenous of the West and the aspirants from the East. However, for this book, no one knew what the next chapter would bear.

Together Yet Separate

Since the initial meeting some two weeks prior, each group attempted to be more visible to the other. No longer existing were the tribe's camouflaged peering and observation from yards away of their new neighbors. No more were there the governours' militaristic walks to ensure their boundary had not been breached. These actions were replaced with a walk by one to the perimeter of the other where, when sighted, they were greeted with a wave and smile. Frequently, these visits included a plate of offerings from the day's cooking. While the offerings of the Puritans were sparse, the offerings by the indigenous were always welcome and provided some needed variation.

While conversation remained a barrier, charadic hand signs proved to be the most successful. It was only hoped that the phrase conveyed matched the phrase intended. A response of a smile or humor was always welcome. A scowl or angry shout meant there had been a misinterpretation, resulting in a deep bow by the offending governour or Puritan. The tribe came to realize this bodily posture to be an act of contrition, and that no ill will was meant. In time, the tribe believed their neighbors meant no harm, and each worked at more accurately conveying their thoughts.

As September ended, a group consisting primarily of tribal women visited the Puritan camp. Upon arrival, the group motioned the women to follow them. Rachael was amongst the group of puritans who followed their hosts. Tom accompanied in both interest and to provide protection if needed.

"Where do you think we are going?" Inquired Rachael.

"That I know not. However, I take this as a good sign," replied Tom.

"Perhaps we shall see their camp. I would like very much to see how they succeed," offered Rachael.

"Are ye inferring that we governours are failing you?" Tom playfully inquired.

"Never Sir, that thought never entered this womanly mind," offered Rachael in equal playfulness.

A few minutes later found both groups at the tribal camp. Proceeding to a far edge of the encampment was the tribe's garden. The women of the tribe pointed toward the garden and offered the Puritan women a closer look at the vegetables and soil.

The offerings of the garden were wondrous. Large melons, succulent tomatoes, engorged gourds. A few feet away were strands of hay, much of it baled in preparation for the winter. All being shown to provide their new neighbors insight on what they could grow in this difficult soil.

A further examination of the soil provided the clue to the success — a smelly clue it was. The Puritans soon learned that these indigenous were using physical waste from animals to provide better growing conditions. A challenging fragrance it was, but the results seemed well worth the negativity.

The tribal women giggled as their neighbors realized what they were seeing and the reality of the smell. As an appeasing action, the tribal women offered two large tomatoes to their guests. The women consumed the first with glee. The second they saved for sharing back at their camp.

Rachael grinned continuously at the sight of the garden and the joy she was experiencing from making contact with another. Her smile was noticed by her indigenous friends, and a few approached her. Cautiously, one of the tribal women raised her open palm to Rachael's face. Rachael continued to smile as the woman cautiously reached out and stroked her cheek. The woman uttered a single word to those around, to which they tittered and smiled.

Unknown to Rachael, the woman had commented on her smooth skin. Rachael was just happy that a slap was not the result of the open hand. In a return of tactile friendliness, Rachael opened her hand and slowly moved it to the hair of the woman near her. The other woman silently stood and allowed Rachael to stroke her thick, black hair. Rachael responded with a smile, and schoolgirl giggles resounded amongst those present.

Noticing a bracelet Rachael was wearing, one of the women pointed to it. Realizing the importance of such a moment, Rachael chose to part with this sentimental bracelet provided to her by her grandmother. Rachael believed that Nana would be smiling at her as she strove to be a good ambassador for these new neighbors thousands of miles from her past. Removing her bracelet, Rachael handed it gingerly to the woman who was showing interest.

Placing the bracelet in her hand, Rachael bowed releasing her hands from the heirloom.

Overcome with tears, the woman reached into her hair and removed two braids made of colorful shells. The woman returned the gesture and placed the braids into Rachael's hand, mimicking the bow. The first act of female bonding between the East and West had just occurred.

Their stay continued for another 30 minutes, at which time both sides waved to the other and the women with Tom returned to their camp, holding onto the large tomato and memories of their new friendships.

At the Puritan camp, construction continued during the coming weeks. The most recent addition was the walls, a necessity for winter housing. Observant by nature, the communication barrier did not deter assistance from the tribe, as the indigenous could see what problems their new friends were about to encounter. The day after a particularly chilly night, when numerous Puritans were again questioning their choice to leave the warmth of their English dwellings, an unexpected visit occurred.

Early in the morning, a group of 10 Indian braves brought with them large sacks overstuffed with hay. Approaching the camp and waiting for recognition, the Puritans and governours were startled by the early morning visit. Seeing that the braves bore large bags instigated curiosity and a trio of the governours who had just recently awoke proceeded toward the braves and with wide smiles waved them into the compound. The braves moved forward bearing their gifts and lay the stuffed bags at the feet of the governours. Examining the bags, the Indians mimicked a shivering motion and pointed toward the overstuffed bags. The governours joy was clear by their smiles and proceeding bows. The Indians grinned, followed by a wave in the manner they had grown accustomed and left the encampment.

In the coming weeks, this courtship of curiosity and friendliness continued. As the tribe members continued to make periodic visits and provide needed supplies, food, and techniques for creating the same; the Puritans, no longer visitors, began to wonder what they could offer the indigenous. Soon one item of barter became evident. During one visit, a few members of the tribe observed the governours cleaning rifles. The braves seemed quite taken by this sight and showed incredible interest. In a show of demonstration, some ducks were disturbed from their roost and an ensuing bullet claimed the birds as they took flight. The ease with which the kill occurred caused intense concern and respect by the tribe members as they realized the power of these pipes of iron. In response to his interest, Peti offered a rifle to the brave.

The group assembled watched with great interest in what would happen next. The very lives of those in the compound were in danger, as a deadly weapon was now in the hands of an unknown. As the seconds ticked, the brave felt the gun and then with a grimace dropped it on the ground as his hand breached the barrel still warm from the discharge.

Barnes retrieved the gun and with his hands pointed to the hot areas. Facial contortions indicated the pain of touching the hot area, and with that, Barnes returned the rifle to the brave.

After a few more moments, the brave raised the gun to the area above the trees, and sighting a bird, he carefully pulled the trigger. There was a hesitation as he realized the strength needed and then the unexpected discharge. The ensuing explosion was more violent than anticipated, pushing the brave's arm and shoulder back. The first shot by the brave garnered him a bird pierced by the bullet. Fascinated by the power of the pipe of iron, the brave bowed and smiled as he returned the rifle to the owner. Those of the tribe present shared with appreciation the power of the iron pipe. All in the immediate vicinity returned the ceremonial bow.

Upon seeing this display, later in the day, Lars called together the Council of Leaders. "Gentlemen," he began, "we have witnessed the introduction of rifles and bullets to the Indian. Yea, while I have no fear at the moment, I dare say that this may not be an appropriate move or strategy. While our friendship is growing and fear of both appears to be waning, I wish not to be destroyed by the weapons of our own hand."

Barnes replied, "Gentlemen, I know we seek safety in all areas of our existence. Our safety is already plagued with a potential food shortage and with the approach of colder evenings and days. We have enough to be concerned without wondering if we shall be shot by a bullet which we hath brought into this world."

The next comment was by the Parson, who inquired, "Do we not have some level of trust for these indigenous? Do we not trust that God will provide and protect?"

"Aye Parson," Lars began, "we do, but is providing an unknown with such a temptation appropriate? With no proven communication, a simple act or mistake can be one for which the Indian will seek revenge. Do we wish to provide the source of achieving that ultimate revenge?"

The conversation continued, ultimately determining that firearms would not be readily provided for the tribes to use and that only with the approval of the Council would a rifle ever be given as a gift. While some assembled argued that food and trinkets are freely provided to the tribe; the governours present reiterated that trinkets do not kill — bullets do.

As their separate lives continued, the days became shorter and the temperatures colder. The previous gifts by the tribe were greatly welcome as the Puritans' first harvesting of hay was many months away and their soil was still grossly incapable of sustaining the 57 of them. Were it not for body heat and a few meager inches of insulation to protect their bodies from the wind, the group would surely have perished. To avoid that ultimate fate in the coldest of temperatures, temperatures which were a few months away, the Puritans and governours continued to build. The houses which were constructed had nearly a cubit of space behind the interior walls to allow for stuffing of what they could find. These recesses were filled with leaves, boughs, animal skins, and ash. While not the greatest barrier, as the stuffing grew, the warmth inside the dwelling increased. Governour

O'Toole had become an expert on this construction and with his guidance, the group had increased the hours of warmth during the nights, which dropped in temperature to a chilled level.

On one trip Tom made to the tribal camp, the tribe introduced him to their leader, an elder named Opechancanough. The pronunciation of his name took nearly 10 minutes to learn. Lucky for Tom, the syllables were quite easy. For many times, Tom repeated with guidance, 'O Pe Chan Canoe', 'O Pe Chan Canoe'. With each attempt, the smiles of the indigenous got broader and their appreciation for their new friend grew.

Upon meeting the challenge of the leader's name, Tom approached and performed the symbolic bow of respect. He was waved toward a seat by the leader and offered a plate of berries. Tom exhibited a large smile and, folding his hands in prayer, bowed his head again to the leader.

For the next several minutes, the two sat quietly looking at each, taking in the details of the other while they consumed the plate of berries. The men were in stark contrast to each other. Opechancanough was a weathered old man whose remaining teeth were permanently discolored. His grayed hairs were unkempt and in patches. His arms and shoulders bore the scars of previous battles with both man and beast.

Tom, in opposition, was a young man whose full head of hair still held the luster of its original color. His brows were bushy and his teeth complete. Were it not for the 60 days of salt drenching, his skin would match his age, as his life had not borne the physical drama of the elder leader. And so it was that at this initial meeting, silence was the language and observation, the activity. Upon completion of their shared meal, Tom arose, bowed respectfully to the leader, and proceeded out of their encampment, returning to his own.

Upon his return, he encountered O'Toole. "Squint . . . I have just met their leader."

"Ye did . . . are we in danger?" joked Squint.

Taken aback, Tom replied, "Not a joking matter! . . . especially for a governour. No, we are not in danger! it was quite a cordial meeting. We shared berries, and little else."

"Why is this?" asked Squint.

"Because we share not the language," laughed Tom. "Yet, by all who are in heaven, I do believe he knew I brought him no harm."

"Aye mate, this be good," began Squint, "were it not for the hay, bacon, beans, and pumpkin, we would surely have resorted to eating bark. Truth be told, the tribe has saved us and I know we will need their saving even more in the coming months."

"Never has a truer statement been made, me fellow governour. No . . . Never!"

And with that, the two continued into the compound and began to place more insulation into the walls of their new home, insulation originally suggested by their new friends.

First Feast planning

It was another beautiful morning in the unspoiled land of Virginia. The air was clear; the skies were blue, and the scent of forest gently permeated the air. Life was good. It appeared that the governours and Puritans had made the right choice in their escape from the Crowne. These were the thoughts of Tom as he rose and greeted his 95th day as a denizen of these new lands. It was on this morning that Tom's plan began. The plan began as an ache, an ache in Tom's stomach as he realized he was hungry. As he grabbed his tattered jacket to fend off the morning chill, he began his walk toward the newly constructed dining area — a structure that also served for meetings and food storage. It was into this area that Tom marched, filled with grandiose plans waiting to be shared. As Tom entered the Hall, he was greeted by at least 10 — some of whom had been assembled since just after dawn.

"Good Morrow governour, glad ye could make out of bed today," joked Ned, a Puritan known for early rising and retiring equally early.

"Well, here I be . . . ready for another glorious day!" replied Tom.

"Too early for a drink of apple cider?" inquired another. "The women-folk completed a batch late yesterday."

"Aye, that and an apple would do this weary body good."

Taking a seat amongst the others, Tom began to nourish his body. As he did, he looked up to see

Lars entering the Hall. Raising his hand, he motioned Lars to the seat beside him.

"Good Morrow Lars, how did ye rest?" asked Tom of his boon buddy and fellow governour.

"Glorious! Glorious was me sleep. Thank ye for askin'," replied Lars as he shook off the final remnants of the night hours.

"Lars . . . I have a plan," began Tom.

"You . . . a plan . . . surely not," joke Lars.

"Aye, that I do."

"Planning and plotting . . . that is what ye do Governour Smythe. From the day I met ye, planning and plotting, plotting and planning . . . doth thou brain ever sleep?" joked Lars.

"Only when I has had too much mead," Tom replied with a laugh; a laugh stifled by a drink of the cider.

"What be ye thinking, mate?"

"A feast."

"Feast?"

"Yes, a feast; a feast on the order of Epiphany, Christmas, and Candlemas. Today shall be our 95th day upon the shores of Virginia. In a mere 5 days will be our centennial, a centennial which deserves recognition. I request that later today, we announce to all that in 5 days, we shall hold a feast. A feast recognizing our new land and our new friends. We shall invite the local tribe and dine with them in the fashion of previous sumptuous feasts. What think thee Governour Bonham?"

"Planner and plotter ye be, and again a most worthy plan ye have plotted. I concur with yer plans me fellow governour. Go forth and Feast!"

With this blessing and concurrence, Tom proceeded to the area frequented by the women behind the dining area, an area where most of the cooking occurred. Several women were already tending the daily pot. The assorted smells emitting were a joy to the olfactory, causing Tom to hesitate and savor the sensorial reward before entering the area.

Sitting at the table shelling nuts and cutting fruit were a majority of the women. Attired in tunics with scarves in their hair, they proceeded with the daily task of ensuring the community was fed. Entering the area, Tom looked about for the one woman who was not readily found.

"Aye governour . . . Good Day to ye," spoke Meriam, the Parson's wife, as she continued peeling a stack of apples.

"And to you, Maid Meriam. A joyous morn to ye all," began Tom." Know ye where Rachael be?"

"Aye governour," replied a familiar voice, entering with a basket of gourds.

Turning towards the voice, Tom answered, "Good Morrow, Miss Rachael. I trust your sleep was well."

"That it be . . . wondrous and peaceful. What brings ye to this area? Care to peel a basket or two of these apples?" joked Rachael.

"I dare say the other men would not appreciate me graciously performing such a task, as they may fear that they be next, therefore, I shall pass." began Tom with a lilt of humor in his voice, "However, I do have a plan I would like to discuss."

"Please be seated, dear governour," replied Bridget, the choirmaster's wife.

"Thank ye," replied Tom as he took a seat at the table. As each of the women's eyes rested on Tom, he began to explain his plan. "If I may, I have a proposal I would like yer thoughts on . . ."

"Pray continue governour," replied Bridget.

"I would like to propose a celebration. As today marks our 95th day upon these shores. I believe this victory should be memorialized for one and all. In 5 days, it shall be our centennial. One hundred days will have passed. We knew not if we would survive . . . what would greet us . . . if any, would greet us. Here we find ourselves with food, with new friends . . . with new hope! Dost thou agree?"

"Aye, you speak the truth governour, pray continue," were the affirmative words of Meriam.

"I propose a feast. A feast of the likes of Candlemas, or Epiphany, or ye verily . . . that of Christmas. Food and festivities. Dining and dancing. And . . . and to provide an opportunity for the learning of more of the customs of our native friends. We shall invite Opechancanough and his braves to dine with us, to drink with us, and to learn more of our ways, just as we learn theirs. What say thee?"

The women around the table had ceased working as Tom mentioned the tribes and Opechancanough. Fear and distrust were innate within the women, and while their faith taught them to trust and forgive, their genetics instilled fear. A fear which could only be described as indismissible.

"Governour . . ." began Bridget, "how dost thou propose to communicate this to our native friends?"

"Aye governour," began another, "offering food as they approach is quite different from planning a future event. How will you communicate this?"

"We shall try . . . no, I shall try," was the answer offered by Tom to those assembled.

"Are ye willing? Can ye help?" asked Tom.

After a moment's lapse, Rachael stood and offered, "Aye, governour, I shall support yer plan . . . nay not merely the plan but yer celebration. It doth truly sound wondrous!"

"And I." "And I." "Aye." These were the replies from around the table.

Having his concurrence, Tom returned to a corner of the compound to plan the Celebration of New Beginnings . . .their First Feast.

For the next several hours, Tom laid out his plan. His plan had two parts. The first would be communication with those in their camp. The second would be communication with the tribe. Tom planned to communicate to the tribe with basic hand gestures and items of food. For the date, he would use a rudimentary calendar. Armed with this thought and plan, Tom began his communication with his fellow governours and Puritans.

Crossing the now-named community square, Tom entered the gathering hut, the largest room under a roof, and the location of all centralized activities. Besides seating and freshly hewn tables, the hut even boasted a bell designated the Assembly Bell. Found within the bowel of Figs was an old bell salvaged from a beached ship. The group had silently appropriated it, and now it served to beckon all as needed. This was a time of need and appropriately the bell was rung. Within 15 minutes, all within hearing distance had abandoned their current task and sat in wait for the impromptu meeting to start. Seeing nearly all present, Tom began.

"Fellow Puritans, esteemed governours, craftsmen, and cooks . . . I bring ye together fer yer approval. As today marks our 95th day upon the soil of this new land, I believe an appropriate celebration of our upcoming centennial might be in order. A Celebration of New Beginnings. A celebration of our new land, our new friends, our new purpose. In the glorious tradition of Candlemas, Epiphany, and Christmas, I seek your approval to have a feast . . . our First Feast. A feast of a type not previously seen in this land. A feast including the best of our past while bringing together our new tribal friends. I propose this feast to be in 5 days, upon our centennial in this new land, and to include all from our camp and all from the tribal camp nearby."

Hesitating, Tom awaited a comment or challenge. Hearing none, Tom continued. "May I have a yea or a nay as to the Celebration of New Beginnings?"

Quiet discussion amongst the various assembled ensued. Questions that Tom believed would happen, did in fact, not. Finally, after a few minutes, Governour O'Toole stood.

"On behalf of the governour's I concur."

A few moments later, Parson Malone stood.

"Aye, on behalf of the Puritans who came to this land seeking freedom, we concur."

"On behalf of the cooks, we concur . . ." came the giggling voice of Rachael.

"This be good, a celebration cannot be without cooks!" replied Tom in a playfully affirming manner.

Shocked by the agreement, Tom asked the final question.

"Doth any man or woman see the need to quell this assembling? If not, let the planning commence!"

The silence was deafening, and with that Tom rang the Assembly Bell in proclamation of the proposal.

"Thank ye, Governour Tom," were the words echoed by many. As Tom left the assembly area, he could hear stray conversations about the food which would be served and how to seat the group.

Having secured approval, Tom gathered some paper, quill, ink, and an apple. Armed with these and his ideas, Tom prepared to leave the camp to begin his communication with the tribe. Before leaving camp, he stopped by the cooking area to retrieve one of the women's bags of candied fruit, a favorite of the indigenous. Not near the level of perfection as those brought from England, these were indeed a suitable substitute where none other existed.

The encampment of the tribe was a brief 30-minute walk. As Tom approached the tribe, he heard the sounds of those gathering to see who was approaching their space. Unfortunately, all of the European descent were not skilled in quietly approaching an area. The crackling of twigs, the sound of boots hitting the soil, the movement of broken rock. All were sounds that the tribe avoided and all which alerted the tribe when another was approaching.

As Tom turned the bend preparing to walk into the camp, his eyes immediately met those of the outer ring of braves. A group quickly assembled to prevent those unwanted from entering their village. Seeing it was Tom, the braves lowered their weapons and beckoned him forth.

Tom walked through the gate and surveyed the area for Opechancanough. On the far side of the camp, Tom saw he whom he sought. Slowly walking to not cause any unnecessary stirring amongst the tribe, Tom approached Opechancanough, waiting for a few feet from him for recognition.

Opechancanough detected the presence of one not of the land and looked up from his conversation. Seeing Tom, he looked into the eyes of he with whom he had been conversing, and with a motion of his hand dismissed him. His face remained stoic, his demeanor unchanged. Turning to Tom, he motioned him to come forward.

Tom approached and when within arm's reach, he extended his hand in friendship. Opechancanough now familiar with this custom, did the same and motioned for Tom to sit.

Sitting upon the rock in the nearest proximity, Tom first offered the candied fruit. For a moment, Opechancanough relaxed his pursed lips and broke into a momentary smile. Tom noticed this brief change and took it as appreciation for the gift.

Tom then began his task of conveyance about the upcoming feast. First, Tom drew a calendar with 30 days on a piece of paper he had brought. Showing this to Opechancanough, there was little reaction, only a brief perception of puzzlement. Tom placed on 'x' on today, to which he stood and moved his hand around in a circle while rotating his body, signifying all that surrounded him was that 'x'. A brief nod by Opechancanough showed some appreciation for the symbol. Tom then took a second piece of paper. He drew 5 boxes with spaces between them. Placing an 'x' in the first box, he pointed to the 'x' on the original sheet. Tom did this motion multiple times, trying to convey they were the same. Opechancanough nodded. Tom then drew a moon followed by the sun in the space between the first two boxes. When pointing to the second box he pointed in the distance and up in the sky. Again, a brief nod; again puzzlement. Repeating the same with the next 3 boxes, Tom tried to convey days in the future. Tom's final conveyance involved the concept of food. Through both pointing at food and drawing rudimentary fish and duck; Tom attempted to convey eating on the 5th day. Upon completion of his attempt at teaching, Tom rose, extended his hand in friendship, and left the Indian camp.

Tom repeated this same routine for the next 4 days, each day showing Opechancanough the calendar squares that corresponded to the current day, the past day, and the future day. With each visit, Opechancanough's understanding of the concept appeared to grow.

Concurrent with these visits, the womenfolk planned the Feast. Some of the necessary items had been brought from England. Others were indigenous to the area. Unfortunately, some would have to be forgone unless Opechancanough and his members brought the items.

Candied fruit was definitely on the menu, as would be dried apples and beans. Bird or beast would be on the menu if the men were successful on their hunt. The presence of fish by those attending from the tribe was almost certain.

The younger ones in the group were charged with nut collection. The collected nuts would form the basis for many treats and dishes. Some never partaken by those present. The abundance of honey assured that sweetened fare would be present for all to enjoy.

The centerpiece of the meal would be the pottage. Ah yes, the mainstay of every robust and celebratory meal. The stew was assured to provide comfort to the stomach and joy to those who partook. Complete with secret ingredients of the preparers, all eagerly awaited the pottage's completion. The temptation would fill the camp with smells of joy for hours to come before the consumption, and when complete, would draw all to its cauldron. The plans were in motion for the Celebration of New Beginnings.

When not conferring with his fellow governours or checking the local feast preparation, Tom continued to visit Opechancanough. At 3 days before the Feast, Tom again visited with the calendar, showing the dates until the Feast with the moon and sun between each day. On the last day, he had drawn a fish, an apple, and stalks of wheat. During this day's visit, Tom once again performed the counting ritual. He repeated the count until day 5. He had Opechancanough count along with him. On the 5th day, Tom visualized eating the apple, fish, and wheat. Opechancanough nodded in understanding.

Twice more, Tom visited the camp and emphasized eating on that future day. Each time, there appeared to be more understanding.

As understanding appeared to increase, so too did excitement amongst the Puritans. The journey had been hard, the perils greater than expected, the loss of life and health a taker of substantial tolls on the spirit and heartiness of the remaining. A feast was indeed needed. Similar to the adrenaline experienced on Christmas morn, the prospect of spending several hours dining elegantly on fruit and meat of the land was the boost needed by all. Wherever Tom went, others congratulated him for his brilliance, and with each day he further endeared himself as an appropriate choice to govern and lead. A far cry it was from the Tom Smythe who left the port of Plymouth those 6 months past. But boost his importance by succumbing to his own laurels — he could not. Tom had to ensure the local tribe attended. An attendance that was questionable by the speaking gap. Would this gap make this First Feast a non-reality?

On Tom's last visit, the day before the Feast, he noticed more activity occurring among the female squaws. He noted an increase in quantities cooked.

It appeared his teachings had been successful. There would indeed be a feast.

Sustenance

The day began like many others. Nature was abundant with a beautiful blue sky, chirping birds, and a gentle breeze with a hint of pine. However, this day also bore an air of completeness, of beginnings, of anticipation. Today was the day on which all would gather in a spirit of friendship and joy. Just 5 days in planning, the Celebration of New Beginnings, our First Feast, was here.

As the hours passed and the hour of the First Feast approached, Tom decided it was time to confirm whether his previous actions had appropriately conveyed the upcoming event. Departing the camp, Tom headed toward the village of Opechancanough. However, after just 5 minutes, Tom's eyes were treated to a wondrous sight! Coming towards him, a line of braves, women, and children were marching forward. The group was carrying baskets, and although covered, the smells were a beautiful gift to Tom's senses. Other members of the tribe carried poles supporting the weight of many freshly caught fish; others carried spits upon which birds of prey were skewered. Tom approached the group, put his hands in the air as a symbol of thankfulness and celebration, and knelt before the coming caravan. Pausing a few seconds, he rose and looked at his guests. A faint smile of appreciation was detected on the faces of the tribal elders, their normal scowls of mistrust happily vacant.

Tom's role now became one of escort. As if rolling out a red carpet, Tom walked in front of the assemblage and parted branches, pushed aside small stones, and readied the path for the food and friends. Tom's glee got the best of him and his mannerisms became more animated as he adopted dancelike moves and added twirls and leaps to his clearing activities. His guests, not sure of the meaning, could only smirk in amusement.

The hard work had paid off, Tom had conceived the Feast, communicated the Feast and at this moment was ushering in the Feast. The sight of Tom walking forward with a tribe of natives would, under other circumstances, be an event of concern. Were they under attack? Would they survive the next hours? Why were so many approaching their camp? These would have been the natural questions of one trained in the military arts, and although the Feast had been planned, a subtle feeling of distrust and caution still permeated the event.

These same feelings of an unnatural act were sensed by the tribal leaders. Is this a trick? What trap has been laid by these from across the great water? Had Opechancanough sought council on this decision? These and other thoughts were harbored by the elders and older men of the tribe as they made their way into the camp of their natural enemy. An enemy with pipes of iron capable of immediate decimation.

Waiting for the group was a gathering of the governours and men of the camp. Two small tables had been prepared outside the camp walls. Upon the approach of Opechancanough and his tribe, Lars strode forward and raised his hands for all to stop. All eyes then focused on Lars, awaiting his next move.

With distinct slow movements, Lars pulled a small gun from his waist, and with slowness and precise movements, he placed the gun upon the table and returned to his place in line. This same activity took place 15 times, as each man removed his weapon and placed it on the table outside the fenced area.

Upon completion of this ceremonial act, 15 governours and members of the Puritan community extended their arms in a pointing gesture, welcoming their neighbors to their camp. This sincere act of goodwill was greeted with marked hesitation by Opechancanough and his tribe. An act that lasted not more than two minutes, but at the moment seemed like far more. The ritualistic disarmament by the governours resulted in a similar disarming by the chief and his tribe. Upon Opechancanough's relinquishment of his ever-present knife, there was an uneasy transfer of knives and bows from the natives to the provided tables; an abandonment of the accouterments carried to protect themselves at all times.

Watching from the gateway, Lars, Tom, and the others were pleased, while still surprised by the honesty and willingness of their guests to disarm. Perhaps their biases and forethoughts were wrong. Maybe the two groups could coexist. Indeed, the Feast was appearing to be a success and a learning experience for all.

Ceremonies complete, their guests entered the camp. The women came forth to meet the squaws, motioning them to bring the food into the preparation area. The children followed immediately, joining into a game of tag with children of the Puritan nation, a testament that children's play transcended all adult-created barriers.

Another handshake and bow by Tom preceded his motioning the leaders to join him and the other governours and Puritan leaders in the center of the camp. An area that now had wood-hewn tables and stumps for sitting. A pouch of tobacco was offered, and soon the group sat smiling at each other while attempting to make conversation with those around them. The conversation, while not understood by the other, involved theatrics and hand motions. However, the resulting smiles were welcome and contributed to the bright and sunny day. For the time being, all was going well.

As in all realities, the theatric smiles and gestures were underpinned by a nervous reality. In the compound's corner, Barnes and Squint stood observing the actions of their guests. "It appears we are safe," offered Barnes after surveying the events of the previous minutes.

"That we be, surprised am I . . . but indeed happy," Squint responded.

"Must say, Tom was indeed successful. Dining with those we fear didst not appear a likelihood a few weeks past," commented Barnes.

"You speak the truth," Squint replied as he watched the discourses occurring.

"The youths know no fear," responded Clement, a Puritan carpenter, as he joined the governours.

"Ah, to have the naivety of youth once again. How are you this fine day Clement?" asked Barnes.

"Happy to be here, and happy to have this wonderful food to enjoy."

"A meal fit for the Crowne, I dare say," casually commented Squint.

"Well, I for one, am glad the Crowne is not present," responded Clement, controlling his desire to elaborate.

"Not sure if they would have traveled this far for a pot o' porridge," responded Squint with a snicker.

"That be true," snickered Clement.

A moment later, the trite conversation of those assembled was interrupted by a gentile feminine voice. "Ah gents, could you help us? . . . the fish are a bit heavy and dare I say, fishy," inquired Rachael as she approached the circle.

"Fish being fishy is a good sign, dear lass. Come on gents, we are called," commented Clement. With that, the circle broke up and moved to assist in the request.

During this discourse, Tom had excused himself from his conversation and returned bearing an instrument, a polished tube of metal. Holding the tube towards the treetops, he beckoned his guests to look through the eyeglass. Their confused looks turned immediately to stunned appreciation, for upon their eye bringing the vision into focus their brain conveyed images as if they were at the top of the tree observing their subject, whether bird or squirrel. Slowly, they shared the experience amongst themselves while their hosts stood gently amused, for it was obvious that none had seen a telescope.

"Wabi Tibik?" inquired a brave to another as he looked skyward.

Nodding, the other replied, "Nij!".

Being joined by another who repeated, "Wabi Tibik!," in a voice that inferred surprise. After looking through the glass, he too responded, "Nij . . ." with a nod.

For the next 15 minutes, the scope pointed in various directions; the viewers uttering words and inflections of surprise unknown to their hosts. After a few more minutes, the surprise inflection subtlety changed in tone. An observer may have also noticed the facial expressions slowly turning from naive surprise to subtle fear. Unknown to their hosts, the ensuing conversation now centered on a realization that these visitors had tools that could challenge their existence. An Indian is taught to excel in the art of stealth; however, if one can be observed from a great distance, the stealth of their actions may not matter. The life of the brave and those around him are in great danger when another has the sight of a god. The braves soon realized that this instrument was a threat not only to their existence but to the existence of all tribes.

How many hours have their actions been observed without their knowledge? These were the fears that slowly were kindled as the interaction of disparate cultures continued.

In the cooking area, a stewing of another sort was occurring. The women of the group were in final preparation. The squaws huddled with their spices as they wrapped and folded the bits of herbal gold into the fare they had brought. Curiosity by the Puritan women brought titters of joy as they gingerly tasted and smelled each new ingredient. An initial sampling of the pottage brought smiles of joy to the tribal women as their stomachs savored the blend of vegetables and wine. Each detected an unusual ingredient, but none could identify the subtlety.

Today's special ingredient was the meat of a fox. Earlier in the day, one of the young Puritan men had been successful in his hunt and returned with a fox. The fox was the likes of which the Puritans had never seen. Upon preparation and incorporation into the meal some hours before, all hoped that this feast would be memorable for all assembled.

As the hours passed, the anticipation grew. Anticipation by the Puritans and governours for the continued success of the gathering. Anticipation by the tribe they had not fallen prey to deception, a trick intent on disarming them and extinguishing their tribe.

Soon the highly awaited visible act of final preparation began. The placement of the main dining table and the arrangement of the eating area. Previously cleared of sticks and leaves, these eating areas were covered with blankets. Boxes and stones were arranged in circles. Logs were rolled to provide seating for others.

The time was nearing two o'clock and, as if on cue, a flock of cardinals, resplendent in their red coloring, erupted from a nearby tree, wings spread as they headed skyward. Upon their flight, the women began bringing trays and pots, plates and forks, bowls, and spoons. The Feast was about to begin.

The movement of the women and food provided cues to others in the assembly. The men took immediate notice and immediately ceased their actions. Their thoughts turning singularly to another instinct. Eating.

Seeing the tables assembled, Tom separated himself from the group and motioned Opechancanough and his braves to follow to the seats provided at the table. The men understood the motion and followed accordingly. Upon seating by the men, the other groups assembled began filling in where they were able. Groups of Puritans, followed by younger tribe members, took a seat. The final group to join the table were the mothers and their children, both Indian and Puritan. Each group sat in preparation for the coming event, a feast for their consumption unparalleled in the previous months. For some, a feast for which they would have no comparison.

The bowls began circulation. The smells aroused even the most finicky of appetites. A pottage overflowing with spice and wondrous meat was brought forth, followed closely by fruits of the region, beans, and bacon. Another wave brought freshly caught fish seasoned in an aged manner. Accompaniments included sauces prepared from generational recipes and jellied biscuits. Waiting in the kitchen for future serving were several ceremonial pies. Each serving of the meal brought a broader smile and a louder exclamation of awe. Courses of bread and drink followed the food distribution. All the while, the children present had to be incessantly reminded to wait until the men had spoken before the food could be eaten. Those few minutes were hours for the hungry youth in the assembly. Several of their eager hands being gently smacked as a reminder to wait.

Upon final distribution of the food, Tom arose and performed the formal welcome and blessing of the food. He had been practicing for days, he would now find out whether his practice would be appreciated and welcomed.

Looking at Opechancanough and then to the assembled tribe, Tom began. "Nuquisi,"— which he hoped was an appropriate rendition of 'Welcome Friends'. "Kwe-kwe Nuquisi . . .Kwe-kwe Nuquisi, wingapo wiroans. Kwe-kwe."

Before completing his welcome, Tom looked into the eyes and faces of those assembled. Amongst the group, Tom detected a few snickers, but no scowls or anger. He continued by raising his arms to the sky and bowing his head for a moment. With that ritualistic act complete, Tom took a piece of bread from his plate, placed it in his mouth, and began the meal while taking his seat. The fellow governours followed slowly, ensuring that the guests would follow. Opechancanough and his braves observed the motions and also began partaking in the food on their plate. All at the gathering began to eat. The Feast was a success. The First Feast was underway.

While enjoying the most succulent of meats, Opechancanough, sat amongst his natural enemies and for a moment forgot that he was dining with those who unfettered could put an end to his nation or at a minimum, deplete their food reserves for years to come. Languishing at the table, enjoying dishes he had not previously experienced, numbed him temporarily. But only temporarily it was, for amidst a bite of candied fruit, he looked across the table and spotted a sight that immediately stopped his actions. Scanning the periphery of the assembly area, he spied a sight, nay, an abomination. Amongst the skins and waste of fruit and meat, lay a white furry object. Standing erect, Opechancanough moved toward the waste pile.

"Sir, is there something wrong?" a Puritan asked, forgetting entirely that his words were not understood.

"Chief, do we have a problem?" asked a loyal brave in his native Algonquian.

"There!" pointed Opechancanough.

The brave rose and followed his leader's finger directed toward a pile of discarded material from the feast preparation. Continuing forward, Opechancanough made his way toward the pile of refuse.

Stopping within a foot of the pile, a wave of anger erupted in Opechancanough. His eyes became orbs and his breath slowed in preparation for a tribal scream. Reaching forward, he grabbed the white fur from the pile, the plumed tail still attached. Holding the skin over his head, he proclaimed to all within his booming voice.

"Wagosh, wagosh! Midjin wagosh! Kitcitwawis wagosh!!"

His utterance had let all know that the meat they had consumed was the meat of a fox. Not just any fox, this was the white fox deemed sacred by the tribe. For the previous year, this white majestic and unique albino fox would appear at times of distress and upon its disappearance, so too would the despair end. The fox had become a sign of hope. A god brought unto this earth, a creature to be revered. Until now. These savages from the lands across the sea had captured, killed, and offered for consumption this harbinger of hope . . . this unique amongst all the Vulpe genus.

Turning in anger, Opechancanough looked first to the sky, then turned to his fellow tribemates. His face was ashen, his lips pursed, his eyes glowing.

"Musquantum Manit!" were the words he uttered as he punched his fist into the air and, in a rapid motion, dashed toward the table of weapons. Grabbing his faithful bow, he pointed a drawn arrow toward his hosts.

The gods are angry, was the cry he had evoked, and in response to that cry, his fellow tribesmen also dashed for the table to recover their weapons in response to the sacrilege which had occurred; a ploy by the white man to further remove prosperity from their shores.

The rush by the natives for their weapons had taken the Puritans and governours by surprise. This rush prevented the Puritans from retrieving their weapons, rendering their defense non-existent. And so, on that late November afternoon, the world stood still as the fate of both parties was unknown, their individual tempers rising, their minds calculating the next move.

Recourse of the native

Anger! Extreme Anger! What was a few moments earlier a wondrous feast had now degraded to two sides in a battle stance against each other. The tribe members were stoic in their stance, eyeballs piercing the enemy, breathing shortened as they mentally brewed their next move. The Puritans and governours were taken aback by the quick turn of events and were not ready nor trained for the quick escalation.

"Mates . . . we . . . we . . . mean you no harm!" one Puritan stuttered unconvincingly in words that were not understood by the aggressors.

Raising his hand, another Puritan began a similar utterance. An utterance which was greeted by an arrow whistling through the air and piercing his extended palm.

"No here,! a brave said in broken English, to which began a chorus characterized by a semi-staccato chant.

"No here! Madja . . . Madja!" was the chant as the tribe members pointed toward the sea.

"No here! Madja . . . Madja . . . Nibe!" shouted more of the tribesman, each pointing frantically toward the sea while waving their instruments of war into the air. Their chants intensified as stomping began and voices continued to rise in unison.

"No here! Madja . . . No here . . . Madja! No here! Madja . . . Nibe . . . Nibe!"

"No here! Madja . . . No here . . . Madja! No here! Madja . . . Nibe . . . Nibe!"

Fear was now the prevailing emotion amongst the Puritans as the tribal chants penetrated their very souls.

Blood dripped from the pierced hand of the one, and screams of pain were heard as barrages of arrows pierced their scared and confused bodies. Instinctive actions resulted in several falling to earth futilely trying to live. Some who fell feigned death, others rushed off into the brush, keeping low to the ground and avoiding the arrows of death. Unfortunately, the arrows were not discriminating as to their target, for several of those who lay mortally wounded were mothers struck while trying to protect their children.

Two groups escaped the circle of insanity. One group totaled seven; the other, three. Besides these two groups, a sole individual escaped. This solitary escapee was the governour who was the conceiver of this event, the one some would view as the reason for the mayhem. This governour was Tom. Not wishing to die, Tom saw his moment before the releasing of the barrage of arrows. Observing the multiple bowstrings being rhythmically drawn, Tom dropped to the ground and scooted at a full tilt into the clearing. Three of the tribe observed Tom's exit. These three immediately gave chase. Upon reaching the cover of brush, Tom stood and sprinted into the woods. With each stride, Tom's mind became clouded with memories of previous escapes. While minor in comparison to the moment, Tom recalled running the streets of Cromwell

Crossing, escaping teachers, principals, or constables. All these memories clouded Tom's perception of the current reality. As he ran Tom had to remind himself continually that this escape was real — his very life depended upon it. This zig-zagging journey became his most important dream — his dream of survival. This dream was far more important than previously held dreams of freedom and tolerance. Tom's dreams of yore had never been coupled with an escape from death. Yet that was the dream Tom was pursuing as he careened through the woods, breaking twigs and branches; notifying all of his path.

Coming to a clearing, Tom instinctively stopped. This momentary lapse prolonged Tom's life a bit longer. In his fright, Tom had not realized he was heading toward a significant drop in the landscape. This area was normally avoided because of its potential danger, but here it lay before Tom in all its majesty. Tom stood on the precipice of a clearing that ended with a 200-foot drop into a raging stream strewn with rock.

As Tom stopped, turned, and assessed a new direction, he immediately felt a pain; a pain that stopped him from proceeding further. In slow motion, Tom turned; his sight now meeting the eyes of three braves. One of the braves was returning his bow to his side, after precisely releasing one of his arrows into the body of Tom. It took but a few moments after the arrows struck Tom's femur that Tom dropped to the ground.

For the next few moments, Tom lay on the ground; his arms mentally straining to remove the arrow tip from his thigh. Mentally, Tom imagined his hand grasping at the arrow and pulling it from its crevice within his fleshy thigh. In reality, no such movement occurred. Minute by minute, as Tom mentally sought to remove the invader, the poison which coated the tip surged through his body via the bloodstream. Each inch through which the poison passed became unusable and began its death. Within minutes, Tom's entire body would begin to decay from the inside, robbed of the taken-for-granted lifeblood.

Immediately after the entry of the poison into Tom's punctured body, Tom's mental faculties began shutting down. Tom's mind remained active during his final 15 minutes of life. As Tom lay there, his mind returned to Cromwell Crossing, to his Aunt Polly, to the bed that he had sold. He thought of Candlemas, the planned reunion with his Aunt. Thoughts of Darwin, Hopkins, and Higgins passed through his consciousness for a final time. The memory of the bottle with his note to Polly . . . and . . . and . . ..

Near the end of these thoughts, Tom mentally waved a solemn goodbye to this world. In reality, his final salute to his earthly existence would be a penultimate blink followed by a closure of his eyes, and then silence.

***   ***   ***

Back at camp, as the mayhem was beginning, one member of the group of three had noted Tom's departure. That individual was Lars. When the barrage of arrows began, Lars, along with Puritans

Clarke and Antwerp, dropped to the ground, waiting
for what seemed like forever for their escape window.
As the confusion intensified, Lars and the Puritans
crept to the edge of the clearing and, in the confusion,
were able to duck into the woods. At the point when
they sensed it was safe they began to slowly follow the
path Tom had forged. After following the path for
nearly 20 minutes, Lars stopped, fixed his eyes and
ears toward the upcoming clearing, and announced
his conclusion. "I'm sure that's the direction he was
running!"

Upon arrival at the precipice, Lars and his
group also peered over the edge into the river's rocks
and rapids. Not immediately seeing Tom, the group
peered in all directions. It was then that they detected
a human shape lying unmoving near a worn and
twisted log. Approaching the body whose face was
resting in a needle-filled hollow; their eyes widened as
they confirmed their fear. The nearly deceased figure
was that of their friend and governour . . . there lay
the mortally wounded body of Tom.

Lars raced to his mate, looked into his closed
eyes, and proceeded to remove the arrow. Hoping
for a yelp or a twitch or a grimace or encouraging
movement, Lars instead was greeted by stillness and
the faint whiff of death.

Looking to the heavens, Lars looked up and
emitted a guttural moan, followed by tears. Not just
any tears, but a soul-wrenching, body-racking, earth-
moving torrent. Lars had lost his mate.

Lars' anguish was not unnoticed.
Unfortunately for the party of three, as Lars grieved,
the party was being surrounded. In a moment of

silence between the emotion, a twig crack was heard. Looking toward the source, the group saw a band of Indians looking intently at them with arrows pointed their way. Arrows which in the next moment would pierce their very skin, providing passage for the same poison which had killed Tom.

It was on this day that Tom and Lars departed this world almost a year to the day that they had become fast friends in the confines of Cromwell Crossing House No. 2 some three thousand miles and seemingly the same number of experiences away.

Soon after Lars and his party consumed their last breath of this earth, a tribe member and his young son approached the deceased bodies of the four. Looking down at them, a few words were murmured, "Papa, why do they not move?" inquired the young one, not quite 7.

"The medicine god has filled them with poison . . . they shall never move again!" the father proudly proclaimed to his confused offspring.

"But why? How will they walk in the woods with their little boys?" asked the inquisitive lad.

"They wish not to walk in our woods. They only wish to destroy your land, so you can no longer play, so you can no longer hunt, so you can no longer fish. Is this what you want, to stop your life as it is?"

"Oh no father, No . . . not at all! Thank you for stopping these men," uttered the boy in his first proclamation of distrust of another. Moving forward, the father and son left the dead and proceeded to their favorite fishing hole, leaving the four to the forces of nature.

⁂   *⁂*   *⁂*

The third and largest group who had fled for survival unknowingly took advantage of the sacrifice of the others. As the arrow barrage began, several of the Puritan colony instinctively rushed to attack their new enemy. Rushing forward, they grabbed bows and knives, initially ignoring the wounds and lacerations to which their bodies were being subjected. As these men fought with their last ounces of energy, five of the Puritans and two of the governours ran in the opposite direction, taking advantage of the distraction. Not initially a group, three were followed by another two, who were followed by another two. These seven ran back toward a remote supply area not quite 3 minutes from the camp. In this area, supplies had been removed from Figs but had not quite made it to the encampment. Fear filled the eyes of the seven, their lungs devoid of air, their brains of cohesive thought. Panting, crying, quivering in fear, their minds slowly took in the assault they had viewed. Not knowing how much time they had or if they had been followed, they immediately began gathering supplies to sustain them for an unknown duration in an unknown location. The seven included Governours Barnes and Peti, both exposed to military means from a young age, four Puritans, and one Rachael of Ivywood, a frequent companion of Tom. While the five Puritans grabbed bags of food and items for immediate survival, the governours grabbed items for shelter construction and cooking. Their stay had been less than 10 minutes, but as they prepared to exit, they heard the muffled sounds of a foreign language approaching from the feast area. Not wishing to end their time on this earth, the seven looked at each other and ultimately followed the lead of Barnes. For it was he who made a motion with his finger in a circular motion above his head and pointed toward the forest with a finger to his lips.

With this direction, the group exited the shelter, provisions in their arms or cradled in sheets of canvas. Barnes led them out of the supply tent and after confirming none of the indigenous were in the immediate area, led the group to the North toward the deep woods.

The group hiked for nearly an hour, passing markers they had learned from previous expeditions. Quietly, they passed the barren knotty pine, the large rock at the brook's edge, and the three towering hemlock trees. Further they walked and hours passed. As they walked, the sun set lower and lower. The silence was deafening, but Barnes made sure that he walked where he broke or disrupted the least earth. In a few places, he intentionally stepped over a gnarled growth forming a natural fence. He hoped this would distract further any who may follow. At this hour's end, the group stopped and listened. They listened with an intensity that could save their life.

Nothing. Aside from a now-detected cricket or squirrel, there was nothing. Barnes could only hope that his military training surpassed the life lessons generationally passed within the tribe from grandfather to father to son.

Making a motion for the other six to join him, he spoke in a near whisper. "We must prepare the sleep tonight. Two must be awake at all times tonight. Do I have two volunteers?" inquired Barnes.

"I'll watch the first session," offered Peti.

"I shall join him," offered a Puritan known only as Tybbs.

"Excellent . . . thank ye . . . and who shall join me in late night to sunrise?"

"I'll be glad to help," offered the quiet and doe-like voice of Rachael.

"Me Lady . . . I'm sorry, but in case of an immediate fight, I would prefer one of our men to be watching. I trust you understand," offered Barnes in his military persona voice.

"I do . . . but I'm still willing," Rachael replied.

"Who shall join me on the second watch? "inquired Barnes.

"I shall join you, governour," came the voice of Woodfer, another Puritan present.

"Thank ye, Sir . . . And now, let us prepare for the evening."

Preparing in quiet, the group erected a small lean-to for sleep and ate a few berries and biscuits. As their life truly depended on it, their conversation was replaced with listening. Listening to the tree branches scraping, listening to a distant brook, listening to the rabbits scampering. With each motion and each sound, a heartbeat stopped. It would be a long night.

Rising in the sky was a full moon. The enormous orb illuminated all beneath it, its luminescence producing flickering shadows and peripheral hoaxes. While the five attempted sleep,

Peti and Tybbs sat with rifles in hand, listening to the nothingness.

Nothingness was the total of what occurred in the first hours of moonlight. Nothingness that caused the hours to drag on, a nothingness that proved to be welcome.

Come two hours past midnight, Woodfer and Barnes approached Tybbs and Peti. Replacing their seats upon the rock, they began a 4-hour shift lasting until sunrise.

Pre-dawn has its own challenges to the mind. Whereas moonlight can cast deceiving shadows, a subtly rising sun bathes those same apparitions with a different light. It was these imagined peripheral movements, these sounds exaggerated by silence, and the realities of the expansive world of insects and rodents, which challenged the guards in these early morning hours. Each crack and each sound was mentally analyzed to ensure the safety of the others would be preserved. The guardians of night and day would never look at a forest the same way. Each during their period of sentry would question why. Why had they left the warmth of England, why had they journeyed thousands of miles, why were they not curled in sleep? Why had dawn not arrived? Several hours later, the glorious sound of movement began. Not the feared movement of the tribes, but the movement within the shelter of those rising to a new day.

Over the next hour, they quietly disassembled the camp while partaking of some marginal sustenance. Aged biscuits and diluted drinks could hardly be viewed as an enjoyable meal, but upon its consumption, the group prepared for another day of journeying toward safety. They knew not where they wished to go, but they surely knew where they wished to not return.

The rest of the morning brought several miles of walking and multiple breaks to ensure their movement was not being followed. The walk brought different mental exercises, each unique. Some thought of their past and their unknown future. Some thought of families left behind, and whether they would be doomed to die or would they become a part of a future family. Others revisited their thoughts of the previous evening, thoughts conceived in the dank, dark, and lonely night. The thoughts of the governours bore additional burdens. Looking at the previous events, they wondered how they would be viewed historically. Would their existence and identity be forever lost? Lost in the endless annals of history would be the mystery of the event they partook in the day prior — that First Feast. What clues would recreate the names of the deceased and the names of the survivors? Within the next day, would they still be among the living? As these questions were being mentally asked, hours passed, and the group progressed hundreds of steps North, toward areas not previously viewed, at least not by them.

Sustained by these mental gymnastics, the party of survivors continued North for the rest of the day, repeating another evening of sentry duties and fear. As day 3 of their flight began, thoughts of how long entered each of their singular minds. How long would they need to walk? When would they be safe? When could they begin their life again?

As they walk further into the interior of this pristine land, the 'how's' and 'when's' were replaced with 'why's'. The 'whys' were more of a challenge and required a more creative mental response. These 'whys' were the true tests of their faith. At the end of the day, the final remaining 'why' was 'why had God allowed them to live?'

It was during each of the parties' individual accounting of why they had survived that they universally noted the forest becoming less dense. A short time later, a clearing and stream emerged. The stream's shores were littered with brambled branches, the stream itself holding many rocks. However, it was not the beauty of the scene which caused a universal gasp amongst the seven. It was not the beauty of the clearing, nor the branches nor the stream, which caused each of their brains to abandon their previous all-consuming thoughts.

The view they saw which provided the herculean interruption was a set of eyes looking at them from the other side of the stream. Eyes that belonged not to one of native ancestry, but to one of European heritage. Eyes from a one whose facial features bore the hair color and structural characteristics of those who were viewing.

As their eyes and the eyes of the other met, a singular thought encompassed each of their beings. A thought which brought warmth, glee, and utter abandon.

For each now knew that others existed.

Back in England—new world, new colonists

The war with Spain was ending and the work of expansion was beginning anew. Amongst all of England, there remained none as eager to return to the seas as Richard Grenville. Sir Richard had regretted his decision from the moment he approved his nephew's sailing to the West. Richard Jr. was a mere boy in his uncle's eyes, and it was only in a moment of weakness that he agreed to allow his nephew to join a group intent on locating the missing from the storied Roanoke site and providing them the supplies promised by John White. The captain had been a member of the Roanoke landing and had left his brethren to return to England for more supplies in 1587, promising to return before the year's end.

The necessity of rescuing the rescue party was an unforeseen sequence of events. Sir Richard wished to lead this effort, as he felt responsible for his nephew's well-being in that land so many thousands of miles and days away. Through all this uncertainty, the outcome of the voyage on which Richard Jr. had embarked was still not known — had the Roanoke site been located? And if located, were the colonists safe?

Preparing to return to Virginia, Sir Richard Grenville was dealt a fatal blow when the Crowne — in particular Queen Elizabeth — believed that his talents were better served closer to the motherland. Sir Richard fought, argued, conjectured, and attempted manipulation. However, all manner of discourse and verbal marksmanship ended short of Richard's intended goal. Refusing to abandon all hope, Sir Richard ultimately met up with his friend and fellow explorer, Captain John White. White was planning a return trip to rejoin his wife and family. What was unknown was the timing lag between the two parties. Grenville, being proficient at adjudication and the art of logic, appealed to White to expand his journey to include the search and return of Richard Jr. Captain White agreed, and the proposal was made and ultimately accepted by the Queen. Because of this and other faithful services; her majesty had bequeathed upon Captain White the title of Governour.

As the voyage now included parameters of the unknown; the detailed work began. White and Grenville consulted with previous captains who had made the voyage. They were trying to identify options for a landing spot and route. These discussions occurred with Captains Cavendish and Raymond of the expedition in which Sir Richard took part in piloting the Tyger, and with one lesser-known Captain – Carmine McGuilocutty. McGuilocutty was invited to this meeting because he was one of the few Captains who had successfully returned from the land heralded as Virginia. As the discussions continued, it became apparent that nearly 200 Englishmen, women, and children had ventured out West never to be heard from again. Fortunately for all, Captain White had been a part of several of these ventures.

The first venture discussed was the July 1584 exploration under the command of Amadas and Barlowe.

"Doth there be a need to discuss this expedition at length?" inquired Governour White.

"I say no," responded Captain Cavendish," for this journey did not leave any Englishmen behind."

"Noted," concurred the governour; "however, please ensure we have the maps created from this venture . . . these may help with our planning."

"It shall be done, your governourship," confirmed Captain Raymond.

"Next we shall review Sir Richard's journey of Spring 1585." The governour began, "I am familiar with this expedition, having seen Richard's maps and discussed his findings at length."

"Sir Grenville has provided us invaluable detail . . ." began Cavendish, "although detail as this is expected of one with his experience."

"Aye . . . drawings and charts of Ococan, Ottorasko, and Roanoke. These will be of great value in planning," commented the governour in an audibly impressed manner.

"Governour, are ye sure you can find the landing site of those 100," questioned Raymond, "I dare say based on me memory and these maps there be more islands than I recall. I meself am getting a wee bit confused."

"Respectfully gents, it be confusing. Seeing these maps, and remembering those lands . . . I be not sure I could find the landing site of another. Woods often look like other woods. Inlets at times appear no different from others," commented McGuilocutty speaking for the first time.

"McGuilocutty is it?" questioned White.

"Aye, Sir," replied McGuilocutty in a rarely respectful tone.

"Did thee not note distinguishing trees, rocks, or hills?" inquired the governour. "Did not yer years teach you to look for these markers while yer crew was safely landing your vessel?"

"Aye, I thought I had been successful, but nearly two years later . . . I be not sure. These maps . . . they be not providing the assurance a captain should have."

"So be it, but I have faith McGuilocutty that if ye ever saw these locals again, that yer seafaring memory would return and land yer craft appropriately," challenged White in a gentle, but firm tone.

"Aye, governour," McGuilocutty replied once again with respect.

"And then there be me last voyage, I believe I could find the spot with me eyes covered and me hands fettered," began the governour, "aye, that be where me family remains . . . and to there is where I must return." "I can see it as if it were just yesterday, a hill in the distance with a sole tree at its highest loft. A lesser hill to the right and one to the left. The leftmost one with tall grasses, the rightmost one with scrubby brush. And mates, the most distinguishing of all the features made by the heavens . . . some 6 rocks, one as tall as I to the side of the beach."

"Yer memory is notable," exclaimed a surprised Cavendish.

"I remember it well, especially those rocks. The children in our group would spend the day scaling them . . . yelling that they were scaling Olympus . . . ah, the memories, like yesterday," mused White.

"And then . . . 100 yards back was the clearing. Aye, what a glorious piece of God-provided earth. Already cleared by nature and flat; yea in those 10 acres there be not a single stump . . . must have been an area of planting many moons prior. That be where our buildings stood . . . and the fence. That glorious fence hewed of oak . . . I can see it now," began the governour as his mind returned to land long ago and far away.

"And me wife Toma, and gorgeous daughter Elle, and me . . . me . . . granddaughter. . . so little, so fragile," began White publicly weeping before those assembled. "I shall see them again, I shall rescue them, they shall return!" The last words a shout emphasized with a slam of the table, sending a resonating boom echoing throughout the room.

"And so we shall . . ." added Cavendish as if ending a prayer.

The group chatted for a few minutes about details just discussed and the notable features of the barrier islands. It was then, after a few moments of silence, that the eyes of the room rested on Carmine McGuilocutty.

"Captain McGuilocutty . . . you Sir have been quiet in these discussions. What of your journey of not quite 2 years past? Did ye not take Sir Richard Grenville's nephew to these same lands?" asked White as he returned the discussion to the original topic. "You have voiced what you do not remember . . . what does thee remember?"

"Aye Sirs, I do recall some . . . for it was Grenville and 6 others who would serve as governours. Additionally, there be 53 Puritans searching for that which Puritans search."

"How many remain?" inquired Cavendish.

"We were lucky and only lost one... one governour, one Titus Mongier passed when the ship be but a few days from land . . . buried at sea was he."

"What would that final count be?" inquired the governour.

"66. 59 Puritans and 6 governours," replied McGuilocutty.

"That be 65 unless ye be counting the anchor," laughed White.

"So it be . . . so it be. Me mind and the math are not what they used to be," replied McGuilocutty in an embarrassed manner.

As the conversation continued for nearly an hour more, discussions turned to what could have made the previous voyages more successful and how to avoid these restocking trips to England. The group also discussed a topic none wished to dwell on, the discovery of the bones of the 15 who had ventured over in '85. The group avoided this discussion for fear that a similar fate had befallen those currently residing across the Atlantic, outside the blanket of the Crowne. These unknown lives created a sense of urgency. The group determined that speed was of the essence, and to facilitate that speed, a visit for final financing was to be held the very next day. Part of the group would meet with one Mr. W. Hoare, a respected financier and frequent provider of funds for Crowne activities.

The next morning, John White and Captain Cavendish walked into the office of Mr. Hoare's at #2 New Street in Plymouth. They were curtly greeted by Miss Chilsom, Mr. Hoare's administrator.

"Gentleman, how may our office be of assistance to you?" Miss Chilsom asked.

"We would like to discuss a financial matter with Mr. Hoare . . . is he present?" inquired Governour White in his normal authoritative tone.

"Whom shall I say is calling?" Miss Chilsom asked of the gentlemen.

"You may tell Mr. Hoare that Governour John White, a captain, and explorer of the West, would like a word with him."

"Yes Sir, please be seated," Miss Chilsom responded matter-of-factly, as having met the Queen herself had made her immune to those of the royal or famous persuasion.

Retreating into an inner office, Miss Chilsom returned less than five minutes later with Mr. Hoare following closely behind.

"Gentlemen, a pleasure. Would you like to join me in my office? I appreciate your considering me for this discussion."

With that greeting, the trio retreated to Mr. Hoare's office.

"Brandy?" offered Hoare.

"A bit early, but I'll take a snort," replied the captain. "Good for me aged bones."

"None for me, thank you," replied White, politely passing.

Upon pouring a drink for himself and the captain, Mr. Hoare passed the glass to the captain and with his own, settled into his chair for the ensuing discussion.

Governour White spent several minutes laying out the proposal, the need to return to the lands out West, and what the party would look like in terms of ships, members, and supplies.

Several minutes into the discussion, Hoare's eyes got larger, setting down his drink, almost spilling it.

"Are you ok, Sir?" asked the captain.

"Ah yes, but as you spoke, I am remembering a lad who sat in that very chair about 2 years ago!" began Hoare his voice increasing in excitement as he retold the story. "His name was . . . To . . . Tod . . . Tom . . . that's it, Thomas Smythe. He was seeking 100 shillings to finance his dream of heading West. Aye, the lad, he did have quite the grandiose ideas . . . quoted Raleigh several times! Must say, he reminded me of myself at his age."

"100 shillings. I cannot see how that would be enough for passage across the Atlantic," commented White.

"Oh, that be just a portion of the cost. The lad had ingenuity. He had sold items, was willing to work extra jobs . . . the lad had spirit! Yea, he was so positive and headstrong that I could not refuse him. I knew I would never see the money again, but sometimes you have to support the young and ambitious. Doth your journey potentially involve this lad?"

"That it may. There have been two groups who have never returned, and from your recall and the timing, this lad Tom Smythe was probably a part of the group who accompanied Captain McGuilocutty on the ship Figs."

"Well gentlemen, as your journey is approved by the Queen, let me know how much you need and I shall discuss the terms with her majesty next week at our regular meeting," Hoare responded as if meeting the Queen was a non-event and one which anyone in the kingdom could partake.

"Thank you indeed, Hoare," responded the governour.

"And White, if you find the lad Tom, please tell him I remembered him and still respect his spirit! You may also pass on to him that his loan is forgiven. Please tell him this is because of his bravery and gallant performance befitting that of Sir Walter Raleigh himself!"

"That I will do, and again Hoare, thank ye again for your continued generosity in support of the Crowne."

Rising and opening the door, the captain and governour left the office, bid a pleasant day to Miss Chilsom, and headed into the sunlight in search of further confirmations. Over the coming weeks, the trip came together. The ships would be the Hopewell and Little John. Captains White and Cocke would command the vessels supported by a crew of seasoned professionals.

The banner which proudly flew from the Hopewell's bow proclaimed the campaign's theme . . . 'The Crowne forgets not her own'. A formal campaign was created as the Crowne's regality needed some restoration after the near-war years of the Armada and the redirection of many assets toward that effort. The Crowne believed that those in the kingdom needed to know that these hundreds of denizens who had left the shores of the motherland had not been forgotten to perish in some unknown land. The voyage would return to the last known spots of occupation and search for those identified as lost. If found, the lost would be offered a means of return. If they chose to stay, provisions of support would be offered. Amongst the list of the lost included Virginia Dare, granddaughter of Captain White; Dyonis and Margery Harvie; William Dutton; Emme Merrimoth and one Thomas Smythe. Additionally identified on the manifest of McGuilocutty's vessel were the names of six fellow governours including one Lawrence Bonham, an instigator whose name was recorded in the logs of several local constables.

Advertisement of the campaign was far-reaching, including the names of the lost. The news of the Hopewell, Little John, and their crews caught the particular attention of one Polly Helmbright of Cromwell Crossing, the aunt of Thomas Smythe. Polly heard the news from a neighbor who had heard it from a messenger resting his feet en route to locales East. When she heard the news, her heart lept in excitement and fear. Excitement at the prospect of hearing again from her nephew. Fear, in the event, she learned the worst. Since waking in that empty house some 2 years ago, she had never fully put together the pieces. She had received a note delivered to her in a bottle. At first, she thought it was a joke. Where would Tom get that kind of money? As she pondered this, more of the pieces fell together. Selling his bed, working at the Cantery, talk of selling his mum's ring. The last piece of the puzzle was the half-burned list of which the total had survived–100 shillings, a year's wages for the lad. That would explain his ability to go west; however, Polly never had figured out what else Tom had sold or earned to produce that sum.

Talking to others in Cromwell Crossing, Polly learned more about Governour White and his plan. In a moment of uncharacteristic bravado, Polly woke one morning, dressed in her finest, and borrowing a neighbor's horse and cart, she rode to Plymouth, the purported home of Captain Governour White. Arriving mid-morning, she inquired of the locals as to his residence and, as luck would have it, she learned of the location. Heading there, a mere mile from her location; she hesitantly approached the manor and knocked.

"Ma'am," inquired the gent who opened the door after some delay. "I be looking for one Governour White, esteemed Captain, sailor, and explorer," began Polly.

Not disclosing his identity, the governour asked, "Do I know you Ma'am? Are ye a bill collector . . . sent by one to collect a debt?" inquired the one who answered the door. The governour was in an unusual mood, which resulted in this very uncharacteristic, almost playful question.

"Uh, no Sir, just a mere aunt looking for her nephew."

Returning to seriousness, "Nephew, who be yer nephew, and is there a reason you believe I know of his location?"

"If I may Sir, my name be Polly, Polly Helmbright and I heard you will be returning to the lands across the great ocean. I believe me nephew, Thomas Smythe, ventured there some 2 years past . . . never to be seen since that fateful day. If there be any chance that you see him on your journey, please tell him he is missed and his return desired."

"Smythe . . . Smythe, that name doth not ring a bell, but otherwise, you are correct, I am returning and 2 years ago, one Captain McGuilocutty did venture to those same lands. It be possible your nephew was amongst those on his sailing. Ma'am, I will keep Mr. Smythe's name on my mind, and if perchance we meet, I shall convey your wishes."

"Gramercy! Thank ye . . . Gramercy Sir! Safe voyages to you and your crew!" With this reinvigoration, Polly turned and began her journey back to Cromwell Crossing, surprised at her bravery and feeling relieved.

Closing the door, Governour White mused a moment on what had just occurred. For a moment standoffishness and separatism were cast aside, gallantry was discarded, and humanity reigned. In its simplest form Governour White had just been a part of a novel interaction. An interaction of commoner to world explorer. Yes, this was the new England. This would be our destiny, this is our campaign.

The very next day, the final plans were laid.

Sailing Westward

May 22nd, 1590, would be the date of record. Picturesque and worldly was the view that morning; a scene worthy of the masterful brush of Brueghel. The weather was seasonably chilled, the time early. As the sun rose in the eastern sky, ships Hopewell and Little John departed for the lands West. A wealth of experience mastered these vessels. The Hopewell alone would tout the talents of Governour White, Captain Cocke, and Master Hutton. The Little John would be under the command of Captain LeMont, a seasoned captain who had learned his arts from multiple journeys with Sir John Hawkins. Accompanying LeMont was his Master Mate, Nicholas Johnson. These brave leaders had amassed 12 trips to the Western Lands.

Unfortunately, the grandeur of the morning was lost on the nearly 80 sailors ensuring the safe passage of those aboard these two ships. The seasoned ensuring accuracy, the novice enthralled by the newness. For all, after each day, there would not be a return to firm land for at least 60 days from this very day. For it was these plebes, probes, and pages who nervously wound the ropes, tracked the hours, and attended to their entrusted tasks. During these tasks, when not fully engaged, their minds would periodically wander to thoughts of 'why'. Some asked why were they leaving England on such a long trip? Others, why did they not listen to their friends and family when warned of the dangers? Still more would ask, why did they not hug their mum longer? Why . . . why . . . why?

Knowing this full well, the experienced sailors, pilots, and masters had the additional duty of keeping the minds of the crews on their assigned tasks. A wayward thought at the wrong time could jeopardize the entire crew and future voyages of the ship. A line not connected, a hole uncovered, a fouled anchor cable; each could shorten a voyage or doom the ship to its place of remembrance, the memorial within the Halls of St. Charles.

Assured that all had performed their pre-sailing checks, Captain Cocke began his litany of commands. Concurrently, Captain LeMont began the same drill on the Little John.

"Hatches batten."

"Aye, Sir," replied the Master.

"Sails shortened."

"Aye, Sir," confirmed another. This discourse ensued for another 10 minutes until the issuance of the penultimate command.

"Anchor aweigh."

"Aye, Sir."

And with that, Captain Cocke issued the final command, "Westward Ho."

"Aye, Aye, Sir," replied the Master to a confirmation made of him hundreds of times in the past. However, in this case, the command began the start of a journey significantly longer than those previously experienced by most.

Upon completion of the departure commands, the captain turned to the governour stating, "May the Fates be kind, and the waves gentle."

With that wish, the mighty Hopewell leapt forward, joined by Little John. It was their first unfettered tugs that met with no resistance. The ropes connecting them to the dock had curtailed all previous escape attempts. Now, however, with their ropes gone, their stately sails were unfurled, providing the propulsion for the journey. The further from the dock the Hopewell and Little John and their contingent journeyed, the fewer the immediate duties for the captains and their fellow leaders. In a world devoid of problems, smooth sailing would not just be a casual phrase — a nautical greeting — but an accurate depiction of the journey. Only the gods of the sea knew what challenges lie ahead. As the Hopewell and Little John entered deeper water and the operations of the ship became more routine, the governour was afforded more time to refine strategies. Strategies that in reality needed no refinement because they had been part of every breath he had taken since returning to England. Ye, for these previous years, White had been plagued, almost haunted, by almost hourly thoughts of whom he had left behind. While the assembled group a few weeks past had created the formal list; those items noted were more indelibly carved in White's brain. White's mental list was far more detailed and permanent than any paper document annotated with quill and ink, more secure than any sealed with wax of the Crowne.

Ah the lands of Virginia, the current resting place . . . no . . . no . . . residing place of those left. Young, old, singles, families, the Archards, the Prats, the Viccars. The uncertainty of their fates was painful enough, but not nearly as devastating as the unknown regarding the governour's own wife, daughter, and infant granddaughter Virginia Dare. It was these souls waiting for the return of their husband, father, and grandfather, which turned each day into one which would not end and each night into hours of sleepless darkness awaiting a decrease by one the days till return to his beloved. Yea, not only a return to him, but a return to the open arms of the motherland. The good governour could not forget that Queen and Country paid for these voyages. Were it not for the Crowne and their initiatives, he may never see his family again; although one could argue, if not for the Crowne, the original venture would never have been. Performing these mental gymnastics did little to appease the anguish of separation. However, now . . . finally . . . the Hopewell was moving toward his wife, his daughter, his granddaughter. If the Fates be kind, in a few short weeks, he would once again be placing his feet on the same soil he departed those 33 months past.

Because of the conversations of the previous weeks, the governour was not the only respected explorer with family across the seas from the motherland. In early conversations with Sir Grenville, the governour learned of Sir Richard's equally urgent need to return to locate his nephew and ensure his safety. It had been as a result of these conversations that the current journey had been expanded to address not only the 107 left in Virginia, but another 59 left nearby. At least the hope was that the two groups were nearby. Cartographers and

memories were both equally challenged to recreate routes and identify a location strategy.
Unfortunately, Captain Carmine McGuilocutty was more bravado than explorer, and creating accurate maps was not his forte. McGuilocutty had repeatedly argued that he could find the spot where he last saw the younger Grenville; however, no offer was extended for him to join the current expedition. Seems McGuilocutty was intent on performing another crossing; however, the Crowne wished not to imply that this charlatan McGuilocutty be mentioned in the same sentence as the explorer royalty of White and Grenville.

Several hours into his daily challenge of why and subsequent mental torture, Master Hutton came upon the governour in the galley. "Aye governour, can I join ye?"

"Surely, I trust you be not here early for the grub."

Snickering, "No Sir, had several of these crossings, I have no desire to lie on the bonny ocean bed weighted down with those, shall we say . . . biscuits."

A conversation began between Hutton and the governour on how this crossing came to be. White reiterated that while planning this journey, his path crossed with Sir Richard Grenville. Resultant of this and later meetings, they became aware of McGuilocutty. Unknown to most, McGuilocutty had performed a rogue journey also two years prior arriving in July of that same year with a group of 59. During talks, the group discovered that McGuilocutty's financing had come from Sir

Grenville who, like Governour White had a desire to provide supplies and encouragement to the hundred left behind. What was discovered in the discussions between White and Sir Richard was that Sir Richard had been successful in one area which Governour White had not. Sir Grenville had received approval from the Queen to send a ship to the newly found lands of Virginia. One may never know the truth, but it may appear obvious to some that the Queen placed White's obligations to England above those due to his family. Why else would the captain be denied ensuring his family's health over protecting the Crowne and her colonies? Sir Grenville decided to try another approach, one which ultimately succeeded. Sir Richard had offered his nephew in place of himself for service to the Motherland. Success was based on the proposal that his nephew and an unknown captain of dubious distinction would make the voyage to restock the provisions of the 107 left. Assistance to the colony would be provided by volunteers who were seeking a brief respite. Wishing to keep all factions within the Crowne's purview happy, and thereby productive, the Queen agreed to this proposal. Wiser minds would know that the Queen did not expect these 'assistants' to return. However, when a substantial portion of the volunteers chose to not return; another journey could be partially justified in seeking these additionally lost souls. For expeditions to continue, a human element beyond global acquisition was needed. Resultant of this meeting, Richard Grenville Jr., an aged carrick monikered Figs, and one Captain Carmine

McGuilocutty were to begin their journey end of May 1588.

Throughout this litany of recent history, Hutton sat amazed. It was as if he possessed privileged information into the workings of the Crowne. Savoring every word, he begged the governour to continue.

Content with a lack of notoriety, and desiring to acquaint himself more with fishy-smelling lads than fur-bearing lords; Carmine McGuilocutty later was heard to reiterate that he was not impressed nor desirous to answer the initial meeting summons with Governour John White and Sir Richard Grenville. He had humorously told of being taken in by the grandiose nature of Richmond Palace. Because of this experience, McGuilocutty chose to bathe and don a jacket for the second meeting of the parties. A choice that all who knew McGuilocutty could attest to was contrary to his daily countenance and actions.

As the upcoming trip was being planned, McGuilocutty had been able to provide additional details of his journey. It was from this and subsequent discourses that Governour White and Captain Cocke learned of Thomas Smythe, Lars, Timothy O'Toole, and 59 Puritans who volunteered to assist in any way needed. Unfortunately, the two parties never met. Several opportunities were made during the weeks after arrival in which searches for those left were conducted. The total lack of success and no sign of others prior led McGuilocutty to the decision to return before the beginnings of inclement weather. Upon his return to England, he had quietly returned to his less public life, the polar opposite of the other captains who had ventured to the colonies of Virginia.

These were the memories of the governour and the captains. These both common and disparate images and actions comprised the daily torment of John White.

Unfortunately, these memories did not diminish in the coming weeks, as the crossing continued. For it was one monotonous day after another, one storm after another, one aching head or stomach after another. Each day began the same and ended similarly. Captain White's family were somewhere . . . on earth or above was the unknown.

Unlike Captain White's mentally monotonous existence, Hopewell and Little John's journeys were not without adventure. Respect for the governour, others had not. On at least two occasions, the Hopewell was challenged by privateers hoping to acquire her provisions. Firepower, experience, and ingenuity prevailed, allowing the Hopewell and Little John to cross the Atlantic with their supplies intact. During these battles, Governour White could be said to be overly aggressive, for he viewed each attack, each delay, as a personal challenge focused directly on denying him a reunion with his dear wife and family.

With each challenge, with each mile, the time of ultimate reckoning came closer. What was the state of the village left? Had the crops been successful? How were the relations with the neighboring tribes? Is his family healthy? Would the Crowne be pleased with the expansion effort? These were the mental questions asked. It was only when worn out, and when his future was nearly not his own, that his mind went to that dark corner and utter the deadly word . . . 'if'.

What if the colony had not survived? How had they survived, if they had been unsuccessful growing crops? Had they angered the indigenous tribes, if so . . .? What if his wife and daughter and granddaughter were not alive?

It was this final inquiry that would awaken the governour at night; awakened by his own guttural yell wrought from his dream of the unimagined.

Startling those around him, it took only one explanation for this uncharacteristic action — this yell — by such a great leader. Uncharacteristic — yes, but both human, and understandable. So understandable that upon an initial inquiry by some brave soul, it was never spoken of again.

42 days into the voyage, the normalcy was continuing. The novices on the crew were now acting as yeomen. The one area of degradation was the food. Having reached the level of consumption fit only for rodents, tempers flared, and equipment broke, all challenging those aboard. A challenge that was deemed as a typical expedition, and not worthy of note for the seasoned leaders aboard.

As a manner of maintaining sanity, the governour had committed mental matches of the flora, fauna, boulders, and buttes. He had assembled his own and others' images into a map of the landscape, a map which he hoped was still accurate for landing Hopewell and Little John. Cocke had drawn maps based on personal memories and the discussion with McGuilocutty. It was from these maps and mental images that the plans for discovery were continually confirmed, clarified, and expanded. Failure to perform these mental exercises would surely have resulted in nothing short of madness.

Throughout the journey, the day may change, but the conversation did not. Intense was not a strong enough word. As if trying to codify the fluidity of memories, the conversations repeated the same, whether they were between White and Cocke, or Cocke and Hutton, or multiples of the group scrutinizing one last time the drawings provided and created. Slowly, with each passing day, the mighty Hopewell and Little John came closer to the point of origin.

The best case had been formulated and documented. The inlet chosen would be the same White had chosen 3 years past. As the ship neared the harbor, the spyglass would detect leaping and jumping for joy, for the inhabitants would have their provisions, the Dare's would have their father, and Toma would have her husband.

A second scenario would have the Hopewell picking the wrong inlet, resulting in search expeditions, each one week in duration. One to the north of the location, one to the West, and a final to the south of the location of the landing location. A scenario not desired, as there would be at least one month of searching, but if successful, would result in the reuniting of White with his family.

A final scenario would involve moving the Hopewell North and the Little John South to multiple locations similar in appearance to the original landing location. Once anchored, they would execute a plan similar to the second scenario. This option could involve a minimum of 3 months of searching. None of the current contingents relished the thought of spending 3 months on their feet traipsing through forests in an unknown land. Staying put for 3 months, and establishing a camp for 3 months, were different options. However, searching for 3 months was not the desired outcome.

It was these options that were calculated and re-examined, taking the place of the monotony of the seas and the lack of other diversions. Like a dream which would not end, there was rising in the morning, remembrances of map details, conversations on map details, a tour of the vessel, discussions of the ship, eating, discussing the return, more tours, more discussions . . . more . . ..

Then it came, the day no one spoke of. For the most seasoned of sailors knew that seeking affirmation of when the water would turn to sand and the sand to soil and the soil to trees, was often the damnation of their plan and a plea to Neptune to plague the intruders of his realm. And so it was on the 61st day of the journey, the 22nd day of July, that one Hiberian Moses, a squat sailor of Irish descent, a novice to both the water and the Hopewell, asked that fateful question.

"Cap, when doth we see the land foretold . . . when do we leave this godforsaken water and return to the land we were meant to walk upon?"

The captain, himself eager for a sight on the horizon, could only respond.

"Any day mate, any day..."

And with that, the die was cast.

The Landing

For those present, they would remember the events of the early afternoon on the 23rd of July 1590 forever. It was on this day that the horizon began to change. During the greater part of the day, the skies had been overcast, the wind knots above normal, and periodic mist growing by the hour. The experienced sailors on board knew something evil to be brewing. It did not take long for their eagle eyes to spy that which they were expecting. Looming in the very direction the vessels were heading was a blackened morass, spewing lighting and causing waves of extraordinary height and force. Closer and closer it came to the two ships as if they were being sucked into the vortex. By evening, the cook announced food would not be served and the lads on board had long ago begun preparing their lashings to weather the night ahead.

"Ah, quite the Noreaster, Cap," commented the governour with a glint in his eye, as he remembered some of the great storms he had weathered.

"Tis stronger than I would have believed," began Cocke, "with land nearing, storms this strong be not what ye normally encounter."

"So ye believes we be close to landing?"

"Aye, but I dare not make mention to those below, would only serve as a distraction," commented Cocke in a matter-of-fact tone.

As the conversation continued, a sailor came rushing up to the two men. "Governour . . . Sir, ye is needed below."

"Aye, lad, I shall be below in a moment."

Upon disappearance below by the sailor, the governour turned, wished the captain well, and followed the path the sailor had taken.

Seems the distraction was more frivolous than strategic. The galley cook wished to know whether the governour would like something to eat since the impending weather would likely cause disruption or total cancellation of the evening's fare. The governour's decline was in itself a statement as to the quality of the food and his decision to skip a meal instead of a repeated punishment of his innards.

As the storm continued, the lightning illuminated the western panorama. It was during one of these flashes that solidity was seen for a brief second. The viewer couldn't be sure, but when the lightning repeated a second and third time, its illumination showed a strong possibility of a mass of solidity in the distance.

"Lad, fetch me the glass," asked Elize to the assistant boatswain nearby. The requestor was one Armando Elize, a pilot first class of the Hopewell. The requested glass was from the personal collection of Governour White, a gift from Sir Walter Raleigh.

After a few brief minutes, a soaked sailor came running with his hands and cloak protecting the glass. Damaging the glass would be the ultimate offense, and one for which walking the plank could be the result.

"Here boy, pass me the glass," the Master urgently requested, reaching out his rain-soaked hand.

Receiving the glass, the Master immediately raised it to his eye, scrutinizing what was visible for only seconds at a time.

There it was. A single flash confirmed the outline of an earthly body rising from the sea. Immediately following, a second flash confirmed that water ended in the distance and the rolling waters migrated from seascape to landscape. The third flash of light confirmed the Master's vision.

With that, the command which those assembled were awaiting . . . a command showing the nearing of the end to their 68 days at sea. A command echoed throughout the entirety of the Hopewell and across to the Little John.

"Land Ho," cracked the voice of Elize.

As if the lid of a jack-in-the-box had been released or the energy of a compressed spring let go, the energy of the current storm could barely challenge the fury which erupted on the Hopewell and Little John. With each crash of thunder came an equally loud howl of delight. The end was nigh. Soon those aboard would be touching terra firma. Their legs would no longer be subjected to the constant rocking; nor their hearing assaulted by the crashing of waves. Their noses no longer poisoned by the constant smell of water, dampness, and salt.

It was in this moment of ecstasy that the captain had to refocus all onboard.

"Aye lads, hear me now and hear me well!" began the captain, as he bellowed over the storm.

"Not one of you will make it to shore if you don't remember what you have learned. We be sailing nearly blind. The wind, the rain, these be no friend of the sailor. Pay heed of yer duties. The storm doth not appear to be weakening, and as ye know, we cannot anchor till the winds die down. While I appreciate your glee, return to yer post and keep yerself, yer ship, and yer fellow passengers and crew safe."

Turning towards the approaching land, the captain resumed his watch as did the crew slowly return to their duties; duties which, as reminded, would ensure the safety of all.

The winds which were assaulting the Hopewell and the Little John were relentless. For each yard forward, the winds drove the floundering ships back, or worse, almost in a collision with each other. Were it not for the focal point just seen, the storm would have knocked the ships off their course.

The commands from the boatswain were constant and reactive. His voice ensuring that the sails remained undamaged and the masts solid and unbroken.

"Upper sails down!"
"Mainsail down!"
"Storm sail port!"
"Storm jib ready!"
"Jibs, watch!"
"Bow forward!"
"Shrouds taut!"

These commands continued for the next hours. For each force wind that threatened to upend the ships, the master strategist, the boatswain and his pilot ensured they had a countermove. During the ensuing match of man against nature, the captain remained in the wheelhouse, focusing intently on the progress. Albeit slow, the mighty Hopewell and Little John made progress as they broke through waves and approached closer to the shore.

During the ensuing activities, the governour elected to stay below and not interfere with the more than capable hands of the captain. It was during the intense rocking and constant disruption of all manner of boxes and barrels that White detected a presence in his room. Sitting at his desk, he noted a sudden chill in his spine and the feeling that he was being observed. Pivoting, his vision spied his dear wife Toma standing across the room.

Not being a believer in spirits or that of the unreal, John shook his head vigorously and returned to work, reconstructing for the 104th time the strategy he would use and how he would address the options that beset him.

While recreating the number of hours a walk across the island should be and approximately how many steps it would be marsh to marsh, he heard it.

"Jooohhhnnn . . ."

Turning again, he saw nothing, shook his head, and returned to the calculations and notes which had plagued his existence for these many months.

"Jooohhhnnn . . ."

Again, the same sound. The wind? Surely the wind is whistling at a precise pitch to mimic his name. The governour rationalized these noises were the result of his mental and physical stresses.

"YYoouurrr heeerrreee . . ."

The same voice, although this time from another corner of the room. A quick turn revealed his lovely Tama attired in a flowing blue dress with a white cap upon her head; her face unnaturally white, her hands ivory.

Noticeably flustered, John stood. Mentally trying to assess what was occurring. He heard another sound just behind him. That sound caused him to quake to his very soul. For that sound was a baby's cry.

Visually leaving his wife he turned to see his daughter Elle holding his granddaughter Virginia. The child was whimpering, the daughter's eyes piercing.

"Take Care . . . Taaakkkkeeee Care . . . Trust None . . . Truuuussssstttt . . .," the words slowly reverberated until they were no more.

And with that, the vision of the Lady Tama ended her conversation as John watched unbelievably, her body walking through the wall proclaiming the final warning. Turning around, he found himself alone as Elle and Virginia had vanished.

Rushing to the door, his eyes were wide, his body quaking, his skin soaked. Seeing no one worldly or other, he grabbed a wall to avoid being pitched forward and returned to his quarters.

The governour spent the remaining hours of dark assessing what had occurred and what it could mean. Were his wife and daughter awaiting his return? Were his wife and daughter no longer of this world? Was this all a vicious trick induced by lack of food and overage of ale?

Governour White had no answers and could only spend another wakeful night awaiting an answer. Dawn arrived and with it, the last remnants of the storm. The exercising of the sails the previous night had exhausted the crew. However, at first light, the fact that the mainmast, sails and jib were intact was evidence of their success.

"Fine work . . . fine work . . . me fellow sailors," exclaimed the governour as he entered the main deck. Looking westward he saw their goals. The expected shoreline was nearing and now visible to the naked eye.

After assessing the position of the Hopewell in contrast to what he viewed through the spyglass, the governour inquired. "Captain, yer plan for anchoring? I see we be approximately 3 leagues out from the outer islands."

"That be me calculation. I had planned to approach slowly, seeking the inlet we are to take and then slowly sailing the bay in search of our landing spot. Me plan is to anchor within half a league of our planned landing location. As ye may recall, the bottom can be dangerously shallow in the bay. Grounding our ship would not contribute to a safe venture home, although I'm sure it would cause a brief laugh if word of it got to Raleigh."

"Aye, I agree Sir," echoed the governour.

"If the saints and souls are willing, your feet may touch ground this very day," replied the captain in encouragement to the governour.

"Saints and souls, eh?" spoke the governour under his breath in a barely audible tone.

"Say something, Sir?"

"Oh nothing, nothing at all," replied the governour as he turned and contemplated again the events of the previous evening.

The rest of the morning was inconsequential as compared to the evening before. The governour made final preparations for the post-landing activities. Once again, he committed memories to paper. Repeatedly, he checked and rechecked mental references to confirm that the images, stories, and perceptions were the same now as they were then. Amidst this mental housekeeping, Captain Cocke entered the room.

"Sir, have ye a moment?"

"Certainly, captain, whatever would thou like to discuss?"

"You, Sir . . . if I may."

"Me, whatever would you like to talk about me for?"

"Well . . . your health, Sir."

"Fit as Achilles, why doth thou ask?"

"You . . . you seem a bit distracted, Sir. If I may continue."

"Pray continue . . .," responded the governour not sure of the course this conversation was taking.

"For lo these past months, beginning at this journeys mental inception, the reunion with your family was paramount . . . yeh if I may . . . your North Star. And drive ye did . . . ah, more than I hast ever seen. Planning, plotting, drawing. Confirming with others, finding facts, digging nuances. Aye, Sir Robert Carey could do no better a job."

"Excuse me, dear captain, I applaud your insights into my drive, but is there a reason for this assemblage of fact?"

"Me pardons, governour. My concern lies with your current appearance. If I may, you look worn. You do not possess the same drive present in previous months. Indeed, you look to be a part of the man which was. If I may speak bluntly, I fear your abilities to lead rationally and ensure the success of our mission. Please know I would be remiss if I didn't make your governourship aware of the perceptions of I and others on board."

"Pish posh, man. I, you, and this crew here have just spent 67 days at sea. We've consumed food questionable for vermin and just weathered a storm that has taken the last remnants from most. I can assure ye, that when me feet touch that ground, it will be as if I have quaffed from the cup of the Fountain of Youth. My step will quicken, my mind will be of Copernicus, my eyes of an eagle. I appreciate ye concern, but fear not . . . we will be successful in this quest."

"Thank ye for your ear Sir . . . the Fountain awaits," replied the captain as he turned and left the governour. He believed the conversation had gone well and was thankful that he had not unduly annoyed the governour. At least not visually.

Frustrated with the conversation which had just occurred, the governour sat on the edge of his bunk and uncharacteristically laid his head back down. The nearness of the completion of the journey and the emotions of the conversation was indeed taking a toll. A toll not usually experienced; a toll that required an unplanned nap.

"Governour! Governour! . . . there be trees . . . trees there be," were the words that awoke White from his slumber.

In response, the governour bolted from his bed, leaving the cabin, and ascended the stairs to the deck in what appeared to be a single spry leap. There it was! Denied for these previous months, the sight of land was visible to the naked eye. Aye, not the land of industrial England; this be the land of prior years' memories. Trees and greenery. Hills and hoards of the avian variety. Not a stack in sight; nor blackened coal fumes tainting the blue of the horizon. Aye, in nearly an instant, the governour uncorked the Fountain. Immediately his demeanor returned to that of his youth.

As the Hopewell and Little John neared the shore, the eyes of the governour and captain scoured the shoreline for familiarity. Those trees entwined in the letter "V". The welcoming rock — larger than expected — whose placement was a mystery. Those dead trees of memory presenting a portal to the forest. Where were these memories of yore, those sights committed to paper? Would there be an indicium of success?

Floating forward, any of these would show where to make the first breach of the outer islands. Upon successfully navigating the inlet, a brief passing of nearby cays and keys would bring the Hopewell to the beaches of the land christened Virginia.

Spying an inlet and some trees which he construed to be a letter; the governour gave the command to sail forward.

Navigating the inlet was slow and treacherous, for each subsurface impediment could permanently wound, if not moor the Hopewell. Slowly she moved, navigating the too narrow path, a path which seemed to bring back memories. Yea, memories and fears of a time many months passed. The replication of the cringes and fear brought comfort, for as the governour experienced each memory again; realizing that he may be much closer to being reunited with his family.

What seemed like an eternity ultimately ended. The Hopewell and Little John navigated the inlet, avoided the cays and kept themselves intact. Taking in this success, a welcome command broke the silence.

"Drop anchor." A command of dreams. A command of finality. The command which all aboard had desired for months. With this anchoring; the Hopewell ended their journey some 800 feet from shore. The task of journeying from the ship to the land and beyond lay on the shoulder of Captain White and those who were preparing to join him. It was their task to begin the journey which they had been waiting for these many months to begin. A journey forged in the mind of many; a journey begun on the shores of Plymouth those many months prior.

Slicing through the water, resting atop crests that were far calmer than those encountered during the previous 24 hours, the landing party in their longboat progressed towards the shore. Noticing how far different from industrial England these shores were. These shores were a beauteous sight of lush trees and caramel sand beach. Birds flew in the air, returning to the trees to erupt in melodious tones. Deer could be seen in the distance, and if one looked a lone coyote. The entirety of the scene spoke of serenity.

Violating the serenity was the captain's longboat with a crew of six to support the leadership. The elite aboard were adorned in coats, pants, and freshly shined boots. Heavily worn clothing and torn canvas were the attire of the sailors. The officers and dignitaries carried rifles; the others bore knives. In the true spirit of an oxymoronical act; these very rifles were the ones that when discharged would foul the air with both a smell and sound foreign to the bucolic world. These longboat passengers, through their own actions, would begin the transformation and elimination of the view that they held to be so beautiful.

Reaching the shore, as if reading from a script; their next action would place their feet on solid soil — terra firma.

First Feast – reprise

As the governour's longboat touched the land, the last drops from the deluge fittingly ended, moving from the land to the sea in reverence to the parties' arrival. White took the lead in departing the landing craft first. Following behind were Master's Mate Hutton and Captain Cocke. Remaining on the craft until the governour and captain and their mate departed were sailors Millette, Taylor, and Harding. The longboat's arrival and touching of soil, the first soil that was seen by the governour and his crew in 66 days, necessitated the oft-repeated act of kissing the ground and thanking their Lord for a safe journey. Previous expeditions would have marked this moment as a time of contemplation, a time of pause as their eyes took in this land so far from the motherland and warmth of the Crowne.

Not so for this landing. The governour and his crew had a job to do and as quickly as they departed the longboat and bowed their heads in a mere minute of thanks, they began progressing over the beach towards the forest. With the mental alacrity of one taking exams from the university, the party began comparing the reality before them to the maps and drawings they had viewed and discussed ad nauseam for the past months. As they walked across the silent sand and entered the fringe of the trees, they heard movement ahead. Another step sent a deer rising and bolting further into the forest while several ducks rose from their roost and headed skyward. The sudden noises initially startled the men, which instinctively resulted in the return of the ducks to earth after being pierced by bullets from their guns. If the crew had selected properly and located the exact site of their previous embarkation, the gunshot would surely have caused interest amongst any inhabitants within earshot.

Realizing this, the trio stopped and listened intently for indications of voices or steps made not by animals or the like. After a few minutes of intent scrutiny, the reality of the silence and the need for continued exploration came to bear.

"Aye governour, hear anything, do ye?" asked Hutton in the hope that the governour's ears were more discerning than his own.

Intently listening, White finally responded. "Not even a twig snap . . ." replied a dejected John White. With that, the group returned to the beach, where they set their plan into motion.

"Shall we prepare for the first foray?" inquired the captain.

"Aye . . . and that will be one day of hiking and a return day. Is that correct Captain Cocke?" responded the governour.

"That it shall be," confirmed the captain. "Let us gather our provisions and begin while the light is still kind."

For the next hour, the group assembled provisions for the overnight expedition. Included in the provisions were equipment for fishing and hunting. Here on land, far away from the Hopewell's biscuits, eating food of a more desirous nature could occur. Gathering rations, tarps, and journals, the group prepared to set off into the forest.

"Master, oversee the ship's repairs . . ." began the captain. "When we return, if we be unsuccessful, we shall sail again to the North."

"Aye, Sir . . . may I make one request?" inquired Hutton.

"Certainly . . . what be your request?"

"If ye find a bounty of fish . . . if ye please bring a few extras back. A man can only survive so long on those rodent-infested biscuits."

Laughing, the Cap responded, "Fish . . ., I'll bring ye crab, the finest which has ever graced yer gullet. Huge crabs. Crabs with claws that can tear a man's arm if not careful. Aye, I'll bring ye a feast worthy of our 60-day voyage."

With a few remaining laughs and the sun hanging in the afternoon sky, a group of 5 ventured toward a natural opening in the forest, an opening some 100 yards from the shore. Walking for an hour, the ground became marshier, and the sounds of water closer.

"Well lads, the trees are familiar, as is the terrain; but I see no sign of our brethren's visit, do ye?" asked the governour.

"Not a mark . . . where shall we proceed?" asked the captain.

"To the north," replied White.

Turning from a westward direction to a northern one, the group continued to traipse through lush green forests. Periodically, the forest would end and the group would walk upon the open marshy ground with calmer water lapping at the earth. As the hours proceeded, the men became more acclimated to the fauna that was the Land of Virginia. Virgin wilderness, squirrels, ducks, and lizards graced the pristine land. Aside from some periodic breaks for water or to rest their feet, the group proceeded North. Relaxation or admiration of the surroundings was not on their agenda.

Continually as they proceeded, each had the same mental gnawing — had they seen this before? The land seemed familiar; however, no sign of those they sought was evident. It had been determined that in the short 2 years since these paths were walked that they would still exist. The paths would not have grown over and the structures and gates built would remain. As was lamented by the governours, no sign of occupancy recent or past existed.

"Mates, prepare our tents." The order from the Master was directed toward two sailors who accompanied the group. In short order; tarps were laid, coverings established, and sleeping gear prepared.

During the day's journey, the group had shot several ducks and a squirrel. These were prepared over the open fire. A bottle of whiskey completed the evening meal.

The conversations were sparse, for the men had their bellies filled and their senses dulled. Within two hours, all were sleeping the sleep of the dead. Morning came early as the sounds of the forest reached their ears . . . ears that had become accustomed to the continuous sound of waves and their watery dilution of all surrounding sounds.

A cawing bird, angry at their tents fouling his land, chastised the group in the early morning. The governour was the first to rise, eager to find his family, and disappointed that he had slept beyond the first light.

"Captain, Captain . . . a beautiful day it looks to be . . . are ye ready to begin?!" inquired White, eager to get started.

Sleepily, the captain rolled over, and in a true militaristic manner suddenly bolted to attention, ready to respond to his governour's question. "A . . . A . . . Aye, Sir," was his sleepy yet respectful response.

Within the hour, they had torn down the camp. The group harvested some fruit from a nearby tree and began day two of their expedition. Before departure, Governour White expressed his thoughts. "I believe we should walk further inland, but heading South toward the Hopewell."

"Splendid idea, my governour," was the response of Hutton. With this affirmation, the second day of searching began.

Unfortunately, day two proved to be like day one. Forest, marsh, lapping water, vocal creatures, and nary a trace of European life.

By noon, the group was within sight of the Hopewell and they returned to their point of origin. Greeted by enthusiastic shipmates, the momentary excitement was immediately quelled when a similar reaction was not returned in the explorer's expressions or voices.

"What do you plan now?" asked a sailor who had spent the morning repairing damaged wood upon the hull of the Hopewell.

"I believe I shall walk a bit further, and see what God places before my eyes," responded the governour, in an attempt at a whimsical response. "Captain, please join me. I plan on returning before dark."

"Aye, Sir," responded Cocke to the governour's request. With that, the two ventured further down the marsh and sand heading South.

As nothing on the Northern end of the land had been discovered on the previous day, the spyglass had remained sheathed. Not so today. Just over an hour into the trek, the governour and captain emerged from the forest and laid eyes on the water surrounding them on three sides. Climbing a dune on the sandy shore; the governour stood against the pristine blue sky and readied his spyglass. White's trained eye began to slowly and methodically scan the horizon. With clocklike precision, the entirety of the immediate horizon was scanned. Foot by foot, mile by mile, the governour moved the glass, eastward, westward, east . . ..

A sudden stop, an adjustment of the glass, and upon a reconfirmation — a proclamation. A proclamation that was made in disbelief. "Land? . . . Captain, there be another island a mere 5 miles from this very island."

With the glee of a schoolgirl and the speed of youth, the captain and governour ran — yea, literally ran to the Hopewell. Their enthusiasm of the captain and governour was immediately read by all. Quite soon, all on the Hopewell and Little John knew that success, some success, some unknown success, was near.

Unable to prepare the Hopewell for movement in short order and re-anchor in daylight, it was agreed to start the journey at first light. The renewed possibility of success fueled the adrenaline of the group. An adrenaline that was characterized by an evening of singing, playing of accordion, and guitar. After a bit of whiskey, there was even some entertaining dance by the younger and more inebriated.

At first light, the order was given to move the Hopewell to the land a few miles to the South. Luckily for all, anchoring and embarkment were not as challenging as the maneuvers of the previous days. Upon completion of the transition to the nearby island, the calm waters of the bay allowed the longboat to cut effortlessly through the waves and enable a landing without incident.

As the longboat got closer, the images seen began to match perfectly those remembered. The governour and captain could hardly contain themselves, as they pointed out landmarks documented prior and discussed for months. Before them lay the scruffy pines that resembled mouse ears, the tall fronds reminiscent of giraffes lounging by the water, even the rock upon the hill resembling a well-worn cap. These same landscapes, which previously were part of distant memories, were now resurrected and coming to life before their very eyes. This HAD to be the same location landed those years past.

As the longboat exited the surf and touched the land. The land consisted of an apron of sand with forestry starting and progressing denser past the eyes view. It was a particular area of the forest that caused interest to all. Not only interest, but intense excitement! For before them lay an area immortalized in memory, drawing, and tale. Upon their gaze lie a profoundly English structure. A fence. A segment of the wooden fence some 15 feet tall rested in a transitory state from the sandy beach to the greenery of the pines.

Approaching the fence, the lack of voices dismayed the group. The barren area distinctly lacked humanity, nor any sign of life. Most troubling was the scene behind the fence, for as they approached the structure and looked behind, all that remained were the remnants of a fight. Wood was littered about, structures knocked over, fence sections torn, chests opened, contents ransacked, clothing half-buried in the ground, dishes askew.

The sight from which Governour White had departed in August of 1587 had been found! However, the governour had not expected to see such a violent upheaval — a sure sign of a struggle. A struggle that relocated the group he had left. Where had they gone? And for how long had they been gone? Had many, or, any, survived? These were the thoughts that now barraged the governour.

Those with the governour noticed immediately the change in his demeanor. His manner had gone from calculating and demure to frenzied and near hysteric. Their attempts at calming were in vain and within a few minutes, Governour John White began racing through the woods, searching frantically for a sign.

Racing about, he searched the clothing rends, shields of plywood, and belongings dropped in haste. Where were the signs telling the rest of the story?

Would they find any clues? Would they be able to find anyone who could tell the tale?

And then. A sign.

Not 100 yards from the vacated camp; an unnatural sight awaited explorers of the land.

A pile of bones. A pile of bones with a driftwood board affixed to the base. Etched upon the board were six letters . . . letters of abandonment . . . of fear . . . of destiny. The letters spelled the sole word . . . 'Apauco', a word translated as 'unwanted'.

As a trained soldier, the governour reacted to the site in an unemotional, almost Pavlovian response. Cocking his rifle, the governour engaged his senses to assess whether a current threat existed.

Making his way circuitously around the cairn-like structure, Governour White slowly entered the welcoming yet foreboding woods.

Unknown to those ashore, for the previous hour, two braves had been spying on their party. Hearing their noises, smelling their fire powder, disrupting the silence. The two braves peered first through the bushes and a mere second later towards each other. In unison, the same thought came to their minds; and in that unison, they expressed a powerful word that would dictate the events of the coming days. That sole word was . . .

'Piacano.'

That single word meaning . . .

'They're back . . .'

In Conclusion...

Thank you for purchasing this novel. My most memorable comment was related to one of the early drafts. After reading the first few chapters my father asked the question — "where did this come from?"

This book is dedicated to my loving wife, Trese; my infinitely talented son, Ian; my parents for their endless support; and posthumously to my in-laws, for their unparalleled generosity.